He'd expected Katie Vincent to work miracles.

Deep down, he'd been hoping she'd be able to do more for them, based on all Jasper had shared. Maybe he'd been hoping that Katie Vincent was someone like her dad, and would be able to miraculously solve all of the park's problems.

He could use a miracle.

But he'd been wrong to even let his thoughts go in that direction. And, come to think of it, Jasper had been very careful about what he shared—and even more careful about what he hadn't shared—when it came to Katie.

But, in his heart, Luke wanted this miracle, this woman. The one who felt such responsibility. The one who carried the weight of the world on her shoulders. The one who made him want to scoop her up and convince her all was well with the universe.

But with an animal dying and a park on the brink of disaster, she wasn't the one he needed. He needed someone who loved and worked with animals, like he did.

Someone who understood about a labor of love.

Dear Reader,

Ideas knock on my door all the time. This time, however, the idea growled at me.

Years ago I was at Wildlife Zoo in Glendale, Arizona. I was near the big cats, and one big cat was actually right over my head. See, they had this netting that allowed the cats to jump up and rest right over where people walked. It seemed the black panther was looking down and saying something to me.

My writer's imagination took over. Was he saying "This is boring"? Or "I'm hot"? Or even "You people really paid to come see me?" None of those were good enough. Not for this magnificent creature. Finally, I came up with "Where were you? I've been waiting for you." And that's how *Katie's Rescue* was born. I looked at an exotic cat and wondered about his history, who he'd come into contact with, and who he had loved. And of course, in romance, *who he had loved* is a very important element, wouldn't you say?

Quite a few people helped me with this novel. First, my critique group, who said, "Pam, this reads like a memoir! Put more romance in." Then, there were the wonderful keepers at the Wildlife Zoo and Aquarium, the Phoenix Zoo and Out of Africa who deserve special thanks. Finally, it was Victoria Curran and Adrienne Macintosh who helped fine-tune it and bring the characters, animals and especially the romance to life.

I hope you enjoy reading *Katie's Rescue* as much as I enjoyed writing it. When you're done, visit a zoo and watch the black panthers. They're amazing.

Ideas knock on my door all the time. Lately, there's been a black bear pawing at it. Hmm, I think I'll open the door wide and let my next idea growl... Er, I mean grow.

Have a great day!

Pamela Tracy

HARLEQUIN HEARTWARMING

Pamela Tracy

Katie's Rescue

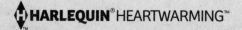

Recycling programs
for this product may
not exist in your area.

ISBN-13: 978-0-373-36636-1

KATIE'S RESCUE

Printed in U.S.A.

www.Harlequin.com

PAMELA TRACY

is an award-winning author, who lives with her
husband (who claims to be the inspiration for
most of her heroes) and son (who claims to be the
interference for most of her writing time). She started
writing at a very young age (a series of romances, all
with David Cassidy as the hero, though sometimes
Bobby Sherman would elbow in). Then, while
earning a BA in journalism at Texas Tech University
in Lubbock, Texas, she picked up writing again–this
time it was a very bad science-fiction novel.

She went back to her love and was first published
in 1999. Since then, Pamela has had more than
twenty romance novels in print. She's a winner of the
American Christian Fiction Writer's CAROL award
and has been a RITA® Award finalist. Readers can
find her at www.heartwarmingauthors.blogspot.com
or www.pamelatracy.com.

To Sonya Bateman
who richly blesses everyone
who comes in contact with her.
BTW, your mother loves you!

CHAPTER ONE

"HE'S GOING TO die unless *you* do something!"

The "he" in this case was not human, but that didn't make the situation any easier.

Leaning against the wall in a crowded college hallway, Katie Vincent frowned and wished she'd ignored her cell phone's ring. But she hadn't and now could only ask, "How did you get this number?"

"The lawyer."

Never trust a lawyer, especially not a semi-retired one who'd kept her dad as a client because of old times' sake.

"The panther you sold me," Luke Rittenhouse practically growled, "isn't responding to anything I've tried. Based on Aquila's weight loss, he probably won't last another week unless you do something."

The man sounded annoyed, worried and bossy all at the same time.

Katie closed her eyes. This wasn't the first time she'd been asked to make a difference in Aquila's life. But now Katie was no longer an adolescent girl who thought herself indestructible as well as indispensable.

"Mr. Rittenhouse, I'm at work. It's the beginning of the semester, and I don't have any vacation coming. Plus, I have responsibilities with my younger sister. You're asking the impossible. I don't work with animals anymore. I can't help you."

"You don't have a choice. I've gone over all the paperwork, and according to what you signed, you have to improve his condition or you're in breach of contract."

Breach of contract? Unfortunately he might be right. She'd wanted to settle her father's estate as quickly as possible, so when Luke Rittenhouse had asked her to guarantee her father's performance animals' health and abilities, she'd agreed. She'd not hesitated to put it in writing. Bob Vincent, her father, animal trainer extraordinaire with almost three decades of experience, took great care of his animals—better care of his animals than he'd taken of his children.

But improve Aquila's condition? Katie closed her eyes again and tried to remember exactly where Luke Rittenhouse lived. She was pretty sure it wasn't Texas.

"Are you still there?"

"I'm still here, but, Mr. Rittenhouse, I can't do anything for Aquila. I stopped helping my father more than a decade ago. I wouldn't know what to do. I don't even keep a pet and—"

"I'm not letting Aquila die. Not if I can help it."

Katie seriously doubted that Aquila was dying. He was only twelve years old. Panthers, in captivity, usually lived into their early twenties.

"I need you to come to Scorpion Ridge."

Katie almost dropped the phone. "Are you nuts?" she said, getting the attention of the few students scurrying late to class. "Scorpion Ridge? What kind of place is that?"

"It's in Arizona."

"I'm not coming to Arizona. I—"

The man had no trouble finishing her sentences. "—signed a paper guaranteeing all of your father's animals were in good health."

"My father's animals *were* in excellent condition," Katie exclaimed. "Not only did my father's vet, as well as yours, examine each and every animal before the sale, but we hired an independent consultant to attest to their health. No way can you claim—"

"Lady, I'm telling you, nothing we've tried has worked. Aquila is dying."

Katie paused as the memories washed over her. She'd been eleven when Aquila and his brother were born on her father's property. She'd cried for a straight week after their mother, an always standoffish black panther, rejected her two cubs. So Katie went to work alongside her father, bottle-feeding, seeing both Tyre and Aquila open their eyes for the first time, rubbing their heads, watching the silky gray babies turn black, soothing the cubs after the vet took blood samples, cleaning up after them. Anything her father asked, Katie had done because she loved those cubs, especially Aquila.

Later, her father had said she'd done "too" good a job with Aquila. The cat wasn't supposed to be a pet; he was supposed to be a performer. But in the end, the truth couldn't be changed. Aquila loved her, liked her father, but wouldn't perform for Jasper—her father's right-hand man.

Tyre, Aquila's brother, was a typical panther and much like his mother, disdained captivity and prepped to attack. He didn't care for anybody. When her father started training him, Tyre performed but only because his reward was food.

"Are you still there?" Luke demanded.

"I'm still here. What's wrong with Aquila?"

"If a cat can be heartsick, I think this cat is. He won't eat, he barely moves and he won't perform. We've tried just about everything. We've fed him live game. We've put enough toys in his area to make him feel he's gone to stalk-pounce-chase heaven. But so far he just lies there. I can't watch him die." His voice softened, giving Katie hope. This man wouldn't give up on Aquila. He'd find a way to help him.

A way that didn't involve her.

"Mr. Rittenhouse. I can't come to Scorpion Ridge. Plus, I have a sister to take care of."

"Isn't your sister in college?"

So, Mr. Rittenhouse had done some homework.

"Yes," Katie said, "but in some ways she needs me now more than ever."

There was a long pause. Finally, he said, "Look, I have sisters, too. But I also have a responsibility to these animals, plus my employer and employees. Right now my number one priority is keeping Aquila alive. And, apparently, I need your help."

Katie didn't say anything.

His voice grew firmer. "Aquila was the inspiration for my purchasing your father's menagerie, and I'm sure you're aware I paid top dollar."

Yes, Katie knew to the penny what the man had paid for each animal and for some extras. He'd made a wise investment. George, the brown bear, had appeared in more than one movie. The camel, Kobie, could untie a knot in a rope. Ollie, the orangutan, waved and blew kisses.

Aquila, however, had been the reigning prince of Bob Vincent's menagerie. He could jump through a ring of fire, dive into a swimming pool and he actually danced to Cyndi Lauper's "Girls Just Wanna Have Fun."

Katie hadn't always agreed with her father's ideas of what his animals should do, but Aquila's affinity for dancing was entirely Katie's doing. Most of Bob's animals had been good dancers, at least to Katie's music.

Well, maybe not the snakes.

Luke went on. "If he can't perform, then I made a bad deal. One I cannot afford to keep. There's a six-month reversal clause for breach of contract, so I'm going to have my lawyer contact your lawyer..."

Katie opened her mouth but no sound came out, and she sank to the cold, hard, tiled floor. The reversal clause would be for the whole kingdom, not just Aquila. She didn't have any place to put four large animals. Her father's house and land had been sold, allowing her to pay his bills and bury him. The money from the animals had allowed her to pay off her debts, get Janie into college and move into a decent apartment.

As for the lawyer, she barely knew him. Plus,

from what she remembered of her dad's lawyer, he'd be on the side of the animals.

Not that she wasn't, but… Two deep breaths later, she managed to croak out, "Mr. Rittenhouse, are you aware I've not been in contact with Aquila for years?"

"Yes, Jasper told me."

Katie all but collapsed against a wall and tried to ignore the students hurrying down the hall. She could have been one of them, if not for her life experiences and responsibilities.

"Jasper's with you?" she whispered.

"Yes."

The man had to be nearing eighty. He'd been like a grandfather to her once, and yet Katie had never looked into how he was doing after her father died. He and Bob had worked together for almost thirty years.

Guilt tapped her on the shoulder *again*.

"It was Jasper who suggested I call you before I called my lawyer," Luke said. "He's sure that Aquila would remember you and pull through."

Pulling together every ounce of stamina she could manage, Katie said, "Mr. Rittenhouse, wild animals aren't supposed to pine for people. Besides, I don't think you realize what you're asking. Last time I worked with Aquila, I was a kid. I'm a different person now."

"Yes."

She didn't know if he was agreeing with her or encouraging her to go on. No matter, Katie had a feeling the man on the other end of the phone didn't think much of the different person she'd become.

"Mr. Rittenhouse, the animal kingdom is no longer my world. I have no desire to work with animals again…."

She didn't mention she also had no desire to sacrifice her job, schooling or endanger herself or her family. She didn't say any of these things because if he worked with animals, he was a showman, and he accepted the sacrifices and ignored the risks.

"Lady, I don't have the time or willingness to play games. I've gone over the sales agreement for Bob's Backyard Animal Kingdom, and I'm real comfortable with my rights. You either show up here within twenty-four hours to help with Aquila, or my lawyer will begin proceedings to enforce the reversal clause."

"Twenty-four hours? I've already told you, I have a job. I have a home. I have a little sister to take care of."

"Just give me two weeks. Bring your sister along if you have to. Help me with Aquila. Then you can go back to whatever you're doing now. Two weeks. Jasper said you could do it. See you in twenty-four hours." He hung up.

Katie stared openmouthed at her cell phone until the silence of the hallway caught her attention. Thursday-morning classes had started and students were either cocooned safe inside their rooms or were already in the student union or out in the parking lot. As an interpreter for the deaf, she belonged in statistics class with her student, and no doubt both student and instructor were growing concerned. Her student, all of nineteen and extremely bright, could read lips, but this particular instructor spoke English with a heavy accent. More than once Katie had signed, "One hungry student" when the instructor had really said, "One hundred students." The instructor also tended to speak louder whenever he looked at the deaf student, which made the class giggle.

Katie didn't like the man.

Well, this might be her last day in Mr. Hungry Student's class. Luke Rittenhouse had backed her into a corner. And since she'd already gotten in trouble for breaking the "Thou Shalt Not Let Thy Cell Phone Ring During Class" rule, it looked like the perfect time for a change.

Too bad Katie didn't want one.

LUKE HUNG UP the phone and walked to the far wall of his office where a dry-erase board displayed his five-goals-in-five-years plan. Standing in front of it, he reminded himself that people who didn't take risks were often people who stood still. Bridget's had stood still for way too long. His job was to change things for the better.

NEW ACQUISITIONS was number five on his list, and the only one with a check mark next to it.

That had been *his* risk, the one that kept him awake at night worrying.

The purchase was supposed to be a step forward, but it ultimately might be the undoing of the four items above it: EMPLOYEE SALARIES AND BENEFITS, GENERAL OPERATIONS, FACILITIES MAINTENANCE AND CAPITAL RENEWAL. He'd chosen the order of importance. And he'd been the one to act on the dead-last goal first.

He moved to the window and watched as the day-to-day operations of Bridget's AZ Animal Adventure carried on.

At the front of Bridget's, his friend Adam was painting the grand entrance. It was an ongoing work that might never be finished.

He'd met Adam fifteen years ago in a taekwondo studio. Adam, aged ten at the time, took lessons with his twin brother who'd been born disabled. Luke, then a junior in high school, did his homework while his sister Bridget had a lesson.

Adam quit lessons and soon was asking Luke for help with math. Seemed he'd doodled during every math class and was now behind. They'd been friends ever since.

Five years ago, Luke asked for a favor in return.

Even at twenty-five, Adam was still a kid—a kid without a high school diploma, but a kid who could replicate anything he put his mind to. Luke needed his talent and his perspective to design child-friendly attractions. And now thanks to Adam, the entrance of Bridget's had cutouts of animals where kids could stick their heads in holes and become the animals. There were places where children looked in a mirror and suddenly their head appeared above a pirate, or a cowboy. Scattered among activities were animal information charts with lots and lots of pictures. And, of course, soon there would be places to buy souvenirs and snacks even before they walked under the giant Bridget's AZ Animal Adventure sign.

His little sister would have loved it.

For her, Luke's goal was to put Scorpion Ridge on the map and make Bridget's a success. Sure, it was a little off the beaten path, but with an orangutan that read the newspaper and took afternoon tea, an anaconda that weighed over a hundred pounds and a black panther that danced to Cindi Lauper, the number of people willing to drive a ways and spend money could quadruple.

It just needed to quadruple really soon.

As if sensing his owner's unhappiness, Tinker chose that moment to jump off the desk, meander over and plop down on Luke's foot to meow.

"I'm all right," Luke said, bending down and scooping up the full-grown, long-haired, black-and-white cat that was roughly the same size as his shoe. The zoo vet, Fred, said malnutrition had stunted the cat's growth. Luke figured the cat truly liked his compact size; the beast could fit anywhere.

Setting the feline back on his desk—there was already enough cat hair on his clothing to stuff a pillow—Luke picked up his cell phone and called his most treasured coworker. Ruth Moore was almost sixty, weighed two hundred pounds, always wore a pair of reading glasses that matched her outfit and for years had run the place.

Before Luke had turned it into Bridget's, the property had been managed by his uncle Albert, and consisted of nothing more than a roadside petting zoo with a few exotics. And Ruth.

Ruth was straightforward, liked all animals

and most people, and Luke couldn't get along without her. He'd known her all his life, and she'd been the one who'd suggested him for the job of director. She did whatever he asked without question. And, best of all, if he *didn't* ask, she figured out something to do.

She knew everyone in the animal world and definitely knew more than he did about Bridget's. She was his go-to person.

"I'm behind the scenes with my lion," Ruth yelled over the radio. Nothing Luke said could convince her he could hear her without the yelling. "Terrance the Terrible is yawning on command and getting his teeth brushed. We need to film this."

Ever since Jasper, Bob Vincent's right-hand man—and somehow part of the "extras" Luke had purchased—arrived along with the Vincent animals, Ruth had suddenly become idea woman of the month.

"Good thinking," Luke said, just as he'd said to all her ideas for the past month. Though this idea just might be doable and affordable: Luke's two favorite words.

After ending his call with Ruth, he checked to see what his head keeper, Meredith, was up to. Then he opened his scheduler. He had two school tours booked; one had reserved the birthday area for their picnic lunch. A good sign this early in the school year. Scorpion Ridge's nearest neighbor, a college town called Adobe Hills, was 45 minutes away, and Tucson was fifteen minutes past that. So for most, a visit to Bridget's meant planning in advance.

But Luke needed to entice more visitors, desperately, and to get more visitors, he needed the cats to perform.

So far the cougar did a great job of mutilating giant cardboard boxes. And the bobcat walked across the rope from his shady area to a tree—when he wanted. To Terrance, the lion's, credit, he snored and made great noises while he slept. The kids loved it.

But Aquila…so far, nothing.

And Aquila could dance if he wanted! Something that would surely draw kids from all over.

Instead, he glared and didn't move. He was also doing his best to qualify as a spokescat for a weight loss center—a topic the local newspaper didn't mind putting in print. Aquila had weighed just over a hundred pounds when he'd arrived at AZ Adventures. Now he was more like seventy. Ruth refused to go near the animal; it made her cry. Jasper had tried different kinds of foods, tried different kinds of games and when nothing worked, muttered under his breath. Meredith admitted she was running out of ideas. Katie was their last hope. And maybe

Bridget's, as well. If the private society that funded Bridget's ever stopped footing most of the park's bills, it'd go under.

In weeks.

The door to the office opened. Meredith peeked in, looking annoyed. "Katie Vincent just called. She won't be here tomorrow. Apparently they couldn't get anyone to replace her at work. She'll drive out Saturday morning."

"That will put her here either Saturday at midnight or early Sunday morning," Luke figured. "Did she say if she was heading straight here or to a motel?"

"She didn't really give me a chance to ask questions." Meredith smirked. "She simply told me to give the message to His Highness and then she hung up."

Luke grinned and relaxed for the first time that morning. His Highness, huh? He kind of liked it. "Find out what Katie does for a living."

Meredith bowed, something she'd never done before, and Luke just knew he heard a faint *Yes, Your Highness* as she backed out the door.

Before Luke had a chance to return to his schedule, Meredith came back.

"She's an interpreter for the deaf. She attends college classes with students. They couldn't get a replacement for tomorrow's classes. She said if Saturday didn't work…" Meredith's smirk returned, and Luke could imagine what Katie had said.

"So you reached her—"

"Briefly. I get the sense that she's less than thrilled about the sudden career change."

No doubt Meredith couldn't fathom why anyone would choose any career that wasn't with animals.

"It's not a career change," Luke grumbled. "I asked her for two weeks."

If not for his concerns about Aquila's health and Bridget's finances, Luke would have been looking forward to meeting Katie Vincent. It was clear Jasper thought she hung the moon, yet the man had admitted she hadn't had much contact with either him or her father in years.

Still, for Luke, it was hard to get past the fact that she hadn't personally arranged or physically attended her father's funeral, and then had hired outsiders to pack up the kingdom and sell everything. If she'd cared one iota about her dad or the animals, she'd have been on hand and made sure everything was taken care of.

Personally.

That's how Luke would have done it.

When he'd said as much to Jasper, the older man just muttered about bad decisions and hurt feelings.

So what! They were a part of life. What family didn't have their share of bad decisions and hurt feelings? You fought it out, worked it out and forged a bond that couldn't be shaken.

He looked out the window of his office again. The animal adventure had grown a lot since he'd taken it over. His little sister wouldn't recognize it. She'd still recognize some of the animals, though. This place had been Bridget's favorite place in the whole world.

"Someday I'll run this place," she'd told Luke. "You can help."

That had been years ago, before either of them knew what their futures held, when both of them still believed—or at least pretended to—in Santa. But two weeks after Bridget died, Luke had come to say his goodbyes to the animals that had made her happy. Instead, he'd taken one look at the buildings in need of paint, the closed food concessions and the animals with no one to admire them, and he'd said, "What can I do?"

Ruth had instantly made a phone call. Next thing he knew, he'd been filling out papers and looking for an apartment. His new title was director of an animal park.

He now made considerably less than he'd made as director of marketing for a Tucson company. But to everyone's surprise, especially his own, he'd settled into his new job and was good at it.

The degree in marketing helped; his love of animals helped even more.

In just two months, they'd celebrate what would have been the real Bridget's twentieth birthday. Luke's dream was to expand enough so that Bridget's AZ Animal Adventure made money, met his five goals and they could even take one day out of every month and donate the day's take to a charity.

His sister's charity.

The National Down Syndrome Society. But Bridget would never work alongside him, and that's what hurt the most.

CHAPTER TWO

STANDING IN FRONT of Aquila's enclosure on Friday morning, Luke hoped he'd done the right thing by practically forcing Katie Vincent to come.

Really, there'd been no choice if he intended to keep Aquila—and Bridget's—alive.

Surely Katie wouldn't lose her job, not for just two weeks.

But would two weeks be enough for Aquila?

The panther's illness made no sense. Luke had called three zoo directors and one renowned wildlife vet. They all said the same thing. Panthers don't bond with people, so there's no way he could be pining.

Jasper, however, maintained that the zoo directors and renowned wildlife vet hadn't met Aquila, hadn't seen Aquila with either Katie or Bob Vincent.

Luke really hoped Jasper was right.

Because now, along with worrying about Aquila, he also had Katie to worry about. He hoped she'd managed to take time off with pay because she couldn't expect a paycheck from him.

It was her contractual obligation to make sure the animals were healthy. He shouldn't feel the need to pay her.

But he did.

"Katie's a good girl" was all Jasper would say. And, according to Jasper, at one time the animals had been her life. Then she and her sister had just moved away. Luke got the idea there was more to the story. He knew there'd been an accident, and her sister had gotten hurt. He knew Bob Vincent had turned his daughters over to a relative. That's all Jasper would share. Maybe now that Katie was really coming, Jasper would be more forthcoming.

Luke stopped in front of the camels' pen. "How's it going?"

Jasper nodded but didn't say anything. The man preferred four-footed friends to two-legged ones, particularly those he'd arrived with. There wasn't much about animals that Jasper didn't know. He'd traveled with an Australian circus during his prime, but had migrated to America almost fifty years ago when Ringling Brothers leased an act from that circus. He'd been hooked up with Bob Vincent for the past thirty.

Luke knew his type. The man was an animal keeper and would die an animal keeper. It wasn't so much that Jasper loved animals, it was more that he understood them and they him.

Ruth said the animals at Bridget's were the only beings that could rightly get along with Jasper.

Cheeky, the camel, named not so much because of her third cheek but because of her personality, pounded a foot on the ground. It didn't appear she much cared for Jasper paying attention to Luke instead of her.

"Hold on, Cheeky," Jasper groused. "I could feed you all day and you'd still be hungry."

Cheeky seemed to nod.

And smile.

Kobie, the camel that had come from Bob Vincent, ignored both Jasper and Luke. Right now Kobie didn't smile. Dan Reeker, Luke's vet, said animals needed time to adjust after a change.

Unlike Aquila, at least Kobie ate well, played with his rope and did what he was supposed to do. The smile would come later, Luke hoped.

If Bridget were here, she'd have Kobie smiling. She'd loved camels. Most children wanted to see the lion first. Not Bridget. From the time she was little and had seen a baby camel on the news channel, she'd been a fan.

It was an unusual choice. Camels were usually not the friendliest of animals; sometimes they were downright mean. One of Bridget's therapists had suggested that Bridget had chosen a somewhat unlovable animal to revere because she, Bridget, felt somewhat unlovable.

Luke had never managed to forget that therapist's words. They'd been spoken kindly, but the meaning behind the words, to the young boy he'd been, had been haunting.

It was the first time he'd seen Bridget through the eyes of the world instead of through the eyes of a brother.

He'd mistrusted the world ever since.

"You got time to talk?" Luke asked.

"Got a few things I need to do." Then Jasper added suspiciously, "What do you want to talk about?"

"Katie Vincent's agreed to come work with Aquila. She'll be here on Sunday."

Jasper nodded, his face—usually animated—void of expression. Funny, Jasper had pushed for Luke to call Katie Vincent. "About time."

"She didn't have much choice. I threatened to return the animals."

Jasper frowned. "She'd have come around eventually. Too bad you had to twist her arm. Still, it's right that she come home."

Luke frowned. Home? This wasn't home.

As if reading Luke's mind, Jasper said, "Back to her roots. She's a natural with animals. She'll know what to do. Her daddy was wrong to send her away."

"Then why did he?"

Jasper became absorbed with the camels. He looked as though he'd rather be anywhere but here. For days now, Luke had tried to instigate this conversation, but always Jasper found a way out. At the moment, though, he was trapped: two big camels on one side, Luke on the other.

That didn't keep him from taking a step toward Kobie as if a four-hundred-pound camel with thirty-four teeth—weapons really—was safer than straight-talking with Luke.

When Jasper did respond, instead of looking at Luke, he studied one of Kobie's calloused knee joints as if it were the most fascinating thing in the world. "I think at the time, Bob thought it was easier to take care of animals than to take care of animals and kids."

Luke opened his mouth to ask another question, but Jasper—with an agility that came from years of caring for skittish animals—managed to skirt around Luke and walk away, looking older than Luke remembered.

It was something you couldn't stop, aging. Apparently even for camels. Was that the beginning of gray forming on Cheeky's chin? Luke and the vet hadn't even begun to discuss geriatric care.

Lately, they'd been too busy discussing how to save Aquila.

When cats were sick—losing weight and such—they still acted as if they were in perfect health. Because in the jungle, if a cat became ill, it became a target. Nature called it survival of the fittest. But Aquila wasn't in the wild; he was in captivity.

Luke also didn't think Aquila was sick, not really. He was depressed, and not just about the change in venue. With Bob Vincent gone, Aquila missed the person who'd cared the most for him.

Aquila had what Jasper called a one-owner heart.

But Jasper also believed that at one time Katie Vincent had owned Aquila's heart and that she could, with a little work, take ownership of it again.

"I CAN'T BELIEVE you're just packing up and leaving." Janie Vincent, all of nineteen years old, looked both dismayed and intrigued.

Not a good look coming from a little sister who was no longer little.

"The sooner I leave, the sooner I'll be home," Katie said.

She'd expected her sister to be upset at the thought of her leaving. After all, Katie not only paid the bills, but also stocked the refrigerator, cleaned the house and did the laundry. Plus, both Katie and Janie had issues with leaving.

But it was the intrigued look that worried Katie. At the moment, Katie playing cheerleader was the only thing keeping Janie at least halfway interested in being a college freshman—a college freshman with no idea what to major in and who only wanted to take art classes. Without Katie there to push her, Janie could easily walk away from her studies.

"You don't even know this guy," Janie protested. "You're driving across two states and it might be for nothing."

"I know a few things about him."

More than a few, actually. When Luke had made the offer on her father's animals, she had spent hours on the internet researching Bridget's AZ Animal Adventure and Luke himself. She knew he wasn't an animal trainer like their father. She knew that Luke had a marketing degree and had worked at an advertising firm before hiring on as director of Bridget's AZ Animal Adventure. She knew he preferred the words *animal park* to *zoo,* and that Bridget's had had humble beginnings. She knew that Luke had renamed the park after his sister Bridget who'd died from Down Syndrome. She knew that Bridget's name had only been added to the marquee and letterhead a year ago.

"He's perfectly safe," Katie said, "and I'm not doing it for nothing. I have to make sure Aquila is all right."

Janie nodded. A shadow crossed her face, but only briefly before her typical I-don't-have-a-care-in-the-world look returned. "I remember Aquila. He was nothing like Tyre. He was your favorite, like a pet."

"No," Katie said firmly. "Wild animals are never pets."

Janie, more than anyone, should realize that. The scar down the left side of her face was a constant reminder. She wore her hair cut in a style that hid her ear. But Katie didn't need to see the damage.

She remembered it was there.

"Are you sure—"

Katie shook her head. Now was not the time to get into a debate about the past.

A past that would all too quickly be a reality for Katie.

On one hand, she'd love seeing Jasper again. He'd been like a grandfather. It was Jasper who'd drummed into her that wild animals should never be considered pets. Katie's father had thought the same thing, but he was too busy buying animals and training them to take on television shoots to worry about what Katie was doing. He was just happy that she'd inherited his gift with animals and that he could market her ability.

He had plans for Katie.

She was photogenic.

She'd basked in the role of favored daughter, mistaking it for love. Sometimes, at night, Katie would replay in her mind what her father had taught her, how to hold animals, how to tuck them against the skin so they were tight and safe.

Katie had felt safe with her father.

Janie, on the other hand, had seemed to take after their mother—at least where animals were concerned. Leslie Vincent had liked animals but wasn't so crazy about the effort it took to care for them. She'd been the bookkeeper, the organizer, the voice of reason.

And when she died, all reason left. There'd been no gentle voice to remind Bob that family came first, that their daughters still needed a father. So Katie had had to take care of Janie.

Her sister hadn't inherited their father's gift with animals, except when it came to drawing them. She also hadn't inherited their mom's money skills, though she was an expert at getting cash out of Katie. Janie did know, however, how to organize her time so that every minute was accounted for: going out with friends, surfing the internet and watching television.

Janie had a few issues to overcome yet, some Katie took the blame for. Which is why Katie needed to get to Scorpion Ridge, take care of Aquila and get home. Otherwise, judging by the earlier intrigued look, their house would become party central. Complete with an empty fridge and clothes everywhere. And without Katie there, who would cheer Janie up when she was down, remind her to eat when she was absorbed in her latest piece of art, kiss her goodnight?

"I'll miss you," Janie said, following Katie as she carried two suitcases out to her Rav4.

Katie blinked back the tears that threatened. She'd learned long ago that tears changed nothing and only made her look weak.

She hugged Janie goodbye. "Be good, and do your homework."

"Homework, what I live for," Janie teased.

For a moment, Katie considered grabbing a third suitcase and stuffing Janie in it. Yet, in the back of her mind, she knew the separation would be good for them. Six years ago, at age eighteen, she'd fought the system to get custody of Janie, and she'd won. Ever since, she'd kept waiting to mess up and it all to fall apart.

The way her life had fallen apart when Janie had gotten attacked by Tyre.

Because of her.

And now she was heading back to the world that had ripped her family apart.

Katie started the car's ignition, put the car into Drive and with a last wave headed for Scorpion Ridge. It would be a long trip. Dallas, in late afternoon, still had traffic issues. She hoped to make it to Odessa before stopping to get gas and something to eat.

If she could eat.

Then she planned on making it all the way to El Paso before stopping to find a motel. That would only leave her a six-hour drive for Saturday.

She turned the radio up and settled back, trying to let the music distract her. When that didn't work, she thought about the first class she'd interpreted that morning. It had been a lit class with only a handful of students. Katie liked the class, the teacher and the student. She hated leaving him at the beginning of the semester, but since the law required that two translators be available per class, not that much would change for him. He would still have his other regular translator.

Katie turned off the music and instead switched over to an audio book. It worked, just barely, at limiting the unease she felt and also kept her awake. Abilene and then El Paso slipped by, and Katie focused on the evening shadows of the nearly deserted roads.

Her book ended as she drove through a tiny New Mexico town. She stopped for snacks and a bathroom break as she crossed the border into Arizona. The last of the evening dusk turned to inky blackness. Black as a panther...ready to strike....

She selected another audio book, as none of her music CDs could counter her memories of the past. A past she'd only wanted to forget.

At midnight, she figured there was still time to turn the car around. After all, she didn't owe her dad anything. She'd gotten rid of his animals; he'd gotten rid of his children.

He'd claimed at the time it wasn't safe to have two little girls around so many wild animals. He'd stressed the word *wild* as if it meant something.

She'd take a wild animal over Aunt Betsy any day.

But it wasn't the memory of her father that kept her driving to Arizona, it was the memory of a black cat that she'd loved. Aquila.

Scorpion Ridge came into view just as the rooster crowed. Arizona looked nothing like Texas. There were no rolling green hills. Just brown dirt, the occasional somewhat dwarfed tree and lots of cacti.

Eyes gritty from lack of sleep, Katie checked the map and decided to go ahead and see if she could find Bridget's AZ Animal Adventure. It wouldn't be open yet, but maybe that was for the best. She could explore the park when only the keepers were there.

Katie took a breath as she turned onto the street that led back to a destiny she'd never chosen for herself.

LUKE HAD BEEN up since four, crunching numbers and trying to figure out if he had the money to pay Katie Vincent for her time.

So far, it looked like not.

Though really, he'd known that before he'd reached for the calculator.

Plus, what would he be paying her for? How much extra was she willing to do? He needed Ruth's advice.

At six, he left his apartment and drove to work. It was only a five-minute drive, but today it seemed to take longer as he contemplated Katie's arrival.

The new animals he'd acquired from her had been a leap of faith and just one of the many changes Luke had brought to Bridget's.

During his first year at the animal park, before they'd even added Bridget's name to the adventure, his goal had been to make the struggling animal park self-supporting. Back then it had been just him, Ruth, Fred the veterinarian and a handful of volunteers. They'd needed to expand.

He wasn't a natural with all of the animals, so he'd hired Meredith and devoted his time to the animals he knew best.

He'd started with the fifteen burros. He'd redesigned their enclosures, written their history and not only put them on display but added brief rides for kids.

Later, he added mules so the bigger folk could ride, too. And with a little advertising, the burro and mule rides brought a trickle of paying people to Scorpion Ridge.

The trickle turned to a steady flow on the weekends. It was enough to establish hope, but not enough to make ends meet or fulfill his plans to expand.

So he brought his best friend, Adam, in. Adam's price was perfect: a place to live. At night, he answered the phone and acted as a security guard. During the week, he painted. Thanks to Adam, the zoo had artwork scattered throughout: snakes on the snake house, camels drinking from water bottles on the main concession and, best of all, a playground area that was alive with depicted animals.

On the weekends, Adam also sold caricatures of the visitors. Sometimes Luke thought Adam made more money than the burros did.

The kid-friendly atmosphere brought in more crowds, giving Luke some capital to expand—which he'd spent on Bob's animals. The first risk Luke feared wouldn't pay off.

Luke drove his truck into the parking lot of Bridget's and got out to unlock a side gate.

"Hey, boss."

Adam called Luke "boss" just to annoy him. Luke doubted Adam could get along with a real boss.

"Hey." Luke didn't have time to talk. Adam loved art and thought everyone else should, too. Stopping to talk to Adam usually meant a paintbrush in Luke's hand. So he just drove through the gate, closed it and parked near the camel area.

IN THE PREDAWN HOUR, the birds were especially noisy, but the burros and mules clamored in, too. It also seemed the only time Terrance chose to roar was when no one was around, like now.

Luke first headed for his office to drop his briefcase off. Then he went looking for Jasper and Ruth. He found them in the turtle pen, of all places, working on one of the shelters that had somehow fallen overnight. They were a great team when they weren't competing.

"Where's Meredith?"

"She was here a moment ago," Ruth said. "I think she went to check on Aquila."

Before Luke had a chance to respond, static sounded on his radio. Luke reached for it. It was Meredith.

"There's a disturbance at the panther pit. I think somebody's over there." Before Luke could ask her what was wrong, or who, exactly, might be there, Jasper stopped what he was doing, cocked his head and listened a moment before saying, "That's what Aquila sounds like when he's upset."

"I don't hear anything," Ruth protested.

It didn't matter that Luke didn't hear anything, either. He was certain Jasper did, and that was enough to inspire an Olympic-style sprint toward the panther enclosure.

About the time Luke reached his destination and skidded to a stop, he realized Jasper was beside him. Who knew the old man could move that fast?

He was probably thinking what Luke was thinking.

Katie Vincent had arrived.

More than anything, Luke hoped he was

wrong, because if the tall blonde standing frozen in front of Aquila's enclosure was Katie, Bridget's was in trouble.

"Katie," Jasper said sharply. "What's wrong? Are you all right?"

Aquila paced, venting his displeasure with a twitching tail. Even as Luke slowly moved toward the woman, he changed his mind about them being in trouble.

Because the woman, who surely had to be Katie, had certainly inspired Aquila. The cat was agitated, moving, responding—even if Katie wasn't.

She didn't move, not even her fingers that were clenched into fists. Luke moved even closer to her, careful not to make a sound or an abrupt move. He knew how to work with people facing an adversary. His sister Bridget had faced more than her share. Bridget was no stranger to making fists and she'd known how to use them.

Gently, he took Katie by the shoulder and turned her around so she faced him. He waited until her eyes focused on him.

"Are you all right?" he repeated Jasper's words.

She shook her head. Long blond hair went right and left. She was just an inch shorter than he was and pale. Luke's gaze took in her tennis shoes, no tread; her jeans and shirt, not protective; her nails, manicured and painted green; and up to her face.

He'd been right the first time; Bridget's was in a world of trouble. Katie Vincent hadn't been joking when she said he was asking the impossible. Because above the strong chin and too-full lips were her green eyes. They focused on him for only a moment before turning to look at Aquila again.

The expression in them was abject terror.

CHAPTER THREE

KATIE CLUTCHED THE gritty edge of a cement bench and kept her eyes closed, trying to shut out a splitting headache and the voices.

The headache would go away; hopefully the world would stop tilting, too. But she had a feeling the voices were here to stay. The first voice, the one doing most of the talking, was Luke Rittenhouse. At least he didn't sound so annoyed this time.

She carefully opened one eye to a slit.

He wasn't what she expected. For one thing, he was better looking than his website photos suggested and closer to her age. She'd figured he was older. For another, he was looking at her and not at Aquila.

Her father, had she interrupted his day by wimping out, would have put her in the hands of an employee and gone back to work.

"Katie, you all right?" Jasper inched over, right next to Luke.

Katie closed her eyes again. She wasn't ready to deal with this, with him.

His voice hadn't changed. It was still twangy and gravelly and soothing.

"She's going to be fine," the third man said, sitting beside her. This was the only voice she didn't recognize. He felt the back of her head. "Not even a bump."

Somebody else sat down next to her and patted her on the shoulder. She knew it wouldn't be Jasper. He had a master touch when it came to animals but didn't have a clue when it came to humans. Surely it wasn't Luke. Yet, even before she opened her eyes a nano-slit, she knew it was him. He seemed like a take-charge kind of guy.

She was right.

"How long have you been afraid of animals?" Luke asked.

Katie opened her eyes and stared down at her tennis shoes. She wasn't quite ready to meet Luke's gaze. She'd expected a fifty-something, gruff, hard-edged keeper. Instead, she got a thirty-something, rugged, almost Indiana-Jones perfect—a young Indiana-Jones keeper.

"I'm not afraid," she said. "I'm just surprised by how big Aquila's gotten."

From behind her, she heard Jasper snort. Luke just looked at her; his mouth didn't change from a straight line. "Liar," he said.

"It's been more than a decade since I've been around exotic animals," Katie protested, finally looking Luke full in the face. "I didn't know how I'd react when…"

"You mean you didn't know you were afraid?" Luke supplied.

"I'm not sure I *am* afraid. Maybe more like unwilling to find out."

"You aren't afraid of anything, little girl," Jasper said. "What's really bothering you?"

Katie glanced away. It had seemed like such a good idea, to come in alone and assess Aquila without any gawking eyes.

When she'd arrived at Bridget's AZ Animal Adventure, there'd been maybe five cars in the parking lot. A strange-looking man had sat cross-legged in front of the entrance. He'd smiled, asked her name, seemed to recognize it and then offered her a paintbrush. When she turned it down, he'd opened the gate and told her how to find Aquila.

Walking into Bridget's, she'd had an almost ethereal sense of déjà vu.

All she could think, with each step, was how the smell of animals never changed, and how the morning sun seemed more pronounced when there was a vital job to do—like taking care of animals.

Katie had never felt more needed, more confident, than when she'd been taking care of Aquila and Tyre. Taking care of Janie wasn't the same. Katie had been scared to death when, at eighteen, she'd become the guardian of her twelve-year-old sister.

To this day, she was terrified she'd mess up with Janie.

She'd never been scared with Aquila.

Until today.

She looked at Aquila and remembered his brother, Tyre, remembered what a big cat looked like with blood dripping from his mouth onto the ground.

"I'll be all right," she said forcefully. "Maybe it's that I've been awake all night, driving. Maybe it's the worry of being unemployed—"

"We'll find a way to compensate you for your help."

She felt her voice growing tight. "Maybe it's the fear that I can't do whatever it is you want me to do."

"Just get Aquila to eat," Luke said. "That's all we want. He's losing too much weight. If we don't do something soon, we'll lose him."

Now that her eyes were open, Katie could see Aquila pacing back and forth in front of the fence. Every step was agitated. His skin sagged more than it should. His gait was slower than it should be. A decade out of the business and Katie could still spot what John Q. Public would miss.

Aquila wasn't himself. He wasn't holding his head quite as high as normal, his steps weren't as stable. For a moment, she wanted to enter the cage, stroke the satiny fur. Hear Aquila purr.

But after a decade away, she couldn't do that, even if she wanted. It would break every rule her father and Jasper had instilled in her.

And it might break Katie.

But that attitude wouldn't get the job done— and it wouldn't get her home any faster. Aquila might need her, but Janie needed her even more. She couldn't help one without helping the other. No matter what it cost her. "Okay," she said, "I'll try."

She felt a hand land on her shoulder and awkwardly squeeze.

Jasper's fingers were brown and blunt. His nails as short as could be. She'd always believed him to be stronger than her father. Maybe because her dad always seemed to need help, but Jasper, with just a word or the touch of his hand, could get the animals to do anything. "Have you eaten? How's Janie?"

Katie laughed. "You still have a way with words. I stopped about an hour ago and had a doughnut. Janie's fine. She's a freshman in college."

"She okay by herself?"

"We'll find out, won't we?" Katie reached

up and patted Jasper's hand; he squeezed her fingers as he helped her to her feet. She managed not to fall as she repeated, "I'll help, Mr. Rittenhouse."

"You can call me Luke." He didn't look convinced she could really help, though. "How about I show you around Bridget's first? Let you get a feel for the place."

As she fell into step beside Luke and Jasper, Katie tried to tell herself she felt relieved because she was tired, not because she didn't want to face Aquila yet. But she knew the truth—she was a screwup waiting to happen—and welcomed any reprieve that gave her time to regroup.

"We open in an hour," Luke said. "Saturday's our busiest day. We're hoping to get at least five hundred visitors today. That's more than double what we got before your dad's animals."

Katie's headache wasn't as pronounced now as she followed him down a path painted with cat paw prints. "My dad's menagerie made that much of a difference?"

"Yes. Your father's animals and their antics are definitely bringing people in."

"Your website said you had a lion."

Luke nodded. "Terrance the Terrible. He belongs to our veteran keeper, Ruth. He weighs three hundred pounds and is twenty-five years old."

Katie whistled. "That's old."

"In lion years," Luke agreed. "He deserves not only AARP but all that goes with it. He's losing his eyesight. That's what has Ruth worried. Next week he's getting a tooth pulled. Though other than that, he's perfectly healthy—"

Jasper cleared his throat, loudly.

"Okay," Luke admitted. "Terrance also has the worst breath you can imagine. Ruth actually brushes his teeth twice a day, which he lets her do. She's going to film him getting his teeth brushed—"

Jasper cleared his throat again.

"Oh, give it up," Luke said lightly. "You know you like her."

Jasper actually blushed.

"Is it really that exciting to film a tiger being sedated and then having its teeth cleaned?"

Luke laughed, "Oh, Terrance will be awake."

"But—"

"He's the calmest lion you'll ever meet," Luke said.

"He's a wild animal," Katie insisted. "It's dangerous to—"

"Wait until you meet him."

Katie considered protesting more, convincing him of the dangers, but forced herself to stop. She'd been invited here to help with Aquila, not give advice on how to guarantee employee safety.

"My uncle Albert lived and worked here before this *was* a here," Luke continued. "Back in those days it was mostly a place to keep the few animals he had from his carnival days. Then he took in some rescued burros. My sister—"

"Bridget," Katie noted. "I read about her on your website."

He smiled. "My sister Bridget and I came down here every chance we got. Albert believed animals should just enjoy life. At first, he wouldn't even let us touch the burros, but Bridget loved them so much that soon we were riding them. Especially Cheeky."

"A camel," Jasper supplied.

"The next few years were the happiest of Bridget's life. On the weekends, her job was to take care of Cheeky. They were a perfect pair. See, Bridget liked quiet, and Cheeky is quiet. Plus, if something upset Bridget, Cheeky remained calm. The two of them would go out for a ride, and if Bridget got scared, Cheeky would turn around and head home."

"Odd for a camel, I've never considered them friendly. Yet, the way you're talking, it's as if he knew?" Katie said.

"He knew." Luke stopped in front of an exhibit and visibly relaxed.

Yes, the man was a keeper and, like Jasper and her father, more comfortable with animals than humans. He, obviously, was in his element, showing off his critters. What really surprised Katie was what Luke Rittenhouse hadn't said. He hadn't mentioned Bridget's Down Syndrome. Either he was uncomfortable talking about it, or maybe it didn't matter.

"We have two antelope jackrabbits," Luke continued as they made their way back to the front of the enclosure, "but soon we'll have more."

Next to the jackrabbits stretched a huge, fenced grassy area. In the distance, Katie could see the burros. They were busy eating, although a few were kicking up their heels, nipping at each other.

A picture of a burro pulling kids in a cart had been on Luke's webpage, clearly an attempt to attract kids—an attempt that was working.

The before-mentioned Cheeky and her father's camel, Kobie, were next. Luke hadn't mentioned Cheeky's deformity, but Katie had read about it. Cheeky immediately came to the fence and shook her three-cheeked head at Jasper.

"She's fallen in love with Jasper," Luke said. "And he's fallen in love with her."

Already Jasper was slipping behind the fence to check on Cheeky, leaving Katie alone with Luke.

She studied Jasper carefully. Her dad had definitely known Jasper's worth, but that didn't mean he'd always appreciated it. He'd been displeased by how Aquila bonded with Katie, but that had only been one animal. He'd been more than displeased by how many animals preferred Jasper to him, which was why Aquila and Tyre hadn't been in Jasper's care in the first place. Unfortunately for Janie.

Unless Luke was a really good actor, Cheeky's preference didn't bother him a bit, and he knew how to appreciate Jasper.

"Antelope jackrabbits, burros, camels…" Katie said. "You really are staying true to the A-Z theme."

"Not only A through Z, but AZ stands for Arizona, as well. We pay special attention to animals that are native."

"Like a camel?"

Luke simply pointed to the information board in front of the exhibit. "A misguided military venture. I'll tell you about it later when you're up to it and we're not in the sun." He checked his watch. "And not crunched for time before the visitors arrive."

Katie nodded. Her father was all about maximizing an animal's performance. It seemed Luke was more into their history. "So, what D animal is next?"

"The desert tortoise."

"And all this wasn't enough to keep people coming?"

"People came, once. But then it might have been years before they came again. Think about it. A burro ride is fun, but not if the only thing you get to do is watch your kids take that ride. With today's economy and mind-set, we have to provide both education and fun."

She nodded.

"To properly care for the animals and to make a livable wage for my employees, I need gate receipts—which meant I needed bigger draws."

Before Luke could say anything else about money or about the tortoises, his cell phone sounded. When he answered, Katie could make out the words *drainage problem*. Luke wasn't fazed a bit. He barked out a few questions before ending the call.

"I've got to go see about something," he said. "Are you feeling all right? I can—"

"I'm perfectly fine," Katie assured him. She had the sense he'd stay with her if she only asked him to.

"You want to roam on your own, then, and

meet me for lunch, say, so we can talk over what needs to be done?"

"I'll do that."

"You might want to talk to Ruth about a place to stay. Jasper's been like a worried uncle and thinks you should stay with her. Ruth's our senior keeper here, and she has a guesthouse on her property. I guarantee it will save you money. Plus, it's only a mile away." His phone sounded again. With a quick smile, he loped away.

The private tour was over.

Katie texted her little sister a quick note that she'd arrived safe. Then she checked her watch. She had maybe ten minutes before the front gate opened and the day's visitors arrived. She'd rather try facing her fears again without a crowd watching.

Luke's prediction came back to her: *If we don't do something soon, we'll lose him.* Aquila needed her.

It took Katie a few minutes to get her bearings in the park, but soon she was standing once again in front of Aquila's enclosure.

That's when she heard the scream. Her knees locked and before she could sit down, the world tilted.

So far, Katie Vincent was a disappointment. At least in the potential-to-help department. In the beauty department, he wasn't disappointed at all. The couch in his office had never looked so good. Tinker, his cat, didn't agree, though. She gave Katie a look of disdain and settled down on one end, close to Luke.

"She didn't faint because she's scared," Jasper said. "The girl has more grits than that. She must be hungry."

"I hope that's all it is," Luke observed dryly. "She can't weigh more than a hundred pounds." And he should know. When they'd found her in a heap, Jasper had run to get one of Bridget's carts, while Luke had picked Katie up from the walkway and gathered her close. She weighed less than Terrance the Terrible, more than the antelope jackrabbit and about what the full-grown javelina did.

She smelled better than all three.

But he didn't need a woman who smelled good. He needed one willing to roll up her sleeves and get dirty. "She's not going to be able to help with Aquila," Luke said mournfully.

"You can't give up yet," Jasper said. "She just got here."

"And she's fainted twice!" Luke argued.

Meredith came in from the break room and set a glass of water on the table next to Katie.

"Hard to believe this is Bob Vincent's daughter," Fred the vet stated drolly. "Nothing got in that man's way."

"Katie's very much his daughter," Jasper protested. "She was always right there alongside her father, couldn't have been more than four or five when she started, quite the little handler."

"I've seen the videos," Luke said.

"Her father was never one to miss a marketing opportunity," Jasper said. "She was basically in charge of Aquila while Bob worked with Tyre. A visiting journalist snapped a photo of her with Aquila, and it made it into some big-time magazine. Bob got calls from all over."

"Tyre was the aggressive one," Luke remembered.

"Yes, Aquila's litter mate. I told you about him. He's the one who attacked Janie. Bob sold him years ago. Not sure exactly where he finally landed."

Luke remembered the conversation about Tyre. There'd been a few articles written about the attack, as well, mostly of the wild-animals-and-small-children-do-not-mix slant. Not one article, though, said exactly how the little girl had been hurt or why both girls had been sent away—unless Bob Vincent had suddenly bought into that opinion that wild animals and small children do not mix.

Jasper hadn't been exactly forthcoming about the attack, either.

"Maybe you ought to think about doing some videos," Meredith suggested. "A before-and-after feature about Aquila. Get some advertising for Bridget's."

"Katie always took a good photo." Jasper brushed the hair away from Katie's forehead.

"Right now," Luke said drolly, "the only picture a magazine would get would be of her fainting and me picking her up."

"And of a very skinny panther," Meredith added.

"Katie will come around," Jasper insisted.

"She didn't faint before, when you knew her?"

"Not once," Jasper said.

"Could it be exhaustion?" Luke asked the vet.

Fred shrugged, "I think you should take her to the walk-in clinic. Get a real opinion."

"It's not exhaustion."

All three men turned at the sound of Katie's voice. Her eyes, a somber shade of green, were now open. She sat up with Jasper's help. Tinker jumped off the couch, gave an indignant meow and walked over to settle on Luke's desk.

"Then what is it?" Luke couldn't keep the impatience from his voice. Bridget's opened in ten minutes. He'd not done rounds or even checked to make sure his crew was in place. Instead, he'd been saving the woman who was supposed to be saving him.

"I heard someone scream."

"You probably heard a peacock," Luke said. "Do you know what a peacock sounds like?"

She shook her head.

"Are the memories that bad?" Jasper asked softly.

"What memories?" Luke interjected.

"The memories are that bad," Katie whispered.

"Katie, the attack wasn't your fault. Your daddy gave you way too much responsibility, and he should have been watching over you. Give it time. Your confidence will come back to you. Like riding a bike."

Clearly Luke should have demanded that Jasper fill him in on exactly what had happened that long-ago day. Secrets didn't belong in a wild animal park. They could get you killed. "I thought Janie barely had a scar?" Luke said. "You said they got her to the doctor in time. I realize that's why your father sent you to live with an aunt, but your sister is fine, right?"

Katie and Jasper exchanged a look, one Luke couldn't read. Finally, Katie nodded but didn't look convinced.

"Not your fault, little girl," Jasper repeated. "Tyre was always a bad-tempered cat."

Fault?

"Jasper, what are you trying to say?" Luke was losing patience. It was quickly becoming clear that Jasper had left out a few vital pieces of the story, especially when he'd claimed Katie Vincent could deal with Aquila. "I didn't buy a cat named Tyre. I bought one named Aquila. Why would anything be Katie's fault?"

"What he's trying to tell you," Katie said, her voice getting clearer and red spots appearing on cheeks that had previously been white, "is that I'm not afraid of Aquila, or of what Aquila might do. I'm afraid of what *I* might do."

"Lady, you're going to need to be a little clearer because I'm not getting the picture here."

Her eyes closed once more. For a moment, he thought he'd lost her again. Then, almost as if she were talking to herself, she said, "I'd just finished working with Tyre and something distracted me. I don't even remember what. But I left the pen, just for a minute. Next thing I knew there was a snarling sound and screams. My little sister's screams."

"She'd wandered into the cage," Jasper explained, as if Luke couldn't figure it out.

"She thought I was there," Katie said. "Janie always followed me around. Next thing I knew, there she was on the ground and Tyre was at her throat."

"So why is that your fault?" Luke asked.

"I left the gate open."

CHAPTER FOUR

To LUKE'S CREDIT, he didn't offer platitudes. He simply said, "Well, she's fine now, right?"

Typical male.

Unfortunately, he then shot Jasper a questioning look that Katie interpreted as *She left the gate open!*

"Katie was only twelve," Jasper defended.

"And I knew better!" Katie insisted.

"*And* had way more responsibility than you should have had." Jasper said the words matter-of-factly, as if they should be believed and accepted. Judging by the nods of the listeners, after just six short months of being with the park, Jasper's word already held a lot of weight. "And Bob wasn't running a zoo. He didn't answer to the American Zoological Association. He had laws to follow, but those weren't nearly as stringent as the ones we have to follow here because we're open to the public. There were no double gates on Tyre's enclosure, or anything."

Katie protested, "Janie was only six. I was supposed to watch over her."

Luke took back the conversation by repeating, "Well, she's fine now, right?"

Today, at least, Janie was probably more "fine" than Katie.

"She's no doubt stocking the refrigerator and inviting friends over," Katie agreed. "And already planning to trash our apartment while I'm here instead of watching her."

Luke merely harrumphed. *He* obviously didn't have a sister living with—

Katie immediately felt a moment's guilt. He didn't have a sister, because Bridget had died. No doubt he'd love to be worrying about a trashed house instead of a house that was too quiet.

Of course, no man this good-looking, this nice, had a house that was too quiet. He probably had the wife and two-point-five kids.

He wasn't wearing a ring, though. Mind you, her dad hadn't worn one, either. He said it deterred attention from the female demographic.

Katie glanced around the room, wishing she were back home, wishing she'd thought to stop and get a motel room, wishing she were anywhere but here in a small office, packed with Luke, Jasper, Fred the vet and a thirtysomething female she'd yet to officially meet.

And a small black-and-white cat sitting at attention on Luke Rittenhouse's desk.

"I think I just need to rest," Katie finally said.

Jasper patted her hand awkwardly and left the room.

"That couch isn't very comfortable," the other woman said.

"Hey," Luke protested, "it's plenty comfortable when you pull out the Hide-A-Bed."

"Which we're not doing today," the woman scolded, an edge to her voice. "Don't even think about it."

Katie agreed. No way could she sleep here. Outside Luke's office, she could hear the sounds of animals beginning their day. Birds provided background chatter, bison or maybe an antelope lowed and in the distance she could hear the hum of machinery testifying to the presence of humans.

It was like going back in time more than a decade and waking up twelve years old.

A time she didn't want to go back to.

"She needs time to acclimate." This came from the edgy-voiced woman in the room.

"You must be Meredith," Katie said. "We spoke on the phone."

"Yes, I'm one of the keepers."

Jasper returned and handed Katie a glass of water. "I've talked to Ruth. She's on her way in from the horse arena. She says to call her when you're ready to go. She'll take good care of you."

"I just need to get into town, find a motel and get some sleep. Really, I don't want to be a bother."

"We're all about saving money," Jasper said. "Not a bother at all. You're like family."

"Family?" Things were happening too quickly and Katie felt as if she was losing ground she couldn't regain. Worse, people she didn't even know were offering help she hadn't asked for.

Because when people offered to help, they expected something in return. Usually at a cost Katie couldn't afford. She looked Jasper in the eye and said, "Family? You've got to be kidding?"

Jasper flinched, just barely, enough for Katie to see but not the others.

"No," Meredith said, "we're not kidding. You're here to help Aquila. We'll do anything we can to assist you. Ruth only lives a mile away."

"It's the best choice, Katie." Jasper's words were soft, humble.

Katie didn't like being pushed into making a decision. She'd learned the hard way to make her own choices, and not to rely on anyone else—including those she considered family. And here Jasper was, trying to send her away.

Just as he'd done before.

She closed her eyes, remembering Jasper

driving her and Janie to the bus terminal, carrying their suitcases to the cashier dock, leading them to a long line of strangers all looking as though wherever they were heading was worse than where they were at. In all fairness, he hadn't known that Aunt Betsy was an alcoholic who would take the money Bob sent her each month and spend it on everything but the two girls.

Like her, he'd assumed the change would be temporary until Bob came to his senses.

But when the weeks turned into months and then a year...

He wasn't one to cozy up to a cell phone or an email account, at least all those years ago. Of course, she'd not had one, either. And he'd not responded to any of the letters she'd written.

"You'll like Ruth," Jasper said.

"And if you don't like me, you can bunk with Jasper. But I guarantee I smell better." Ruth Moore walked into the office as if she owned it. Everyone visibly relaxed. The vet seemed to take her presence as some sort of permission to leave. As for Jasper, he looked at her with an expression on his face that he usually reserved for his favorite animals.

Katie used to receive that look. Not this trip. She didn't deserve it, anyway. She wasn't going to be able to do what he asked and help Aquila.

In a matter of minutes, Ruth had Katie up and out the door and into a Lincoln Town Car. The fancy car looked as if it should drive presidents, but instead it had a blanket spread across the backseat, cat hair on the floorboards and smelled of cat, big cat.

The green Christmas tree freshener hanging from the rearview mirror was wasted.

Katie shifted uncomfortably. "You know, I'd be just fine at a motel."

"Probably, but my place is closer."

"I could follow you in my car, at least."

"The fainting worries me. Better safe than sorry. We can fetch your car later."

In the animal world, there were two kinds of caretakers: those who got along better with animals than people, and those who could do both. Ruth must be the first kind.

"I appreciate you letting me stay at your place."

Ruth pushed her glasses up higher on her nose and said, "I'll do anything I can to help Aquila. He's a good cat and deserves a chance."

Katie could only nod. She'd pegged Ruth correctly.

And Katie was getting one message loud and

clear. These people wanted Aquila better and they expected her to accomplish it.

A moment later, Katie and Ruth pulled into a circular driveway meant for a dozen cars. Ruth lived just a five-minute drive from the zoo in an adobe home built on enough acres to start her own zoo.

"I used to have Terrance here," Ruth confided. "If I had my way, I'd still have him and maybe more."

"I understand," Katie murmured, trying not to sound disapproving.

Ruth probably didn't have a clue how much Katie understood. Katie's childhood had revolved around how the land would best house the animals and how the paychecks would best feed and care for them. Any extra money was earmarked for the next animal. Not that Katie would have asked for it, but there'd never been talk of putting something aside for her and Janie's college expenses.

Which was another reason why the sale of Bob's estate had been so necessary. Katie had her own bills to pay and had been worried about Janie's college expenses. And for a brief but blessed period, before Luke Rittenhouse's phone call, Katie hadn't worried.

Her father's death had provided a stability the man himself had never offered.

"This place is really too big for me," Ruth went on. "My husband liked to entertain. He purchased Terrance for that reason. He thought Terrance would be a great showpiece. He was surprised when I fell in love with the beast."

"A lion's a pretty expensive showpiece," Katie commented.

"Grant didn't care."

Judging by the size of their house, Katie believed her.

"Is it all right with your husband that I'm staying in your guesthouse? I mean, you don't really know me."

"Jasper knows you. That's good enough for me. Plus, you'll be helping with Aquila. As for my husband, he's been dead for seven years, and I don't miss him a bit. Turned out he got me for the same reason he got Terrance. He thought I was a good showpiece."

"How long were you married?"

"Thirty-two years."

"That's a long time to keep a showpiece."

"He didn't dare get rid of me. After just ten years of marriage, I knew where his bodies were buried."

Looking at the expanse of desert that made up Ruth's front yard, Katie figured the bodies could all be buried right here and no one would ever find them.

"Until we find out why you've been fainting, I don't want you in the guesthouse. You can have one of the guest rooms upstairs and to the right. Take a shower, get something to eat and enjoy a nap."

She led Katie to a room bigger than Katie's apartment back in Dallas. She disappeared for a moment, returning with a clean, albeit too big, T-shirt and robe.

"I'll be heading back to Bridget's. I have a tour to guide this afternoon," Ruth said. "I'm leaving my cell number here by the phone. If you need anything, just call. Now take a shower and get some sleep. You'll feel better in no time."

Then she patted Katie on the shoulder and was gone, leaving Katie feeling very much alone.

"Luke Rittenhouse," Katie whispered, "I hope you're already considering plan B, because if I'm plan A, it's already failed."

THE DAY HAD started atypically with a crisis of the human kind instead of the animal kind. Even so, as Luke finally made it through his morning routine, he took satisfaction in noting that the keepers and other employees were doing their jobs, the gift shop and concessions had their doors open, the front gate was manned and had a line and the animals were being cared for.

At two, Luke stood in line—always a good sign—and purchased a hot dog from one of the venders and made his way to Aquila's enclosure.

"You need to eat better," Ruth admonished Luke as he finished the last bite. He wasn't surprised to see her there, sitting on the bench just watching. She loved all the animals, except possibly the snakes, but the cats were her favorites.

"You get Katie settled in?"

"Dropped her off, showed her the guest room, came back here. I was only gone about ten minutes."

"You could have taken some time off and helped her out a bit." For some reason, he had to know Katie was taken care of. She was so feminine, so sensitive.

"I'm pretty sure she just needs sleep and maybe someone to watch out for her."

Luke hoped sleep would do the trick. As for needing someone to look out for her, he was a little worried about how many times he'd wanted to do just that.

If she'd simply stayed in his office and slept on the couch, he'd know she was all right. Ruth's was a mile away and Katie was there alone.

"Look. Aquila's just lying there." Ruth interrupted his thoughts. She adjusted her glasses, the same light blue shade as the BAA shirt she wore, and squinted as if hoping the view would change. "I liked it better this morning when he was disgruntled, pacing back and forth."

"I'll take either way as long as we can get some weight on him."

"What do we try next?" Ruth wasn't one to give up, but the fact that she even asked the question told Luke that she was out of ideas.

"I'm working on it."

"I believed Jasper," Ruth muttered. "He said she was a natural with animals, even better than her father."

High praise since Katie hadn't yet been a teen the last time Jasper had worked with her.

Ruth's radio sounded before Luke could respond. Meredith's voice crackled over the line. "Ruth, you've got a group of Red Hat Ladies waiting for you at the store."

"Ah, right on time. See you later." Ruth loped off, ready to meet her friends and show them her babies, Terrance and the animal park.

Luke watched her head back toward the front, weaving between the afternoon visitors, stopping occasionally to answer a question or give a direction.

If she were forty years younger, she'd be the perfect woman for him.

The thought gave him pause—what woman *would* be perfect for him?

It certainly wasn't Katie Vincent. He'd truly expected her to have a change of heart the minute she saw Aquila. He expected her to work miracles, the way Ruth did.

Deep down, he'd been hoping she'd be able to do more for them based on all Jasper had shared. Maybe he'd been hoping that Katie Vincent was someone like her dad, and would be able to miraculously solve all of Bridget's problems.

He could use a miracle.

But he'd been wrong to even let his thoughts go in that direction. And, come to think of it, Jasper had been very careful about what he shared—and even more careful about what he *hadn't* shared—when it came to Katie.

But, in his heart, Luke wanted *this* miracle, *this* woman. The one who felt such responsibility. The one who carried the weight of the world on her shoulders. The one who made him want to scoop her up and convince her all was well with the universe.

But with an animal dying and a park on the brink of disaster, she wasn't the one he needed. He needed someone who loved and worked with animals, as he did.

Someone who understood about a labor of love.

He'd learned a long time ago, two years to be exact, that most women didn't understand how much of himself he had to devote to Bridget's. They wanted the "labor of love" to be them, not an animal park— Especially not an animal park that required a 24/7 work schedule.

He'd wanted a miracle for his sister Bridget but that hadn't happened, either. He started to close his eyes when he heard—

"I'm back, and I'm not going to faint."

Standing next to Aquila's wall, she looked better than she had this morning. Not so pale. The jeans were still tight, and the green button-down shirt was even more wrinkled. But this time Katie Vincent had a determined fire in her eyes.

He reminded himself that he could not afford to be impressed with her looks, no matter how much he noticed them, and he was just as determined. "Prove it."

He watched her take a deep breath before she turned to the enclosure and stepped closer.

To the common observer, Aquila, lying on a heated spot in the grass, would appear oblivious of his surroundings.

Luke knew better.

Just this morning, for the first time in a week, Aquila had been active. Even now, Aquila's ears were up—not moving, but definitely at attention. His shoulder blades, too, were raised just a hair. His tail had the slightest twitch. Luke wondered if Katie noticed the tension. He couldn't tell. When she finally did say something, it wasn't what Luke expected.

"He looks lonely."

"Panthers are solitary."

"I know that, but Aquila always had my dad, me, Jasper, somebody stopping by to play with him."

"I don't think it's been that way for quite a while," Luke said. "When I purchased your father's animals, Aquila was the only cat your father still had, and Jasper said none of the animals had been out on a shoot in over a year."

"When I was twelve, my father had seven big cats."

"At the end, he only kept the ones that were making money."

She nodded. "I realized how few animals he had left when I read Jasper's accounting after the will was read," she said softly. "Of course, by the paperwork I couldn't tell if he'd kept the performers or his favorites. But, then, the performers always were his favorites."

"Did you know he was sick?"

"Aquila wasn't sick when—"

"I mean your dad. Did you know he was sick?"

Determination gave way to wariness. "No, I didn't."

"Why did you—?"

"What should Aquila weigh now? About one fifty?"

Luke let her change the subject. "Near enough."

He stayed on the bench and gave Katie time to just watch Aquila. She moved close to the cement wall, oblivious of the people around her and the sounds of an animal kingdom. Eventually she relaxed enough to rest her arms on the top which was just above her waist. On the other side of the wall was an empty moat wide enough to deter Aquila should he decide to jump. But if the animal-enclosure architect had done his job—and Luke had paid him a pretty penny, so he better have—then the wire that guarded the moat would keep Aquila from even thinking jumping was an option.

"He's never had such a big place to roam," Katie observed when the crowds had passed.

"I'm not much of a cage man."

"My father liked them—they were easy and cost-effective."

She didn't sound as if she approved. Unfortunately she wasn't looking at Aquila's new digs as if they were much of an improvement.

The enclosure Aquila resided in now was meant to resemble nature as best it could. Aquila had grass, vegetation and scratching logs. He had a wooden structure with a roof that he could lie under if he wanted shade, or lie on top of if he wanted sun. Best of all, he had a pool.

Luke had a pool, too, or at least his apartment complex came with one. But he wasn't home enough to use it.

Katie remained quiet for a bit, then turned to look at him. "You know, there were people who said we should have put both cubs down. That it was cruel to keep them alive if they'd be in captivity their whole life."

He didn't know what to say, and doubted she'd be happy with his answer, regardless of whether he agreed with her or not. She looked so lost, so melancholy. He was half-afraid if he said the wrong thing, she'd turn and run. She seemed to be looking at or for something that wasn't there. He had a sudden strong urge to stand behind her, wrap his arms around her and say, "It'll be okay."

He'd done that many times for Bridget. And more often than not, the lost expression evaporated into joy.

What would Katie Vincent look like with a joyful heart?

Instead of moving toward her, however, he said, "Aquila could be content here. We started work on this enclosure two years ago, adding to it whenever we had the money. Finally, when it was finished, we went searching for the right cat to fill it."

"Did you know exactly what you were searching for?"

"No, I just knew I wanted another big cat, a bit younger than Terrance the Terrible. We have the mountain lions and the cougar, but they're fairly common in Arizona. I wanted a jaguar. Arizona is the last state with any left in the wild. But I thought I could settle for a big cat that was a bit more exotic, a bit more comfortable with humans and one that came with a history. A big draw for the park. Aquila fit that bill exactly, or he would if…"

She shuddered and he knew he'd hit a hot spot.

"If you take an Arizona jaguar out of the wild and bring him here," Katie said, "soon there will be none left in the wild."

"I agree, which is why Aquila was perfect," he said easily, realizing that while she claimed not to have had contact with wild animals for the last decade, her heart and opinion had remained sympathetic to their plight.

He continued, watching her eyes while he spoke, hoping to convince her that they were on the same side, at least when it came to acquiring animals.

"We rehabilitate here. The animals we keep are ones, like Aquila, who have been in captivity for so long they wouldn't survive in the wild. Plus, I don't have a jaguar, and even if one became available I couldn't..."

When he didn't continue, she said, "Couldn't?"

But he wasn't ready to admit that even should a jaguar become available, they couldn't afford it. So he changed the subject to Terrance, hoping to distract her from a question he didn't want to answer.

"Like Aquila, Terrance is also a big draw and is comfortable with humans, but he was raised as if he were Ruth's child. He still wants to sit on her lap. The kids love him. My sister loved him. He's had the wild trained right out of him. He's leash-trained."

Katie shook her head, every expression indicating she wasn't impressed with Terrance's rearing. A little surprising since usually only the hard-core animal activists were distressed over Terrance.

But her words were curt. "Don't ever think that Terrance is anything but wild. You can take the cat out of the jungle, but you can't take the jungle out of the cat. Doesn't matter the age. Surely Jasper told you this."

"Jasper has, over and over. But when you meet Terrance, you'll see what I mean."

Katie frowned, seemed to shake herself out of whatever argument she'd been about to make and said, "I doubt that. At the same time, I have to admit that Aquila and the others have a good home here, so I'm glad you took an interest in my father's animals. You're like him. He was always looking for an animal's potential, always looking for something to sell. Sometimes it got in the way of common sense, though."

A family joined them and a stroller separated Luke from Katie. As the dad read aloud the plaque in front of Aquila's enclosure, the family crowded close, hoping to see the cat move.

Aquila was as still as Katie, though, both lost in their own thoughts.

"I wish I could have met your dad," Luke said.

"You probably would have got along well." She didn't look at him when she said the words, and for some reason it bothered him.

Even though he'd never met her father, Luke doubted they were much alike outside of their profession. He'd never have sent his children off to be raised by a relative. He, like every employee here, loved the animals, but not over family.

A missed softball game or romantic dinner was one thing. A missed childhood another.

"I—" Before he could tell her how unfair the

comparison was, yet another family joined them and an additional stroller separated Luke from Katie.

The two parents hoisted their little ones up for a better look, encouraging the kids to find the panther. The little girl located Aquila first, although the little boy tried to take credit, too.

"Pretty," the little boy said.

The father of the group dutifully read the plaque in front of the exhibit: *Aquila is from Africa. Although called a black panther, he is really a black leopard. He is fifteen years old and can dance to "Girls Just Want to Have Fun."*

Luke hadn't had time to come up with decent copy for Aquila's inscription, and Adam hadn't yet painted him on the wall in front of the animal park. It didn't matter. Aquila was a draw. Even now the family lingered. Aquila was doing his part, without a single movement, to help keep Bridget's AZ Animal Adventure going.

If only they could keep him alive.

As a privately owned animal park, Bridget's received no state money, so Luke was constantly double-checking the figures. They earned money from admissions and concessions, but the lifeblood of Bridget's was donations given by families, corporations and nonprofit groups.

He needed to keep the investors happy, show them that Bridget's was a well-run, growing operation. He had to support the animals and the people who worked for him.

Her father had had to support the animals, too, but the fact that they'd lived in cages said it all. They were half of the equation. The other half being Bob himself and the attention *he* craved.

Jasper had been his only long-term employee.

When the family closest to him and Katie moved on, Luke sat beside her on the bench. "I went online and found some YouTube videos of your dad."

She didn't act surprised. "There's probably plenty. His second-favorite place was in front of a camera."

"What was his first?"

"In front of a live audience."

Luke believed her. In the clips, he'd watched Bob Vincent brighten under the spotlight and at the attention of the late-night hosts. He hadn't seem to notice that the late-night hosts were more focused on Ollie, the orangutan, who actually served tea; George, the brown bear, who weighed in at six hundred pounds and would join Ollie at the table—not to have tea but to hold hands! As for Candy, the spider monkey, she gathered up the teacups and arranged them on the talk show hosts' desks.

Oh, the hosts were very glad Bob was there—to stand between them and the wild animals.

"You were in a few of those clips, looking very young and very serious."

"I was always scared to death."

"You didn't look it."

"I was taught to never show fear, never run. On that stage, I had an important job, especially with Aquila, who was my charge. I had to make sure he didn't get frightened or feel like he was being backed into a corner. I made sure all my movements were calm and I was as still as possible."

"I only saw a few clips with Aquila. He never left the cage."

"That always pissed my dad off. Tyre wasn't responding to Dad's training. And though Aquila and I were doing great, because of my age and some laws, I couldn't handle him during a live show."

"That explains why I saw Aquila attempting to dance to 'Girls Just Want to Have Fun' in a cage where he didn't have enough room to turn."

Katie laughed, letting down her guard for a moment. "I remember that show. Aquila didn't really get to dance. It was more like he backed up, raised his shoulders, backed up some more and then playfully leaped forward."

"He stole the show with his haughty 'I don't have to act cute, I am cute' attitude."

"That he did," Katie agreed.

Luke had watched the clips, trying to understand the man and his techniques. It only took a few clips for Luke to realize how distant Bob was. He used a clicker to give commands to the animals. He touched them, but not much. And, unlike the animal lovers Luke knew, Bob was more aware of where the cameras were than what the animals were doing.

Katie, meanwhile, had interacted with the animals. She'd smiled while accepting pretend tea from Ollie. She'd gently put a napkin on George's lap and held his hand while she did it. She'd helped Candy, their spider monkey, clean up the cups.

But anyone watching could see that her smile grew wider and her face truly lit up when she was with Aquila. She'd quietly danced right along with the cat, up close to the cage, comfortable in a way her father wasn't.

Aquila was her love.

But she'd clearly not been posing for the audience like her father. She didn't even look at the cameras. She'd not been selling the animals and their tricks to the public.

"You didn't care for it much, did you?" Luke

asked when the family changed their position, vying for a better viewing spot.

"What?"

"Being on television with the animals."

She gave a half grimace. "Why do you say that?"

"In the clips I watched, you were always quiet, elegant and willing to do whatever the animals needed, but you never seemed comfortable."

"No, the lights were always hot, and the animals, except for Candy, were always disgruntled and off their routine. I was always afraid something would go wrong because the people around us weren't animal people. Once, a secretary moved to pet Aquila's mom. She'd have lost a finger if my father hadn't stopped her. We had signs warning people not to approach the animals without talking to my father first, but it's as if people thought the signs didn't apply to them."

The family with the stroller finished taking pictures and moved on. Katie, back to being tense, still watched Aquila. After a moment, she said, "I don't think panthers were meant to be performers. My father should have figured that out with his mother. She was beautiful, which is why he kept her, but she wouldn't be trained. The only thing she did to earn money was let people look at her and give birth to two cubs that made it out of infancy. That's when my father finally made some money on her. He sold the photographs to every magazine and news show that promised a check."

"I've never seen them, but I hear you were in quite a few of those photographs," Luke said.

"Like anything in my father's menagerie, I didn't get a choice. He said 'Smile' and I smiled."

"We don't focus on tricks here," Luke said. "We focus instead on natural behaviors. If an animal wouldn't have the behavior in the wild, we don't develop the behavior here. The only exceptions are the animals, like yours, that come to us with learned behaviors. And as long as it doesn't endanger the animal or people, we appreciate their skill. If a bear juggling lunch boxes will increase revenue so we can have enough food, medical care and personnel, we encourage them to perform."

She nodded but didn't comment.

"By the way, when you let your guard down in those films, like when you were dancing with Aquila, you had the audience eating out of your hands. You were quite good in front of the cameras, and some of those long-ago smiles actually seemed real. I think you protest too much. Maybe working with animals and showcasing what they can do is in your blood. If not, you could have fooled me."

She pushed away from the wall, arms tight to her sides. Looking him right in the eye, she said, "Maybe you're easy to fool."

She stood, muttering something about exploitation and fools.

He formulated a comeback, only by the time he said the words aloud, she was too far away to hear them: "I may be a fool, but unlike in those clips, you haven't smiled once since I've met you."

CHAPTER FIVE

SHE SHOULD HAVE resisted Luke more. Taking time off work, coming here, thinking she could make a difference, it was all a farce.

And, for some reason, Luke Rittenhouse refused to see it or believe it.

The man was nuts.

No, *she* was nuts for even attempting it.

But she couldn't shake the memory of how thin Aquila was and how unstable he was on his feet. After walking away from Luke and Aquila, she'd left Bridget's AZ Animal Adventure, just got in her car and drove. She didn't have a destination. Her only goal was to clear her head.

She had half a mind to just head home to Texas. Her suitcases were still in the back.

But giving up was not in Katie's nature. If it was, she'd never have been awarded custody of her little sister. Most eighteen-year-olds wouldn't want the job of taking on a twelve-year-old.

But instead of Texas, Katie headed into town. She explored the area for a good hour be-

fore feeling comfortable with it. The town of
Scorpion Ridge was one main thoroughfare
of businesses and then a square neighborhood
of houses that either nestled or climbed up the
Santa Catalina Mountains. Close to Interstate 10
was an RV park that spread for miles. There
were a few ranches, some working, some guest.
Katie hadn't noticed any of it this morning.
She'd been too focused on her destination and
too tired to care.

Although a small town, it didn't have the
Saturday-night-roll-up-the-sidewalks mental-
ity. Arizona clearly hadn't heard that October
was supposed to be cold. Instead, the early evening felt like the end of a perfect summer day,
complete with a breeze.

Katie was tempted to get out of the car and
walk, just for the fun of it, but she'd already
walked once today—all the way from Ruth's
house to Bridget's.

She suddenly realized she hadn't eaten since
she'd left Ruth's and it was already six in the afternoon. A tiny strip mall was to her right. She
could buy a sub sandwich and some chips, if
she wanted. It looked as if she could get a hair-
cut, too, for only nine dollars. But not a bike.
The bike store's orange neon sign blinked from
Open to Closed.

Katie couldn't remember the last time she'd ridden a bike.

Checking her watch, she figured that at Bridget's, the staff would have pushed the last of the straggling visitors out the door a couple of hours ago and would now be putting the animals to bed. The park closed at four, which Katie thought ridiculously early. It was Saturday. They should have some evening events, something to draw more people in, make more money. And tomorrow the park didn't open until noon. Even though Sunday was still the weekend!

"We care for the animals and then some of us go to church," Ruth had said when she'd asked why Bridget's didn't open earlier. "The people come after."

Go to church? A long time ago she remembered attending church with Jasper. Her father had been annoyed at what he considered the waste of time.

Ruth didn't act like it was a big deal.

Made no sense to Katie, but so far, nothing about Bridget's AZ Animal Adventure had—especially not its owner, who was way too good looking and way too easy to talk to—and not just about Aquila, either. He'd gotten her to talk about the past.

She'd not done that in years.

She stopped at a red light and pulled out her

cell phone. After punching in a number, she waited for her little sister to answer.

Loud music accompanied Janie's "Hello."

Katie bit back her first impulse, which was to start scolding. She would not accuse Janie of having a wild party. The apartment was Janie's, too, and if she wanted to have a few friends over she could, as long as she cleaned up after herself and kept up on her homework.

The traffic light turned green as Katie tried to make her "Hi" sound upbeat. "I just wanted to tell you how things were going. It's an interesting place. I've met the animal park's director. He seems nice. I've seen Aquila. He *is* losing weight. And…I don't think I can help him."

After all that, she waited for Janie's response, but only got a "Huh?"

Janie wasn't paying attention.

Katie sighted. "I just wanted to let you know things were going well."

"Good," Janie said. "I knew everything would be all right. You get Aquila to eat?"

Katie hesitated. Aquila and Bob's Backyard were not topics she and Janie discussed willingly. Though her dad's death had pushed their bitter memories back into a dreaded topic of current discussion. "It's not going to be that easy. I might need to—"

"Everything's fine here. You don't need to hurry home. Why not take some vacation time?"

Katie turned into the sub shop's parking lot and took a spot right by the front door.

"I don't have any vacation time."

"You deserve to have fun," Janie said. "And you always loved Aquila."

Yes, Katie had loved Aquila. But love was fickle, and Katie no longer trusted it. Katie had been away for so long, Aquila probably no longer trusted her, either.

"I'm staying with one of the women who helps out at the zoo." Katie looked at the number she'd written on a piece of paper. "Here's her number."

"Wait."

Katie stepped out of her vehicle while Janie went to fetch pen and paper. The sub place was half-full. Some of the people inside wore an orange band around their wrist, indicating they'd gone on the train ride at Bridget's AZ Animal Adventure.

"I'm back," Janie announced. "I couldn't find any paper, so I'm using the back of a bill."

Katie closed her eyes. "Which one?"

"Telephone."

Good, she had two weeks before she had to pay that one. But it would definitely eat into her last paycheck. "You okay for money?" Katie asked.

Janie didn't hesitate, "I need to add more money onto my printer card."

"I left forty dollars in the top desk drawer," Katie said, then gave her sister Ruth's number. She barely got the last number out before Janie needed to go. Katie told her sister she loved her and punched End. Katie thought about all the bills she needed to pay. How would they afford next month's phone bill, or next month's rent?

Luke had mentioned something about paying her...

Katie planned to explore Bridget's more tomorrow. Today, she'd only walked from the parking lot to Aquila's enclosure; then without even trying she'd made it to the director's office. Luke had started taking her on an A-Z tour, but they'd only gotten as far as D, the desert tortoise.

When she'd returned, she'd only seen the animals that were on the way to Aquila's enclosure, and then back to the parking lot.

She couldn't draw a map of the place, and if she were going to prove useful and earn some sort of stipend, she needed to at least be able to direct visitors to the restrooms.

Since helping Aquila might not be possible.

LUKE WATCHED FRED from outside the keeper's entrance to Aquila's enclosure. The vet had been inside for a good ten minutes, and Luke couldn't tell anything from a distance. The September sun was setting and the animals were starting to feel frisky as a cool, gentle breeze gave chase. Aquila had marked the space early on, and that smell along with food and sweat stayed with Luke as he tried to be patient. "Well, do you see any change?"

Fred laughed. "Your Katie's been here all of twelve hours and you expect great change."

"She's not my Katie," Luke pointed out. "She's Aquila's Katie. And, yes, I expect great change. The cat actually got agitated today. That's something."

Aquila paid no attention to them. He remained in the grass and refused to react as Fred strategically moved a tennis ball on a stick from the top of Aquila's body to the end of his tail.

"Can't check him out if he won't move, and I don't want to sedate him," Fred said. "His blood work was fine last time I checked. It's his teeth and gums I'd like to get a look at. But my gut says they're fine."

"I don't want to sedate him, either," Luke agreed. "I trust your gut. We can give Katie more time."

Fred gathered his gear. The vet had been another recruit of Ruth's when she realized that, under Luke, Bridget's was growing. Fred had been a veterinarian at a large California zoo before reaching retirement age. He hadn't wanted to retire, but he had wanted a change, so he'd left a megazoo and eight months ago had been hired on at Bridget's.

Fred, like Ruth, had embraced the job because it gave him a place to keep his chimpanzee and his African hedgehogs.

The chimpanzee had died of old age recently. The hedgehogs, however, had grown in number—they had twenty now—and had their own enclosure near the petting arena. Females lived on one side, males on the other. Of all the animals at the animal park, they were the least expensive residents. While they weren't what Luke considered a draw, they served a purpose besides being cute. During school visits, Luke carried one in his pocket and took it out when a student acted shy or scared of the other animals.

"You and Gloria got plans tonight?" Luke asked as Fred headed for his cart.

"Dinner out and then a movie. You?"

"On Monday I'm giving a talk to the Rotary Club. Thought I'd start putting it together tonight." Luke gave speeches all the time, hawking the animal park and its occupants. They were an important part of his job because if Luke spoke well, he'd inspire a group of people not just to schedule a visit to Bridget's but possibly also to donate money.

"Lately, conservation has been a hot topic, and it's the one they requested."

"Take one of the hedgehogs," Fred suggested. Luke wasn't surprised by the suggestion. "Already considering it," he said before Fred could go into all the reasons why.

Fred was a hedgehog fanatic. He'd bought his first hedgehog for his wife, Gloria, who was allergic to animals and half the time allergic to Fred, since he always came home covered in some kind of fur, feather or quill.

His wife promptly turned over the care for that hedgehog to Fred. Hedgehogs might be hypoallergenic, but they were often hosts for fleas. That didn't matter to Fred, but it mattered a great deal to Gloria. She was a nonanimal enthusiast married to an animal enthusiast. So instead, she worked in the gift shop. They would be celebrating thirty-eight years of marriage next month. Same as Luke's parents.

"I'll probably fall asleep during the movie," Fred groused. "I've been here since five. George was a little grumpy and Meredith called."

"George is always grumpy."

"Yes, but it's the end of breeding season and George didn't get any today, so he took it out on one of the trees in his enclosure. He fell. I had to give him stitches."

"Why wasn't I told?"

"Two stitches only. I put it in the logbook. Then, when your Katie got here, I forgot about it in all the hubbub. Don't worry. If it were something serious, I'd have told you. I know what a worrier you are."

"Somebody has to worry." Luke stepped from Aquila's enclosure into the caged entry and then out the final gate. Fred was already in his cart and turning the ignition.

"You need anything before I go?" Fred asked.

"No, everything looks good. The night crew has already checked in. I'll see if Meredith and Jasper need anything before they clock out. Then, I'll check out the snake house just in case."

Luke should also check up on Katie. Twice he'd taken out his cell ready to call her and twice he'd put it away, telling himself she needed time.

After searching for an hour and not finding Jasper, Luke gave up. Jasper was like a chameleon when he didn't want to be found. Neither Ruth nor Meredith knew where he was, and he wasn't answering his cell.

They didn't know where Katie was, either.

Maybe Katie and Jasper were together and Luke shouldn't interrupt.

Probably not. Most likely Jasper was taking

care of his animals and Katie was speeding toward the Arizona/New Mexico border.

"Call me when she gets to your house," Luke told Ruth.

"*If* she shows up at my house," Ruth said. "Yolanda said she made the bed but otherwise the room looked like it had never been occupied. Katie didn't leave a single personal item. Why don't you call her? See what's going on."

He should, he really should, but after the conversation they'd had by Aquila's enclosure, Luke got the feeling that leaving Katie time to lick her wounds was the best recourse. And for that, he'd need more information about her. She was as skittish as a cat trapped between two big dogs. Make the wrong move, and she'd for sure head for the border.

But make the right move, and maybe the animals at Bridget's would return the smile to her face.

He didn't know why making her smile was suddenly important to him. For some reason, Katie Vincent was getting to him. Something about the way she moved, the way she spoke about animals, all she'd accomplished as an adolescent.

Katie could bring Aquila back to health.

And just maybe Katie would do a bit of healing herself.

THE ONLY REASON Katie returned to Ruth's was that she didn't want to appear rude.

The woman had offered her home, she'd even driven Katie there, so to just walk away without saying, "Thank you," or even, "No, thank you" seemed wrong.

When Katie rang the doorbell, Ruth came to the door wearing a robe and big, brown fuzzy slippers designed to resemble lions.

She looked fairly surprised to see Katie. "We were placing bets on whether you'd headed back to Texas or not. Jasper's the winner. He said you'd stay."

"Good ol' Jasper," Katie said. "He's never been much of a gambler, you know."

"I know," Ruth said, somewhat mournfully. "Now I owe him five dollars and have to help clean Ollie's night house for a week."

After Katie grabbed her suitcase from the car, she followed Ruth again to the guest room. "Will I move to the guesthouse tomorrow?" Katie asked.

"No, for just a two-week stay, I decided to just let you sleep here in the main house. I'll leave a spare key on the counter in the morning. That way you can come and go as you please." Ruth eyed Katie's suitcase. "With just one bag, you won't make much of a mess."

"I always travel light," Katie said.

"So it seems. Well, I'm down in the living room watching television if you want to join me. I like to end my evenings with the late-night shows."

Katie's mother had done the same thing, and she'd always felt it was an honor to join her mother on the couch, cuddled up against her soft robe, and stay up past bedtime.

Katie shook her head and put her suitcase on the bed.

At the door, Ruth stopped. "I'm glad I lost," she said. "Aquila needs you."

It took only minutes to unpack. Then Katie tried Janie—no answer—before crawling under the covers. She closed her eyes, hoping to fall asleep before she thought too much about Aquila needing her.

Sleep didn't come.

Instead, she pictured a black panther. When she'd first been sent away, her dreams had often turned into nightmares of a black panther chasing her.

Too often, she'd wake up, covered in sweat, heart pounding, never knowing who she was running from.

Aquila, who needed her.

Or Tyre, who'd caused her exile.

Aquila might never have been as unpredictable as Tyre, but he was still wild. Something

Luke Rittenhouse seemed to have forgotten about all of the animals at Bridget's. And unless she got him to realize the danger and start making decisions with his head and not his heart, someone at the park would suffer the same fate as her sister...or worse.

CHAPTER SIX

DETERMINED TO FIND out all he could about Katie Vincent, Luke tracked down Jasper early on Sunday morning with Ollie the orangutan. Ollie needed a bit more attention in his new home, and Jasper didn't mind giving it. They'd been friends forever. Sitting in a white lawn chair, Jasper read a newspaper while Ollie rubbed his arm occasionally, looking for something to pick off.

Luke knew better than to come close. For one thing, Ollie considered Luke a threat, a challenge to his territory. Something the staff had already picked up on. Luke had been on the receiving end of lots of Orangutan jokes.

Truth was, Ollie didn't know Luke, and right now didn't want to. Ollie tended to beat his chest and stare at Luke, and was well aware he shouldn't stare back. His years managing Bridget's had given him a boot-camp type of training. His job usually went to someone with years of experience at zoos, shelters or at least the Humane Society. Luke's experience all came from the service animals Bridget had, the menagerie of animals he convinced his mother to let him keep, visiting this very place when his sister was young and helping his uncle Albert with the animals that were child-friendly.

He'd never been the risk taker when it came to Uncle Albert's animals. Because of Uncle Albert, though, Bridget had had a place where she felt welcomed, embraced, and where she was allowed to get close to the animals.

Luke wasn't a natural, at least not with wild animals, but he tried, and he was getting better. Louie the Iguana was proof. Louie responded to Luke and only Luke. But then, Louie's favorite thing to do was hit Luke with his tail. Not much of a response, really, but Luke liked to pretend it was.

Jasper stood, folded the newspaper and handed it to Ollie, who promptly sat in the vacant chair, opened the newspaper and appeared to be reading it.

"You want something, boss?"

"Walk with me for a while. We need to talk."

Silently, Jasper fell into step beside Luke. There was no way he was going to initiate this conversation, so Luke had to. "I want you to tell me the parts of Katie's story that you left out."

No response.

Jasper wasn't a talker, but when the boss

asked a question or gave an order, Jasper was the type of worker to respond.

"She'll never heal," Luke pressed on, "unless I can get her close to Aquila, and I can't get her close to Aquila if I don't know what's holding her back."

"It's her sister—" Jasper began.

"Already read that chapter," Luke interrupted. "There's something more."

"Her dad sent her away—"

"Yep, read that chapter, too."

"She hated living with her aunt."

"You sure that's all you want to tell me?"

Luke had known Jasper almost six months. He'd never seen the man retreat from any situation. He'd been stung by bees in George's enclosure. Kobie the camel had near bitten his finger off and still Jasper held on until the situation was under control. He'd suffered Ruth's competitive edge in silence.

But something else was going on between him and Katie, and Jasper wasn't too keen on sharing what that was.

"Why did you suggest I bring her out here, then? You're almost as miserable as she is."

Jasper shook his head.

"Fine. I'll keep after you until you tell me." Jasper didn't look convinced.

"You know I will."

Finally, Jasper said, "I do believe she can help. Cats have long memories and Katie was Aquila's mother. But…I also asked you to send for her because I need to make amends."

Not what Luke had been expecting.

"Amends? For what?"

"For not making her father do what was right and take care of his daughters. I knew those little girls from the time they were little. When Bob sent them away, Katie wrote me asking me to come get her. I knew how bad it was."

"How bad was it?"

"That woman, Bob's sister, didn't care about those girls." Jasper's words were bitter. "She spent the money Bob sent her on herself, and they didn't get enough to eat or good clothes to wear. No one watched out for them, no one cared for them."

To Jasper, who'd spent his life watching out for his charges, caring for them, there was no deeper travesty.

"I showed the letters to Bob. He said that Katie just didn't like it there and that she was only trying to get me to side with her."

"But it was the truth."

"I should have gone after them. Not given Bob the choice."

"Why didn't you?"

"Because every time I tried, the fool woman

moved. I'd write a return letter to Katie and it would come back address unknown. Then, when Bob found out I was trying to write to Katie, he told me that if I went after the girls, he'd not only fire me but accuse me of kidnapping."

Remembering the TV clips, Luke thought about the public image Bob Vincent portrayed: tall, easygoing, debonair. What a farce. While he showed off his animals, his children had been sent away. And all the while, he'd smiled for the audience, pretending to be a great man.

"For the first time in my life, I was scared," Jasper admitted.

Jasper Dunbar wasn't afraid of lions or full-grown bears or grumpy orangutans. But he'd been scared of Bob Vincent's threats.

"But I did call Social Services. They said I was only reporting neglect, not abuse, and they didn't have the manpower to investigate. The only time I ever got someone to look into Katie's situation, they couldn't find where she lived. Hard to believe in this day and age, but true. Eventually Katie stopped writing me at all."

Luke didn't know what to say.

"I've always been ashamed," Jasper whispered, "that I let it go."

Before Luke had time to ask anything else,

Jasper's radio sounded. Looking relieved, the man sprinted for the camel exhibit.

Jasper turned, though, before he opened the gate. "Put Katie to work around the place. Move her closer to Aquila gradually. She'll decide when the time is right. I promise, she won't disappoint you."

There were words unspoken, Luke knew. But now wasn't the time to press.

Jasper's slumped shoulders and heavy-laden steps didn't invite company, so Luke didn't follow.

Luke sighed. If this kept up, Jasper would soon be in the same condition as Aquila.

And Katie.

THE KNOCK CAME just after seven. Katie opened her eyes, looked at the clock and closed her eyes again, trying to remember where she was.

But whoever was at the door wasn't to be deterred. "Katie," came a voice, "Miss Ruth said I was to wake you if you slept past seven."

Katie rolled from the bed, wishing she'd thought to bring a robe, and headed for the door. She opened it to a young Hispanic woman who looked impatient.

"I'm Yolanda. I'm supposed to tell you that work starts at eight-thirty. Ruth let you sleep because she figured you might need it."

"I never sleep this late," Katie said. "Thanks for waking me."

"Miss Ruth said to help yourself to cereal," Yolanda finished, her voice fading as she walked away, "or whatever else you want."

Katie dressed, ate alone at the kitchen counter and, an hour later, arrived at the zoo, determined to find Luke. The same young man was working on the mural up front. Again he offered her a paintbrush. She really wished she could take it. Instead, she headed for Luke's office.

He wasn't there. The door was open, though, and Meredith—looking very comfortable behind Luke's desk—sat going over paperwork and frowning.

Katie watched for a moment. Her father had been strict. No one touched his desk, looked at his correspondence or questioned his decisions. Luke, it seemed, was a different kind of leader than Bob Vincent. But that didn't mean he was at any less risk of a catastrophe.

"Where's Tinker?" Katie said to make Meredith aware of her presence. The cat had been everywhere yesterday.

"Resting. He's really only active when Luke's here." Meredith didn't look up, but nodded in the direction of the couch Katie had been on yesterday. Plain green, obviously well used and with a cat curled in the corner. "Tinker's really,"

Meredith continued, "a one-man cat. He only tolerates the rest of us."

"So, where is Luke?" Katie asked. "Ruth said Luke would tell me what to do."

"He's either in the snake house or with the burros. Those are his areas."

Katie raised an eyebrow in question.

"I told you," Meredith said matter-of-factly, "I'm the one really in charge. Jasper's a great help but a bit too old to do everything. His job is mainly the Vincent acquisitions. Ruth takes care of all things Terrance and helps here and there. She's great with local public relations, too, knows everybody. Luke takes care of the burros and the snake house and is in charge of zoo management. He's the director, which also means he's the public relations spokesperson, the money guy, a grant writer and our marketer. I'm everything else. Luke and I, *we're a team*."

Katie got the idea that Meredith, while being friendly, was also sending a message. Maybe she and Luke were quite a team.

"He showed me a few places yesterday," Katie responded. "But not the snake house."

Meredith pointed at some pictures on the wall. "Middle one. The biggest. That's the snake house."

It was clearly a child's drawing. It featured lots of pink and green and snakes much bigger than Katie was comfortable with. Actually, the snakes were bigger than the snake house.

"Bridget drew that when she was eight. Luke built it pretty much as she imagined it. Adam painted it."

"I guess I'll look for him there, then," she said, trying to sound friendly. "Thanks."

A minute later, armed with two new light blue shirts that read *BAAA, Bridget's AZ Animal Adventure,* and with a map and directions, Katie set out for the enclosure to the right of the gift shop and next to a small arena. The snake house indeed looked like something an eight-year-old would design. In reality, it was a short, squatty snake, more a curving tunnel than a square building. It wasn't made of wood or cement; it looked carved out of clay, light pink and decorated with paintings of snakes and lizards and rocks.

She put her hand against the rough structure. Jeweled eyes and loping tongues made what shouldn't be beautiful, a piece of art.

She didn't hear Luke come up behind her, so she jumped a bit when he spoke, "Adam painted it, so it seems new, even though it isn't. He's good. Really good."

"My sister would love to do what Adam is doing. Her favorite subject is animals. She once drew and colored an elephant on our bedroom wall that the landlord took a picture of before he painted over it."

"I can draw stick people," Luke admitted.

"But you designed this to resemble what Bridget wanted."

He looked pleased that she knew about Bridget's drawing.

"This structure was my first attempt at updating the animal adventure. Adam saw my and Bridget's vision and turned it into exactly what I wanted."

"He *is* very good."

"He's starting to get outside jobs, so I'm hoping he'll finish the front real soon before we lose him."

She nodded, remembering the offer of the paintbrush. Maybe Adam had been serious.

"So," Katie said, "I keep getting mixed messages. Are you just a director or are you both a director and a keeper? Right now you're also a herpetologist. You didn't mention that yesterday."

"Didn't see the need. With you, I'm only concerned about Aquila. Besides, I'm more *becoming* a herpetologist than *am* one. Learning as I go and taking a few online classes. But, yes, the reptiles, mules and burros are my areas. I'm heading for the burro barn now. But if you want, we can go say hi to Aquila. Unless," he added hopefully, "you already did?"

She didn't hesitate. "Not today."

"Then come with me to the burros. After that, you can change your shirt and I'll assign the rest of your day—since Aquila's a…challenge, I figured you might want to work on some other things. You might find, when you get a feel for the place, that it brings back good memories. Pretty soon, you'll be shoveling floors, tossing meat over walls and handing Ruth toothpaste for Terrance."

"The first two I can do, but toothpaste for Terrance, not a chance. It's not good to get that close to a wild animal. I'm surprised you allow it."

He laughed. "I trust my staff. They know and love animals."

Was his heart making him even more blind to the dangers than she'd assumed? She didn't respond, just followed him to the burro barn on the other side of the gift shop. It looked like something out of Old MacDonald's Farm, complete with a petting zoo.

"That's where we keep two sheep," Luke said. "They're not native to Arizona and they're not exotic, but we couldn't avoid the BAAA brand."

Katie followed him through the barn doors to the animal stalls and education plaques. Out-

side the back door were the burro and mule pens
and riding ring.

"This goes back almost a mile," Luke said,
pointing to a dirt road. "The road ends at a cabin
that we rent out for parties or even business
events. I'm heading over there now to make sure
everything is in order." He sounded proud, as if
this place was his baby and he wanted to show
it off. "Come with me?"

"Do you have enough time for me to tag
along?" Her father never took someone for a
tour unless there was something in it for him
or his business.

Luke checked his watch. "Sure, this is the
best time of the day. We get here very early on
Sunday and then open later. About ten, all of us
relax a bit. We also take turns going to church.
Today's my day to stay here. I'll grab another
mule, but maybe I should ask first if you ride?"

She said the words *I ride* before she'd thought
it through. Riding was another pastime she'd
been forced to give up when she'd been sent to
live with Aunt Betsy.

He opened the gate to the arena where a few
mules stood idly. Many of the burros ambled
over to him, and Katie could hear him talking to them by name. Most, obviously, knew
he brought food and nudged their heads at his
hands and pockets. As he diverted the herd, he

separated a mule from the pack and brought him over for her inspection. "Saddle or bareback?"

"I don't need a saddle." She'd loved riding. As a preteen, she'd bought in to the whole Saddle Club books and horse posters for her walls. She'd had to be content with plastic horses, though, because her father hadn't had horses or burros. They weren't exotic enough. He'd been a bit miffed that she wasn't into wild animal posters. He wasn't a cowboy; he saw himself more as a master of ceremonies.

With her aunt, they'd moved too often for her to have time to put much on the walls. Yet another reason why she wished she were back in Dallas. And yet, somehow, even though she'd put up lots of pictures, the apartment didn't quite feel like home.

"That one's Pixie," Luke introduced, then asked, "How long has it been since you've ridden?"

"More than a decade."

"It's like a bike, I hear. You never forget."

She wasn't as agile as a ten-year-old, so she looked around for something to use as a step stool. There were stumps that would do. She took Pixie by the lead rope, but before she moved her, Luke bent down and entwined his fingers together, making a foothold for her. She hesitated only a moment before using what he offered. Then she swung her leg over Pixie and Luke's gentle hand steadied her as she found her position. He was close, so close that she caught the merest scent of aftershave.

It made her long for something long forgotten, best forgotten.

Unaware of her thoughts, Luke hopped on his mule as if he did it every day, which he probably did. His was bigger than hers, and gave a low snort as if saying, "Can we go now?"

"You seem to have a relationship with that one," Katie commented.

"Yes, we've known each other for a long time. This one's Dust."

"Pixie and Dust. Pixie Dust. You name them?" Katie asked.

"No, these are siblings, the last burros my sister named before she died."

"Oh."

"I've babied them, which is ridiculous, but it makes me feel better. Plus, they're a good pair. Reliable, with a good seat. Follow me."

With the slightest nudge of his heels, Luke guided Dust down a trail that almost immediately twisted to the right.

Following him, Katie couldn't help admiring the muscles his blue BAAA shirt didn't hide. Tan chinos covered legs toned and obviously used to hard work. His brown hair stuck out raggedly from underneath a blue cap with the letters *BAAA* on it. He rode with confidence, something Katie wished she had right now.

Apparently she hid her lack of confidence well, though.

"You're good," Luke remarked.

"I learned on movie sets. My father would take George, Ollie or one of the other animals for a part in a movie. I'd come along to help, but there were hours where I had nothing to do. Often, horses were part of the film. I made friends with some of the owners and trainers. Pretty soon, they were teaching me how to ride."

"I'd love to see all the animals and the behind-the-scenes workings of a movie. My sister Bridget would have loved it even more."

"I loved it early on," Katie admitted, "back when my mother was alive. There's a picture of me somewhere, I'm about two, and I'm on the back of this huge Clydesdale and my legs are sticking straight out. Unfortunately, most of the pictures from my childhood are gone."

He seemed to realize that they'd ventured onto a topic she'd rather not explore, and they rode in silence. After about five minutes, they came to a clearing. A pavilion, with benches and picnic tables inside, was on the right side of the trail. On the other side was a play area. Next to it was a small bathroom and drinking fountain.

"What a perfect place for a birthday party," Katie said, getting off Pixie, handing the rope to Luke and exploring a bit. There was a slide in the shape of an elephant, swings that were decorated with monkeys and even a jungle gym made to look like a mass of giant snakes.

Luke stayed on Dust for a moment, then decided it would be more fun to follow her. "Adam created a small-scale replica of what he envisioned. We found someone to build it, and then Adam did the art. Ruth organized a special event that paid for it."

She explored for a moment, touching the swings and climbing up on the jungle gym. She realized she was having fun, and for the first time since she'd come to Bridget's, she wasn't afraid. She'd so rarely had a chance in the past several years to relax and enjoy herself—and even more rarely with a man. She knew she had to convince Luke that he was playing with fire where the animals were concerned, but maybe she could give herself just a few more hours with him....

THERE WAS SOMETHING about the way Katie Vincent moved, something that told him she *wanted* to enjoy Bridget's, that she was willing to try, but all Luke could think about was her fainting yesterday.

If she bit the dust again, he'd be the only one close enough to catch her.

With that in mind, he moved behind her, caught her easily around the waist and gently nudged her off the jungle gym.

"I'm not afraid of heights," she argued.

"I believe you, but I'm afraid of women who faint twice in one day and then think they should go around climbing things."

"Oh," she acknowledged. "Good point."

He followed her back to her mule and said, "If we ride another fifteen minutes, we'll get to the cabin. When my uncle lived there, it was only one room. He didn't need more."

"He never married?"

"Not that I'm aware of. My mom said he would have been a loner except for the animals, but the animals drew people to him."

She looked at Luke's ring finger, her thoughts so obvious that he had to laugh. Although there were times he himself wondered why he'd not met someone, settled down and started a family.

"I'm not married yet. But I'll never be a loner. I've got too much of my dad in me. He's a car salesman."

"I wasn't being nosy—" she started.

To save her any further embarrassment, or worse, to keep himself from asking about her ideas on marriage, Luke turned the conversation back to the cabin.

"We remodeled and added on to the structure. Downstairs, it's like a house. With couches and a kitchen, which we use for parties. Upstairs, we set up folding chairs and a podium for meetings. It's been in use for just over a year. At first, I thought about living in the cabin myself, but it's brought in quite a bit of revenue."

"How long have you worked here?" She waved him off and used a rock near the playground to give her the step up she needed to return to Pixie's back.

When she had her seat, he led the way and answered, "I've visited the place all my life, but with this a full-time profession, this is my fifth year."

"I read your bio on the website. You worked for a marketing firm before taking over this place. Did you really change careers because of a promise you made to your little sister?"

He'd been asked that question too many times to count, but for some reason, he needed her more than anyone to understand it wasn't just that he'd made a promise.

"Because of the promise, yes, but Bridget and I shared a dream. My promise to her made me accountable, and in the long run has made me a better man for keeping it."

She nodded. "I made a promise to my little sister, and I kept it. It's what I'm most proud of."

"What was the promise?"

For a moment, he thought she wasn't going to answer. Then she said, "That I wouldn't leave her with our aunt. I petitioned the courts and won guardianship of her when I was just eighteen. She was twelve."

They rode in companionable silence until the two-storied cabin came into sight. It looked like something off a postcard, complete with a front porch and a scattering of rocking chairs. The big windows, on both stories, offered spectacular morning views. The logs holding the cabin together were dark with age.

"There used to be another structure, not quite a barn but close enough. Uncle Albert kept his animals in it. Until he got the lion."

"That's when Ruth came in?"

"No, this was in the seventies, Ruth didn't get Terrance until the nineties, in a fairly underhanded way. This was a different lion, not quite as tame."

"I can't picture Ruth doing anything underhanded."

"Let me rephrase," Luke said, getting off Dust and coming back to help Katie. "Her husband was the underhanded one." Luke took Pixie's lead rope and led both mules over to a patch of grass. He didn't tie them up, just left them to graze.

"Ruth told me that much."

"She's very open," Luke agreed. "I think I saw him once or twice when I was here with Bridget, but he wasn't the kind of man who gave time to kids. Ruth would have been a great mom. He, apparently, didn't want her to ruin her figure."

Luke stopped walking and after a moment, shook his head. "I can't even imagine that kind of selfishness."

Katie shook her head, too. "I'm surprised she put up with that."

"She's never said one way or the other, at least not in words. More a 'what was I thinking?' roll of the eyes."

Climbing up the stairs to the cabin, Katie said, "You know a lot about her."

He pondered for a moment. "Right now she's my strongest supporter. I turn to her whenever I have questions or need advice."

"More than your family, or do you mean just with Bridget's?"

He realized she was right, he did lean more on Ruth than on his family, not that he didn't love them. "My family is wonderful. I somehow lucked into two people who married for love, stayed together and expect the kids to come to dinner every Sunday."

"Very lucky," she agreed. "That's something I dream of, two people equally yoked, in love and putting their kids first."

He gazed at her, blond hair swaying a bit in the wind, cheeks still a faint pink, either from the blush earlier or perhaps from the ride. He started to reach out, wanting to touch those cheeks, feel her skin and maybe bring a smile to her face.

His phone rang.

It was Meredith. They needed to get back.

Luke looked at Katie, but she was already turning her mule around. "I understand," she said. "At Bridget's, animals come first."

CHAPTER SEVEN

"I FOUND AN arrow taped on the wall I was working on," Adam said to Katie and Luke. "It said, 'Look behind the big saguaro.' And now I'm mad at myself because I didn't go check right away. I worked for a good thirty minutes before I heard him whimpering."

"Let's go."

They picked up Fred, Jasper and Meredith along the way and discovered the "him" was a young black bear, too young to have been taken away from his mother. He'd been left, tethered to the saguaro, at the animal park sometime during the night. He was wounded and scared.

"With those paws," Fred said, already bending down to examine the bear, "I'm not sure he could have wandered off. He wouldn't have gotten far."

"Get my camera," Luke told Meredith.

"No veterinarian would declaw an animal this way," Fred said, anger lacing his words. He was searching through his bag for a sedative to put the bear to sleep so they could move him safely and try to repair the damage.

Katie stared at the bandages, tinged red with the seepage of blood, that were wrapped around the cub's paws.

"Someone wanted a pet, kept him while he was easy to handle and then made a token effort to care for him," Luke said. "They had him declawed, and not by an expert, then figured he wasn't much of a pet."

Everyone was silent in the moments that followed. The bear—who should be pacing, scared, angry, hungry—just lay there.

"I wish I could find whoever did this," Meredith said as she returned, eyes blazing, her fingers clenched around the camera.

For the first time, Katie thought she could like Meredith, really like her.

"Wild animals are not meant to be pets," Katie said with disgust. "Especially not bears. His owners must have had those claws taken off because they were getting scratched while they tried to play with him."

"You're probably right," Fred said. "Bears can't retract."

"Already called Game and Fish," Meredith said. "They're sending someone, probably Jake, but it will be a while. I also called the sheriff. Figured he'd want to be in the loop." She took distance shots, up close shots. Fred bent down and gently took hold of the cub's paws and held them up.

Jasper explained to Katie that Arizona law required them to notify Game and Fish if they discovered an abandoned animal on their property.

He turned to the group. "How long has it been since their last visit?" Jasper asked.

"A week," Fred said. "When the Gila monster was left at the front gate." To Katie, he added, "The only reason we reported in instead of releasing the Gila Monster ourselves was because they're protected, so Fish and Game need to know someone actually managed to catch one, put it in an aquarium and bring it here."

"People just drop off animals?" Katie asked. "They don't stick around to make sure you'll take them?"

"Very few stick around," Luke admitted. "If they do, we tell them we can't take in animals. We're not a rescue habitat. Our budget is stretched feeding the animals we already have."

"Stretched is too kind a word," Meredith said. "Our budget is broken." She dropped to her knees, seemingly unconcerned about how close she was to a wounded bear, albeit a whimpering baby.

"Broken?" Luke said. "That's one way of putting it. And now we have this little guy. He won't be cheap."

"There's only one thing to do," Katie said. "Look at the shape he's in. He's in pain."

"No, we'll offer him a chance," Luke said. "He deserves a chance."

"We don't do anything," Fred broke in, "until Fish and Game get here. This is a crime scene."

KATIE GAZED AT the little bear, unmoving except for ragged breaths and a few whimpers. Part of her wanted to join Meredith, get down on her knees, take care of the baby. But she had to remain dispassionate.

"When he stops being a crime scene," she said, "he's going to require a little more tender, loving care than Fred here has time for. So who's going to give him that chance?"

Meredith moaned, "Man, you're right. I've been telling you, Luke, we need to hire another person. Fred's got Terrance scheduled for a tooth extraction tomorrow. Ruth expects me to work more with the cats, but right now I'm busy with the bald eagle. Then there's Cheeky's ulcer."

"The camel has an ulcer?" Katie asked.

"Yes," Luke said. "Fred's starting him on some holistic medicine. For the first forty-eight hours, he'll have to be monitored."

"Worst time ever," Fred said, "to acquire a

baby bear in this condition. Unless I miss my guess, there's more wrong with him than the declawing."

"Well, we'll all just have to pitch in," Luke insisted.

Fred stared at Luke as if he were nuts.

"I don't know if we can even help him," Fred said. "This little guy is probably four months, but he looks two. He's not been fed enough or probably the right type of food. I don't like the way his back legs are bent. He's going to take a lot of work, and he'll be dependent on whoever takes care of him, maybe for the rest of his life."

"Abandoned, abused, unwanted, hopeless," Katie breathed, suddenly feeling sorry for the bear.

"It happens to animals all too often," Luke said, "but that's not how we are here."

"I'll help." Katie stood, brushed off her knees and faced Luke. She still thought he was crazy for basing all of his decisions on hope, but whether she liked it or not she was here for two weeks. If she was busy with the bear, maybe they'd cut her some slack when it came to Aquila.

Besides, a weak and maimed baby bear wasn't likely to attack anyone.

IN THE END, Katie stayed with Fred while everyone else hurried off to prepare for the opening of Bridget's.

"You putting him on the bottle?" Katie asked. "He should have been weaned already."

"Yes," Fred agreed, "but he also should be with his mama for another year, and whatever his diet has been, it hasn't been right."

A Jeep pulled into the parking lot, and a man got out. Tall with curly brown hair, he sported a Windbreaker that read Game and Fish. He made his way to Adam who pointed to where Fred and Katie waited.

He shook hands with Fred. To her, he said, "I'm Jake Farraday. You must be Katie."

Just over twenty-four hours and already she'd made a name for herself. How?

"I am."

"I'm sure you'll be a great help."

Katie didn't know the man enough to contradict him. Instead, she waited while he took his own pictures, filled out some form, made a phone call and occasionally asked Fred a question. When Jake finally nodded that he was finished, she carefully unraveled the rope tethering the bear to the saguaro. Then Katie nudged the bear toward Fred while Jake went off to find Luke.

"We'll start with oatmeal and applesauce. See how that goes." Fred opened his black bag and took out a syringe. He mixed some kind of white powder with water.

"You tranquilizing him?"

"Yes. I'm pretty sure he's been around people, based on the way he's so trusting of us, but that doesn't mean he won't get aggressive. Even though he's this young and without claws, we don't take chances. He's just as likely to get hurt as we are."

At that moment, Luke drove up in a Bridget's cart with Jake. The two men were deep in conversation as they walked toward Jake's Jeep. Katie could hear a bit of their conversation; Jake was offering to call bear rescue organizations that he knew of, but Luke was saying that Bridget's could handle it.

They didn't need help.

Based on their strapped resources, Katie thought Luke would have been wise to take Jake Farraday up on his kind offer.

Then Jake got in his Jeep and Luke came over to Katie and Fred and helped them load the still awake but groggy bear onto the back of the cart. Fred hopped on, next to the bear, while Katie took her place in the passenger seat next to Luke.

Now she had to make good on her promise.

An hour later, Katie had attempted to feed the bear (who wouldn't eat), organized his play area (which he probably would never get to use) and named him Scoot. She'd chosen "Scoot" because, based on the condition of his paws and legs, that's all he'd ever be able to do.

Poor baby.

She shouldn't have named him.

Against her better judgment, she'd felt the urge to take over the bear's care, see what she could do, do her best to give him the chance Luke believed every creature deserved. But her best wouldn't be good enough. Luke Rittenhouse was living in a dream world.

When the bear fell asleep, whimpering, Fred said he didn't need her anymore, so she went looking for Luke.

She found him again in the snake house, standing in a glass enclosure the size of a small bedroom. The walls were painted with blue skies, trees, a pond. More of Adam's work, no doubt.

No pink inside. Good.

Luke was carefully running his hand over a big green iguana. This must be Louie, the one he'd wanted her to meet this morning.

Through the glass, she could just barely make out the words spoken by a man behind him.

"I'm not sure how the light fell." Katie guessed the man was a groundskeeper, judging from his outfit and tools.

"These things happen," Luke said. "It's not your fault. But I want all of the exhibits checked."

Katie gently tapped on the window. Both Luke and the groundskeeper looked up.

"This is Louie," Luke mouthed, and motioned for her to go to the employee door and come to the back.

When she joined them, Luke told her Louie'd had a close encounter with one of the heating lights in his glass enclosure. The light had somehow come off the wall near the top of the glass and landed on Louie's head. The lizard appeared dazed, but then, to Katie's mind, lizards always had a bit of a goofy expression.

"He's fine," Luke said. The lizard slowly marched—as only a lizard can do—into Luke's outstretched hands.

"You're okay," Luke soothed. "Think of this as an adventure. Just a tiny knock on the head."

"If the lizard nods," Katie said, "I'm out of here."

"Go ahead," Luke told the lizard, "nod."

Louie nodded.

"You're kidding." Katie stepped closer to the glass. "So does he do tricks?"

Luke scratched Louie on the top of the head, gently. "No, not really, but he's great for taking to schools and other events. He rides on my shoulders."

"Are you sure he's unharmed?"

"Lizards tend to be skittish. His natural incli-nation when scared would be to escape and take cover, but he was stuck. That probably upset him more than anything else. I'll go find Fred to make sure he's all right, though. Then I'll put Louie here in warm water, relax him and moni-tor how he acts the rest of the day."

Katie took a deep breath. "When you find Fred, you should tell him to put the bear down."

"Why?"

"He won't make it. We're making him live in pain. I don't think I can make a difference."

"So you'll give up without even trying?"

She didn't like the amazed, somewhat dis-gruntled look on his face. There he was, judg-ing her—again.

"I don't give up easily," she retorted, "but we're just prolonging that little guy's pain."

"His claws were ripped out, not his heart," Luke said. "He can live without claws. You have two weeks to make a difference. He deserves that chance."

"But—"

"Louie here arrived in a box. He'd been at-tacked by something, probably a dog. Fred didn't think he'd pull through."

"This isn't about Louie."

"It's about trying before you give up."

"I don't give up."

Luke raised one eyebrow. "Really?"

"Really," she responded. "I already told you about winning custody of my sister."

"How long ago was that?"

"Almost seven years."

He smiled, as if he knew a secret. "Well, then, it's time to give your all to a new cause. Your sister's all grown up. Use that determination to help Aquila and the bear."

"Fred said he doesn't need me anymore," she admitted.

"Been to see Aquila, then?"

She didn't answer, couldn't, but if he ordered her to, she'd go.

As if sensing the mood, Louie moved up Luke's arm then draped himself across his shoulders like a lumpy scarf, with one long tail to the left and a slowly pivoting head to the right.

He seemed to be shaking his head in disappointment.

"It's time for Louie's bath," Luke finally said. "I told Gloria you'd help in the gift shop today in between your other duties."

"My other duties being Aquila and the bear."

"You got it."

This was wrong. Every nerve in her body was alive, partly with fear. Aquila and Tyre, as cubs, had been healthy, and she'd still failed with them.

Scoot had so many things wrong with him. What if she couldn't help the little bear?

Luke didn't seem to notice her distress. "Follow me, you have to meet Gloria."

Katie clenched her teeth all the way to the gift shop. Luckily, Gloria, who was in charge of the gift shop, was thrilled to see her and put her right to work, dusting the tops of displays. Katie—at a healthy five foot eight—was the answer to a short woman's prayer.

Katie felt a bit like a piece of furniture, stuck in the corner and unnecessary. Exiled, because clearly all she was good for was dusting and selling lip balm.

Gloria, on the other hand, was a study in productivity, answering the phone, ringing up sales and giving directions as people wandered through.

During a lull in customers, Gloria surprised Katie by sharing, "I met your father."

Not a chance Katie's father had visited Bridget's. It was too small, and there was nothing here he could capitalize on. "When?"

"About ten years ago at the California zoo my husband worked at. A rhinoceros had a baby. It became a big media event. Your father showed up and managed to get interviewed by the press, even though he didn't work for the zoo."

Judging by Gloria's pursed lip, her husband, Fred, who *did* work for the zoo, hadn't rated a mention on the nightly news despite the fact that he'd been the one overseeing the event.

"Very driven" was Gloria's comment. "But he loved his animals."

Katie didn't dispute that.

"Anyone else here personally know my father?" Katie asked.

"Meredith went to school in California. I think she mentioned he'd been a guest lecturer for one of her classes."

Small world, and Katie couldn't help wanting to run from the shadow her father cast.

And yet, as the day wore on, Bob Vincent was ironically how Katie came to feel useful again. She might be afraid of most animals, but she remembered everything her father had taught her. And soon a simple question from a child such as, "What kind of animal is this?" turned into story time for Katie. She had antidotes, statistics and even a few scars to show.

Eventually she relaxed, allowing herself to enjoy the job.

"You're good," Gloria said. "When you talk about taking care of Aquila as a cub, your face comes alive."

After that, Katie didn't share Aquila stories. She feared Gloria was right. She'd felt something stir deep inside, some long suppressed desire she'd thought long gone.

It needed to stay long gone.

Every hour or so, when there was a lull, she went to check on Scoot. If he was asleep, she left. If he was awake, she stood at the door to his room, wanting him to see her face. She wasn't the only one. Ruth was there about half the time. Jasper stopped by at least once. Katie wasn't sure about Meredith and Luke. Could be she just missed them.

Later, when Scoot was a little calmer, she'd start opening the door and going in, probably just standing still at first to let Scoot get used to her face and her smell.

Toward the end of the day, Fred came to stand beside her. "I'm going to put a cast on both legs," he said. "Maybe even higher up. His legs are broken. I just can't figure out why. The only good news is he's still got his back molars. Sometimes people take those, too."

Katie returned to the gift shop.

In the last hour, the store did a brisk business, but Gloria finally flipped the sign to Closed. She started tallying the day's sales as Katie swept the floor and tidied.

"It's nice to get done early," Gloria said on

the way out. "People sure like to keep tabs on you, huh?"

Ruth and Meredith had come in, but Katie knew Gloria was mainly referring to Luke. He'd been in and out of the shop all afternoon, always smiling, and always heading for Katie first.

When Katie didn't respond, the older woman said, "You were a good help and a natural salesperson. We did a good business today."

"I enjoyed it," Katie admitted as she followed Gloria out the door. Answering questions about animals had come easier than actually working with animals. Katie was amazed at what she'd remembered.

Standing outside the gift shop door, Katie watched as the last of Bridget's guests headed for the exit. Gloria went over to meet Fred, who was sitting on a bench, cradling something in his arms. Katie couldn't see what type of animal it was, though she did notice that Gloria didn't reach out to pet it.

When Fred sneezed, however, she did reach out to pet him.

Meredith came up on Katie's left and said, "You still here?"

Katie didn't even want to guess at whether Meredith was questioning her about just today or about her two-week commitment.

"I thought I'd head over to check on Scoot."

"Yes, I heard that's what you'd named him. Fred says Scoot's down for the night. Tomorrow he might be more responsive."

"Most animals come out of the sedative and fight to move," Katie said. "His inactivity isn't normal."

"No," Meredith agreed. "This isn't like anything I've seen before and believe me, I've seen plenty. If you're going to check on him, I'll walk with you. Make sure you don't faint or something."

Katie had fainted twice in her life, both times had occurred yesterday. "Ha, ha, very funny. Where's Luke?" He'd been by so often during the day, she'd expected the day to begin and end with him.

Maybe that should bother her.

"Sunday evenings he drives into Tucson in time to go to evening services with his parents and siblings, and then they all go out to dinner. It's tradition."

"Oh," she said, disappointed. Katie wasn't altogether comfortable with the feeling. After all, she didn't expect him to tell her where he was or what to do at each moment—when she wasn't at Bridget's, that is.

Strangely, she hadn't felt like a stranger in Scorpion Ridge today, either—not while exploring the grounds with Luke, not while monitoring Scoot and not while working in the gift shop. And she should have. This wasn't her world anymore.

Leaving Ruth's house this morning, she'd not wanted to come to Bridget's at all. Now she didn't want to leave.

She blamed the bear. Scoot was already getting a hold on her heart.

Meredith opened the door to the infirmary and they bent before Scoot's cage.

Shaking her head, Katie said, "Whoever had him didn't take good care of him. He's underweight and his bones aren't nearly strong enough. Fred thinks he's not had enough calcium."

Meredith nodded. "We're going to spend a fortune getting him back into shape. And he'll always have to be in a shelter of some kind. What an injustice. He's denied a mother's love and then denied the basics of care."

"They deserve more than the scratching he must have given them before they declawed him," Katie said. "Only an idiot would declaw a cub and then abandon him."

"We're going to have our work cut out for us." Katie noted Meredith included herself. "He'll fight us the whole way."

"I'm not afraid," Katie said. "I'll do what

needs to be done, but I still think he should be put down. His quality of life—"

Meredith shot her a look. "—will be stellar if he winds up staying with us. Like Aquila's life will be stellar if you do for him what you're willing to do for Scoot. It's not just the abandoned, unwanted and maimed that need you."

Katie stood and backed out of the room. It was on the tip of her tongue to tell Meredith where to go, but the other woman was right.

There were two animals on this property that needed her.

Aquila was underweight, too.

Human contact would be good for him.

Instead, Katie hurried for the parking lot.

Although Ruth had given her a key, Katie did the same thing that evening she'd done yesterday. She drove into the center of town and headed for the strip mall and the sub shop. No way did she want to go back to Ruth's, where she'd be barraged with questions. Not when Meredith's words still burned the pit of Katie's stomach.

If Meredith had said them, Luke and everyone else were probably thinking them.

She ordered a sub, and while she waited, she called her little sister.

Who did not answer.

They were so new to Dallas, only living there

for three months, that Katie didn't have friends to call and didn't yet have a handle on who Janie hung out with. Janie gathered and discarded friends very quickly. Katie, on the other hand, usually had two to three people she relied on, and that was enough.

She hadn't met her three people in Dallas yet. She had no one else to call.

She ate her sandwich quickly and then headed for Ruth's house, hoping she could quietly make it to her bedroom, lick her wounds in peace.

She'd just entered the front door and made it two steps into the hallway when her cell sounded a familiar ring tone.

"Janie, where have you been?" Katie snatched open her phone.

"I went out for pizza with some friends."

It was on the tip of Katie's tongue to ask what friends, which pizza place and how much did Janie spend? But Janie was an adult, in college, and should be in charge of herself.

So instead, Katie made her way into the living room, dropped her purse on the couch and sat down next to it. "I miss you, Janie, and I just wanted to see how you were doing. Did you finish all your homework for tomorrow?"

Janie's silence answered that question.

"If you fall behind…" Katie warned.

"I have tons of English homework," Janie

said, "and I don't even want to take English. It's time for you to realize that and let me make some of my own decisions."

"Janie, you have to go to college, and you need to have a second degree in something like English. Your future—"

"My future is *my* future, not *our* future. Everything is fine here. Deb and Billy are waiting in the living room. We're going to watch a movie."

"Please tell me you're still attending classes at least."

"Yes, Mom. I'm still attending classes." Janie's words were clipped, and she only called Katie "mom" when she was annoyed or wanted something. Janie didn't even remember their mother. She'd never gotten to call anyone Mom.

Taking a deep breath, Katie steered the conversation away from school, away from confrontation, and started to fill Janie in on her day—Scoot the bear, Luke and the mule rides, Luke and the iguana, Luke assigning her to work in the gift shop—never had she had so much to share.

After she was finished, Janie said, "I have to go. My friends are waiting. I just noticed you called and wanted to make sure you knew that everything's fine here."

"I'm glad you called. Love you."

Hitting the off button, Katie looked up to find Ruth's eyes on her.

She'd obviously come from the room next to the living room, which housed her office.

"I take it that was your little sister."

"Yes. She hasn't quite figured out that college is supposed to be her life."

As Ruth headed for the hallway and to what Katie assumed was her bedroom, she said, "Very few kids know what they're doing. Most are lucky if they make it out of adolescence without making a mistake they live with the rest of their life. But that shouldn't stop them from living."

CHAPTER EIGHT

YESTERDAY'S ADMISSIONS HAD limped along at a crawl, which made Luke worry when he reviewed the list of items Fred said they'd need for Scoot.

It was time to call the press, take a few more pictures, make a story. Maybe even make a story out of Katie Vincent and her history with animals. Then connect it to how she was working with Scoot. The story might go viral, might bring people in.

Jake from Game and Fish was all for exposure. He added that it might not just bring in the tenderhearted, but possibly also guilt whoever had tried to make the little fellow a pet into coming in.

So that morning, after the staff meeting, he asked Katie to follow him to his office. As she sat on the couch, he said, "I'd like you to talk with the press about Scoot."

"Meredith would be a better choice."

"You were at the meeting this morning. You know how much we need the money. Meredith is nothing new in the Scorpion Ridge community. You are. It would be a big help."

She pressed her lips together. He went back to his paperwork and pretended to ignore her.

"Both his front legs in casts," Katie muttered. "Neither strong enough to bear his weight, and that's on top of the declawing."

"You're right. Scoot's been treated dismally."

"He should be at a bear rescue."

Luke looked up, surprised. "Why? What do you know about bear rescue facilities?"

"I know they have more time to dedicate to a single species. That would give Scoot an edge."

At least she wasn't telling him—again—that Scoot should be put down. That wasn't an option. It wasn't in Luke's nature to give up just because a person or an animal had a handicap.

"Let's see what we can do here first."

When she didn't say anything else, he prompted her, "Which one do you want to work with today?"

"I hate Mondays," she muttered.

"I love them. Now, which one?"

"I'll…I don't know."

"Gotta make up your mind."

She stood quickly, grabbed the BAA backpack she'd been given and left his office. He heard her going down the stairs and slamming the door at the bottom. He counted to three and then went to the window.

She made it all the way to the gift shop. She stood there, not moving except to clench and unclench her fists.

He looked at his watch, then at her and back at his watch. It took her seven minutes to return.

"Tell me what to do today."

He put on his hat, gave Tinker a farewell pat and beckoned for Katie to follow him down the stairs and out into the morning air. Her fists were still clenched.

Almost immediately a peacock screamed. Katie jumped a bit, but then straightened, just barely loosening her fists.

He liked this Katie better than the fainting one. He knew he was pushing her, maybe too far, but he had no choice. Luke had less than two weeks to get her into the enclosure with Aquila. He didn't have time to waste.

He'd had another heart-to-heart about her with Jasper this morning. The older man had repeated what he'd said yesterday. "Get her in with animals. Make her want it. She'll come around. She's already thinking about it."

"Maybe I shouldn't work with Scoot or Aquila. I did a good job in the gift shop," Katie offered. "Ask Gloria."

"Monday's our slowest day," Luke said. "I

don't need two people in the gift shop, and it's Gloria's regular job."

"So my job today, really, is pitching in wherever you want me, whenever you want me?"

"Yes—between the times you're with Scoot or Aquila. Consider yourself my right-hand man."

"Fun."

"Yes, it will be fun." He purposely misunderstood her.

"Most directors don't involve themselves so much with the animals, but you make a point of it, don't you?"

"I wish I was even more hands-on," Luke shared as they walked. "But right now Bridget's needs a director more than a keeper. As director, I don't have enough time to bond with most animals. It's my job to make sure all the *i*'s are dotted and the *t*'s are crossed when it comes to permits and animal care—not to mention having to be the spokesperson and fund-raiser for Bridget's. Like this evening, I'll be giving a talk at a Rotary Club meeting."

"Here in Scorpion Ridge? Is this town big enough to have a Rotary Club?"

"I'm not sure. This one's in Tucson. Their motto is 'Service Above Self.' I have to turn this visit into donations for Bridget's."

"You've talked about needing money before. It's why you purchased my dad's animals."

"And why they have to make money." He looked her full in the eye. "Honestly? I spent money we couldn't afford on them. It was a gamble. Now I need to make it pay off."

"Surely George the Bear could—"

"Arizona's full of bears."

She nodded and kept following. He'd made his point, but for some reason, he didn't want to send her away just yet. With her, he could be himself; she understood him. Selfishly, he wanted to hold on to that a little longer. Besides, she hadn't got the full tour....

"You haven't seen all the animals," Luke said, nudging her through the snake house door. "Saturday you were too busy passing out, and yesterday you were either with Fred or stuck in the gift shop."

"Okay, okay. I'm coming. By the way, I didn't enjoy passing out, but I did enjoy yesterday, working at the gift shop and with Fred."

"Good. Let's start with the mules and burros, then. You liked those yesterday, too." They didn't spend much time with the burros because Luke had already been to see them this morning for an early morning ride.

He didn't mention the ride they'd taken together yesterday, and neither did she.

Maybe tomorrow she could come with him again.

Next they checked on the mountain lions, then the giraffes and onto George the Bear, who lay in his enclosure, resting.

"He's smaller," Katie breathed.

Luke started to answer, but Jasper's voice came from behind them. "He's actually five pounds heavier than when Luke purchased him. You've just not seen him since you were twelve, Little Girl. You're bigger."

Luke watched Katie's expression. For a moment he saw what Katie must have looked like all those years ago before being sent off to live with her aunt. He saw the "Little Girl" Jasper spoke about. For a very brief moment, she was relaxed, happy, ready to embrace if not Jasper, then at least the day.

Animals did that for her, no matter how much she tried to deny it.

But, even before she turned to face the older man, a wall came down and she went back to being I'm-only-here-for-two-weeks Katie Vincent. Shutting everyone else out. Shutting him out.

"I'm twenty-five," Katie reminded Jasper.

"I know how old you are," he responded. "George is sixteen. Do you remember when we got him?"

"He was just a baby, not even four months.

Dad got him down from a tree in the front of someone's yard."

"And you played with him." Luke stood next to her, so close she could feel the heat from his body. His eyes were on her, dark brown, warm, questioning.

But he wasn't thinking about her, not really. She knew that when he said, "Even before Aquila, you learned how to treat a baby wild animal with George."

"George was easy."

"No, he wasn't," Jasper disagreed. "His claws were dangerous, and sometimes when you were playing with him, we couldn't take you away from him without George becoming aggressive toward us."

Katie didn't remember that part.

Jasper continued. "Your dad was thrilled, though. Not only did he get his picture in the paper the day we rescued George—and even for weeks afterward—but he got a new bear. The bear he already had was over twenty and had been trained by someone else. George was the first bear your dad got to train."

"Janie wanted to sleep with George. She thought he was a teddy bear Dad got just for her."

"And you," Jasper said, "wanted him to live

in the house and be your around-the-clock play-mate."

"And I," Luke cut in, looking at his watch with concern, "just want him ready for the noon show."

"George is fine," Jasper reported. "He's just slowing down some, and somewhat confused by Arizona's warm weather."

"What show does he do?" Katie asked.

"He does some acrobatics, and since it's September, we're doing some tosses with school lunch boxes and backpacks."

"Why don't you bring Ollie over and do the tea party? That was always everyone's favorite."

"Because," Luke stated, "during shows I have a one-man-per-animal rule. If we have Ollie, there has to be one keeper whose only job is taking care of Ollie, and one keeper in charge of George. Jasper can't do both."

"Finally, a rule that makes sense. You're entirely too easygoing here."

Jasper and Luke exchanged a look.

"I'm serious," Katie insisted. "There are lots of areas where you're a bit too lax and—"

"We have tight rules where they're needed," Luke said. "So far, neither Ollie or George has bonded with any other keepers."

"The only real keeper you have is Meredith," Katie retorted.

"I'm real," Jasper protested.

"But you're only in charge of my father's animals, right?"

Jasper looked indignant and Luke held up a hand to stop Katie before she said anything else. "Meredith is the most educated keeper, but we have plenty of experienced animal handlers, and we also have students from the university on study programs. Experience takes time."

"You're running out of time," Katie said.

"With Aquila, yes. Which is why we need you."

With that, Jasper headed to the back of George's enclosure, leaving Katie feeling perplexed and Luke looking annoyed. Luke marched off, so Katie, not knowing what else to do, followed him as he continued his tour.

It took three hours for Luke to make his way around the zoo, and at each enclosure, Katie expected her immobilizing terror to return. But Luke's presence soothed her, and it was hard not to catch his infectious enthusiasm.

THEN THEY CAME to the snake house.

She moaned, and for the first time in hours, she felt a trickle of fear.

Luke led them through a door marked Employees and to a hallway just big enough for two people if they walked close to each other.

Katie stayed in the main room, leaning against the wall. She wasn't ready to go behind the exhibits yet.

Sensing her anxiety, Luke lingered with her. After a couple of minutes, he asked, "Your dad had snakes, right?"

"Two. A big anaconda and a boa. I didn't go near them."

"Why not?"

"At first, my mom said I wasn't allowed. They were the only animals she felt that way about. And my father considered them his, and his alone. They were easy to care for, I remember him saying."

"My first pet was a snake," Luke shared. "I caught it in the backyard. It was a little garter snake. 'Bout scared my mother to death when I brought it in the house."

"But she let you keep it."

"Had to. Bridget, only four, fell in love with it, too. She wasn't scared to touch it or anything." Luke smiled at the memory. "Mom could never say no when it came to my little sister."

"Sounds like you had that problem, too," Katie said.

"Guilty," Luke responded.

Just then, Meredith showed up, giving them a look that said, "Why are you just standing there?"

Katie took one step in the right direction. She could do this. When Fred arrived, almost on Meredith's heels, Katie got the idea that whatever they were about to do was important.

Luke led her down a hallway that curved around the backside of the snake and lizard exhibits to a big box. Katie knew right where they were: behind the anaconda room.

The now-empty anaconda room.

Rexette, the anaconda, was now out of the faux pond in her room and in the box.

"Good," said Fred. "If Katie can help, I'll go back and check out Kobie one more time."

"What happened to Kobie?" Luke asked.

It was Meredith who answered, though, as Fred hurried past Katie. "Jasper was feeding Kobie a carrot. Cheeky got jealous and bit Kobie."

"Bad?"

"Not too bad, I think," Meredith replied. "But Jasper intervened and Cheeky hit him with a softball-size chunk of spit. It knocked Jasper off his feet. Fred made him go to your office to rest for a bit. He's going to have a black eye."

Luke shook his head and motioned Katie to take Fred's place. She took a step in Luke's direction and looked down into the box. Rexette was huge.

"And we're going to?" she queried.

"Lift the box," Meredith retorted. "Unless you're not strong enough."

"I thought you only had Arizona animals?" Katie tested her corner of the box, amazed by the weight.

"This one called Yuma home for a while," Luke said. "I get calls from people wanting to get rid of big snakes at least once a month. I said no to this one, too." He took his position and said, "Lift."

As they moved from the back of the snake house to the outdoors, Luke shifted the box so he carried most of the weight. "But sometimes you follow your gut," Luke said as they slowly walked out of the building and into the sunshine, careful not to jostle Rexette. "I had this feeling if I didn't take Rexette, she'd be released into the desert and die without water, or be released into the canals. Not good."

"Don't let him fool you," Meredith said. "She's one of his favorites, he wanted her the minute the kid brought her in."

"You have to admire a teenager who wants a good home for his snake."

"You have to admire," said Meredith, "a director who can't say no to new animals."

"She's a love of mine," Luke agreed. "But—"

"No buts," Meredith teased. "I've seen you

talking to her, telling her she's a pretty girl and rubbing her head."

"Like you do with Yoda," Luke pointed out.

"Not true," Meredith argued. "I never tell Yoda he's a pretty girl. Plus, Yoda needs me. I'm the one who convinced him that his slight limp doesn't matter."

"Who's Yoda?" Katie asked.

"A wolf," Jasper answered, joining them by moving in and helping Katie with her end, "one that thinks he's more dog than anything else."

Meredith gave Jasper a "What are you doing here?" look. He ignored her, so she continued the story. "We got him two years ago when he was found on the side of the road by a trucker. He'd been hit by a car or something. Guy thought he'd found a dog at first."

"He's what used to be called a hybrid," Luke said. "Now they're known as wolf dogs, but Yoda's been raised outdoors, with our wolf pack, and is in no way a dog."

"I'm going to disagree just a bit," Meredith said. "He's the only one we've been able to put on a leash, and he obeys commands like Sit, Stop and Go Get It."

"He obeys *your* commands," Luke drawled.

"True, I work with him all the time."

"Some animals just make their way into your heart," Luke said.

Katie thought about Aquila, remembering the bond between them and challenging the fears that she'd allowed to root for more than a decade.

As they walked from the snake house to the arena, Luke talked about the Yuma teen who'd somehow managed to order an anaconda online and convinced his mother to let him keep it. "When it hit two hundred pounds, it required more space than their spare bedroom and a good-size blue plastic pool could provide."

"You think?" Meredith said snidely.

Luke shot her a disapproving glare.

Meredith just smiled. "Then its appetite increased, and said mom became very antisnake. That, combined with the sixteen-year-old's sudden interest in girls, meant the snake had to go."

"He still comes to visit Rexette," Luke said, "and he donates money for her care. I'm hoping when he hits college, he'll be one of our student volunteers."

They'd made it to just outside the snake arena. To Katie's surprise, the fear she'd experienced outside the snake house had evaporated and she'd carried the snake box without a second thought. Thanks to Luke.

"Kid at first thought she was a boy snake," Luke shared, "so for the first year of this Eunectes Murinum's life, it answered to Rex. Then suddenly a new name was needed."

"How did he discover the truth?"

Meredith answered, "The girl anacondas outweigh the boys. She matured too quickly to be male. Once again, the female demonstrates her superiority."

"And," Jasper added, "ate her way out of house and home."

"Snakes don't eat much. They're very cost-effective," Katie remembered.

"I think," Luke said, "it was the *way* the snake ate more than how much that bothered the kid's mom."

Meredith laughed right along with Jasper and Luke. Katie wanted to join in but hesitated too long and the moment was lost.

There was already a small crowd around the snake arena, which Meredith said was typical for a Monday. Most eyed the box, about the size of a coffin, with suspicion. Others looked alert, as if the snake might suddenly shoot from the box and attack them. There were a few that simply appeared interested.

"Howdy," Luke called as he stopped outside the arena's gate. "I hope you like snakes."

There were a few "Yeahs" and a few "Nos" and some who didn't respond. Maybe they weren't sure. Like Katie. She gazed down at

Rexette, challenging herself to touch the big girl today.

If she did her job without fainting, Luke wouldn't threaten to give Aquila back to her.

Katie just wished Rexette was a bit smaller.

Meredith gave Katie a look that clearly asked, *Are you chicken?*

No way did Katie want this woman to think she was afraid.

Jasper gave her an encouraging nod. "I need five volunteers," Luke said to his audience. There might have been fifteen people, either leaning against the fence or sitting on the stadium bleachers. If five volunteered, the audience would be just a handful.

Three hands immediately went up.

"Okay," Luke said. "I'll take you three and then Meredith and—" he looked from Jasper to Katie "—one of you can volunteer."

"Snake give that man a black eye?" someone in the audience wanted to know.

"Nope," Jasper said, "the black eye came from a jealous camel. I'll take this old man—" he gestured to the snake "—over a camel anytime."

Right now Katie didn't want a snake or a camel. "What are we doing?"

"Carrying the box into the middle of the area, lifting Rexette out of the box and showing her to the audience," Luke said, as if he were talking about a common garter snake.

He made it sound so easy, and for some reason, she didn't want to disappoint him.

The three volunteers hurried to stand alongside the box. Luke pushed open the gate and they all slowly and carefully moved to the center of the area and gently put down the box.

Luke opened the lid, confident and ready. Katie peered inside, worried and ready to run.

Rexette didn't pay attention to either of them; she didn't move at all. Her olive-green body with black blotches was coiled and relaxed. Meredith took the narrow head. Rexette's eyes, set high on the top of her skull, were open, unblinking.

Two weeks. I just need to get through two weeks of this.

At the moment, she wasn't sure she'd make it through two moments. The snake looked slick, oily even, and the thought of touching it had Katie searching for a place to sit down.

But the three volunteers had moved to the middle. Jasper made for the tail.

"Jasper's already had one mishap this morning—" Meredith began.

"I'm strong enough to take you," Jasper said to Meredith, taking the last position. "I may be eighty-one, but you know what they say."

"What do they say?" Meredith asked.

"Eighty-one is the new seventy-one."

The audience laughed. They thought the exchange was part of the show, and that Katie was pretending to be scared.

Eighty-one? Jasper was eighty-one?

Katie searched his face and beside the angry mark left by the camel's spit, she saw the evidence of age in the lines and thinned hair. She noted his hands, a bit more gnarled than she remembered from her childhood. But they still looked as strong as the days when he reached down to lead her to an animal. He'd never let her fall.

Not until the very end.

Jasper caught her staring but misinterpreted her anxiety. "You don't have to do this," Jasper said.

"I can do it," she said.

Meredith and her three helpers were already lifting the snake. Luke had been telling the audience Rexette's story, the same one he'd told her earlier. He paused, watching her, and she realized he'd planned this to show her she *could* do it.

She'd be here for two weeks. She'd already committed to Scoot. She knew that the burros and mules would be a major assignment that she'd be able to cope with. And now she knew she could handle a snake.

After all, this one wouldn't bite anyone's ear off. Not like a leopard.

No, instead, it would swallow them whole. Panic threatened to take over again.

But Luke was there to make sure no mistakes were made, she reminded herself. He was so sure it was safe, he was inviting civilians to help out, come close to the snake, touch it, even carry it. One of the reasons his insurance was ridiculously high, to be sure.

She could only hope that no one in the audience noticed that she was holding her breath and about to faint.

What *she* noticed was how Luke stood close to her, talking to the audience but walking with her. He never stepped more than a foot from her side.

If she fainted, he'd be the one to catch her.

CHAPTER NINE

AFTER REXETTE'S SHOW, which Katie got through without fainting, Luke decided to assign her to the burros and mules. Alone.

"What?" she asked suspiciously. "You're leaving me? By myself?"

"Temporarily," he answered, smiling. "I usually spend my afternoon with them, but you being here frees me up. I need to see what I can do about drumming up publicity for Scoot."

"Thank you," she said softly.

"For Scoot's publicity, or for leaving you alone?"

"For leaving me alone with animals I can handle."

He looked at her, admiring her green eyes. They'd followed him all day, reserved yet uncertain. The combination intrigued him. She held herself back, yet he could see the longing.

But for what?

She'd spent most of the morning being angry, annoyed and/or hesitant.

For the first time today, as they came to the

mules and burros, she started to relax and smiled at him.

"You can handle whatever you put your mind to, Katie."

She nodded, then turned away from him and toward her new task. He watched her—the sway in her walk, the way her hair moved in the October wind—and wished she'd turn around again. He wanted to see that smile once more, aimed at him.

He was enjoying her company, entirely too much. He spun on his heel and headed for his office.

He hoped she kept smiling because Mondays were usually a low-gate day, which meant they spent a whole lot of time cleaning the stalls and grooming the animals, as visitors were few and far between.

He tried to work on a publicity strategy, but his mind kept wandering back to Katie. All afternoon, he found excuses to drop in on her. Every time Luke stopped by to check on her, she was fine. Her smile never got bigger, but neither did it go away—at least it didn't until Meredith suggested visiting Aquila.

It was about an hour before closing, and he'd brought Meredith along to give Katie a break. The keeper had had her own agenda. Katie stiffened. "I'm good here."

"You are, very good, but the mules and burros aren't dying."

Katie's cheeks had pinked from the sun. Her hair was pulled back in a ponytail. She didn't look elegant, as she had on her arrival. She looked as though she was working at something she enjoyed. "Everything's fine *here,*" she assured him.

He wished he believed everything was fine, but attendance was down, even for a Monday. He never worried at the number of people who attended Rexette's show. The snake crowd was fickle. But two hours later, during George's acrobatic display, around the same number had shown up.

A bear juggling Winnie the Pooh lunch boxes usually drew more.

"Meredith is here to relieve you. Have you eaten?"

"No."

"Then let's go. We can stop by and check on Scoot, too."

She didn't protest, just grabbed her backpack—brand-new and with BAAA stenciled on it—and fell into step beside him.

Meredith just shook her head as they walked away.

"Scoot's been asleep most of the day. Fred put him under about an hour ago and worked on his toes. Hopefully this will make the little guy feel better."

"Good. I just hope they catch whoever did such a poor job of removing his claws."

The infirmary had an office attached. Fred kept much of his stuff there. Outside the front door were a few picnic tables. After checking on the slumbering Scoot, Katie headed for one and Luke followed, noting that her smile was still gone and her tenseness had returned. His face must have alerted her to his concern.

"I'm okay, really," she insisted, sitting down and taking out some food. "I just get upset. Animals can't tell you what they need, and when they're that young…" She frowned, staring at her food, which surely couldn't be the object of her consternation because she was eating one of Yolanda's famous tamales. Luke was devouring yet another hot dog.

"So, how much did Aquila and Tyre weigh at birth?" Luke asked.

She gave a rueful smile. "Just over a pound, and Aquila was smaller than Tyre. My father called him a runt."

"Some of my favorite animals have been the runts."

"I didn't realize until later," Katie shared, "that Dad took over with Tyre because Tyre was tougher. Aquila, now, he whimpered and whined. He wanted his mother. Tyre didn't care who fed him as long as he *got* fed."

"How long before you became Aquila's mother?"

"Maybe a day or two. I couldn't stand him being so alone, so helpless. Nobody wanted him, it seemed, but me."

"He definitely was the luckier cub."

"Jasper said that a lot at the time." She looked back at the infirmary. "Jasper said that I learned how to mother from my own mom, and that as long as I followed her example, then she was with me."

She paused, looking at Luke with wonder. "I'd forgotten that until now."

"Sometimes our memories return when we need them most."

She looked at him, brow wrinkled. "Trying to be a poet?"

"No, trying to understand you."

"Good luck with that. Half the time I don't understand myself."

She stood, half-finished with her meal and with a new look in her eyes, one he couldn't read. "I promised Aquila I'd always be there when he needed me. Guess I didn't keep my word."

"You're here now."

"And pretty useless." She stood, tossed her

trash in one of the bins and said, "I'm heading back to the burro pen."

"I'll come with you."

She didn't seem happy, but she didn't tell him no.

He followed her to the burro pen and stuck around to help close the exhibit. She cared for the burros and mules while he handled the petting zoo.

Ruth came by. "I've a Red Hat event tonight," she said to Katie. "Yolanda's leaving soup in the refrigerator for you. You think Jasper will be okay this evening, watching Bridget's on his own with his injury?"

"It's just a black eye," Luke assured her. "Besides, Fred plans to stick around to keep tabs on Scoot."

Ruth nodded. "I'll call Yolanda and tell her it'll be just one for dinner tonight."

"Or," Luke said, not giving himself a chance to rethink the offer, "you can come with me to talk to the Rotary Club in Tucson. You ever been?"

"To Tucson or to a Rotary Club meeting?" Katie asked.

"Doesn't matter," Ruth said before Luke could say which. "Both are fun. I'll tell Yolanda she's free tonight. We'll have the soup tomorrow. You can come over if you want, Luke."

"I can take care of myself tonight," Katie insisted. "There's a good sub place in town and—"

Luke wasn't sure if the sudden rush of disappointment he felt stemmed from losing the chance to put her in greater contact with animals, or because he wouldn't have her company. He suspected the latter.

Ruth shook her head. "You've eaten there every night."

"How did you know?" Katie managed to look surprised and guilty at once. To Luke's way of thinking, both expressions were beautiful on her.

"The woman who manages the sub shop is a Red Hat member," Ruth continued. "She comes here every Monday and we have lunch together. When she saw you today, she mentioned that you'd been in her place."

"Small town," said Luke. "No secrets."

"You should have told me," Ruth scolded. "I wouldn't have expected you to eat twice last night. I did wonder why you made such a face at Yolanda's cooking."

Katie laughed. "I don't think I've eaten so much in years."

"Well, you do need a little meat on your bones." With that, Ruth walked away.

"She likes you," Luke said, motioning at Ruth's retreating figure. He brought the conversation back to the talk. "I'm taking a few animals along and can always use a helping hand. Consider it part of your work assignment. And, although the Rotary Club will feed you, I think your bones look just fine."

"Which animals are you taking?"

"One of Fred's hedgehogs. I don't believe you've met them yet. The hedgehogs always get the 'Ah, how cute' message across. I'm taking Louie, plus a king snake, and if you come, I'll bring Yoda."

"Can't you bring Yoda without me?"

"Because Meredith trained him, Yoda responds better to a woman's voice. If I'm going to convince these men not to shoot wolves if they come near livestock, Yoda has to be at his best to seem worth championing. Plus, wolf-dogs are unpredictable. I'd like to have someone along in case I need help."

"I'm the wrong woman. Why not just take Meredith?"

"Meredith, Jasper and I take turns with the graveyard shift. Tonight's Jasper's turn, but Meredith is on call just in case."

"Which means tomorrow is your turn," Katie reasoned. "Because Jasper must have done it last night if you went to visit your family."

"See," Luke said, "small town."

In the end, to Luke's surprise, Katie agreed

to accompany him. Wearing one of the BAAA shirts and carrying a BAAA backpack, she looked like a keeper. She acted like one, too... for the most part.

She took charge of the hedgehog with no fear whatsoever, and pitched in with Leo the snake, where she stoically controlled her fears.

Yoda, however, clearly put her on edge. Luke guessed it was his size—Yoda was huge, and similar in height to Aquila. In Katie's mind, Yoda had a lot in common with the big cats: predator, apt to attack, able to maim.

Yoda, of course, sensed this and immediately fell in love with Katie and only wanted to be near her.

Eventually they loaded all the animals into the van and climbed in themselves.

"So, what do you think of Bridget's so far?" Luke asked as they drove out of the parking lot and headed for the interstate. "Bridget's is a pretty cool place, huh?"

Her lips went together in a thin line. He waited for her to scold him about where wild animals really belonged, but she didn't.

"I'm glad Aquila and the rest wound up at your animal park. You take good care of them, maybe too good." She had to get one jab in, though. "Remember that they're wild animals—not pets, not friends."

"Jasper says that a lot, too, but he seems to believe that applies to everyone but him."

"Jasper's different."

"You want to tell Meredith that?"

In the back, as if part of the conversation, Yoda howled.

"He disagrees with you," Luke decided.

"I wouldn't bring him to a public place. Maybe if he were still a baby, but too much could happen with a full-grown wolf."

"Yoda is the only wolf we ever use, and Meredith's been working with him—"

"You can't take the wild out of the animal," Katie argued.

He decided not to argue back. Besides, she wasn't the only one who thought Yoda should be left alone. Fred worried every time anyone went near the wolfdog. As a rule, Luke didn't take Yoda to public talks, but this time, Yoda as an ambassador might help to preserve his species. Besides, he was pretty sure her argument had more to do with her own confidence than the danger of the animals.

After a few minutes of driving, Katie offered an olive branch. "So," she said, changing the subject, "do you miss your marketing job?"

"Not a bit," Luke declared. "If I were stuck in an office with four walls and manufactured air,

I'd never see an anaconda shed or have a baby bear pee on my leg."

She nodded but didn't smile as he'd hoped.

"Tell me about your job," he probed. "Meredith says you're an interpreter for the deaf."

"This is my second year and first real full-time attempt."

"Stealing you away for two weeks must not have helped your job security."

"No, it didn't."

"What's your favorite part about being an interpreter?"

"Getting to know my clients, making sure they're aware of what's going on and that they feel part of their community."

He nodded. "You'd be good at that. Gloria says you're a natural in the gift shop, telling stories and making people laugh. And today with Rexette, you made the crowd feel at ease. No one was afraid."

"I'm the only one that's afraid, apparently."

"Of Aquila?"

"And what he can do," she said softly.

He left that alone for now. "Did you choose interpreting because at one time you were worried your little sister might lose her hearing and you wanted to help her?"

Katie shrugged and looked out the window. "There were some concerns about Janie's hearing, mostly concocted by my twelve-year-old imagination and a healthy dose of guilt. But we knew within weeks that her hearing was fine. Until I was twelve, I figured I'd work alongside my father. After we left my father's place, I figured I'd do whatever it took to survive."

"Why was that necessary? Jasper said you had problems with your aunt."

This time she didn't shrug. Her shoulders tensed, and her lips and jaw were rigid. Jasper was right. Whatever had happened with her aunt had been traumatic. So Luke went back to his original question. "Tell me more about how you became an interpreter."

"Janie and I often went to church with a girl from our neighborhood. Her grandmother took us. The church had a ministry for the deaf. On Wednesday nights, the preacher taught hearing people how to sign. My sister and I always got there early because the church provided a meal. But once I started attending the sessions, I learned sign language quickly and I realized I was good at it. Soon, if the church or someone in the congregation needed an interpreter, they asked me."

"And that was enough to get you an interpreting job?"

"Oh, no. There was schooling and credentials. The church actually paid my way. All they asked as payment was that I used the skill in a good and helpful way."

"That's a pretty generous church."

"Aunt Betsy said that since I'd always interpreted for them free of charge, I'd more than earned the tuition they provided. She said they'd used me and should offer me back pay. She even threatened to sue them. But she was drunk and they didn't take her seriously."

His opinion of Katie rose. She'd been in an impossible situation and not only had she made the best of it, but she'd taken care of her little sister and carved out a career for herself, too.

The way he had.

Luke hit the turn blinker. Tucson, its sky already deepening to the blue-gray of early evening, spread on either side of Interstate 10. He found Speedway Road and headed left.

Katie had tensed her shoulders again, so he changed conversation tactics. "The Rotary Club meets for dinner at this wonderful Mexican restaurant. You'll love it. My family has been coming there for years."

"And they let animals in?"

"We have a special permit."

Luke watched her as they parked in the back of the restaurant under some shade. Leo and Louie were fine in the cab of the truck. Katie picked up the hedgehog and followed him, waiting as he went to check on Yoda, hovering close enough to see what he was doing but not close enough to be involved. Yoda was standing, ears up, alert.

"I'll leave him out here while we have something to eat," Luke said. "It's cool enough, he's secure and he's comfortable."

After a moment, he jumped from the rear of the truck and guided her to the front door of the restaurant. She walked slowly, clearly appreciating the restaurant's ambience. He stuck to safe topics. "So, what's your favorite kind of food?"

"I'm pretty happy with just about anything. I like food."

"Come on, everyone has a favorite."

"I'm not fond of spicy food. I'm into everything else. I have a healthy appetite."

She wasn't lying. Twenty minutes later they were sitting at a table with four Rotary Club members, and she was on her third bowl of chips. Luke, who'd grown up with two sisters who were always watching their weight, was quite impressed.

Maybe it was the crowded room or because they were away from Bridget's and on neutral territory, but Katie finally relaxed enough to smile. She'd tucked the hedgehog into her backpack and bantered with the four men. She spoke to them about Bridget's, how his staff was helping animals that had been dropped off, abandoned. She even almost bragged about the snake house. When one man confessed that he'd never been to Bridget's, she just smiled and promised him a tour.

In fact, she continued to smile the rest of the evening. Luke was impressed. But the real test was yet to come.

LUKE HEADED OUTSIDE to fetch Leo and Louis while Katie waited inside, unsure what to do with herself. He came back in and stood up in front of the group of twenty-some men who made up the Rotary Club. The guys actually looked as though they wanted to hear what Luke had to say. And if he happened to entertain them, too, all the better.

Katie wasn't sure what she'd been expecting, but Luke didn't put on a show like her father. He was there to sell preservation; her father would have been there to sell himself and his animals.

Meanwhile, she walked around with the hedgehog, and helped with Leo as Luke preached about the snake's value in keeping the vermin population down. Louie the Iguana kept a regal pose as Luke walked around the room with him, all the while talking about how iguanas were too often the pet of choice for people who didn't have the money or time to care for them properly.

Then he brought in Yoda. Katie plastered herself against a wall in the back of the room near the door.

"He's a hybrid," Luke explained, "Part wolf, part dog. Just like with Louie, someone wanted to make him into a pet and it didn't work. There are plenty of rescue places, but they're full. If we hadn't taken him in, he'd have been put down."

Yoda gave a low, quick bark, as if adding his opinion about the possibility of such a dastardly deed.

As Luke headed to the front of the room to conclude his talk, from out in the hall, so close it sounded right by the door, came a bark.

Someone with a dog—a big dog by the sound of it.

Yoda's ears went up and his lips curled back.

She'd told him the restaurant was no place for a wild animal.

Luke issued a sharp command, which Yoda might have obeyed if the door hadn't opened and a German shepherd hadn't lunged into the room, ready for a fight.

Dog against wolf, the wolf won.

Wolf against man, the wolf definitely won.

Luke tightened his hold on Yoda's leash, but Yoda turned and bit down hard on Luke's hand.

Yoda broke free and Katie acted.

LUKE FELT YODA'S teeth break into his skin, and the pain almost took him to his knees. He tried to hold on to the leash, but Yoda yanked and was gone.

The dog's owner—a kid—was screaming for his dog. The Rotary Club members were scrambling to get the shepherd out of the room. Luke was already draping his shirt over his bleeding hand and searching for Katie.

There. In the back. Somehow she'd gotten Yoda by the leash and cornered him, a chair between her and the wolf dog. He was snarling and she was giving orders.

It only took seconds before, amazingly, Yoda obeyed her.

The men got the shepherd out of the room. Katie waited a few moments, took Yoda to the van and soon came back to help Luke.

One of the Rotary Club members, a doctor, was already binding Luke's hand with a clean cloth napkin from one of the tables.

It was easy for Luke to ignore the pain as he watched Katie miraculously take charge of the audience with a "something has to happen at every presentation—that's why they're called wild animals" speech.

Next, she ended their talk on a high note. The kid got a free guest pass to Bridget's—his dog, however, was not invited. The audience got a story to tell their families once they got home, and Katie emphasized that this was a workplace incident and the wolf had no malicious intent. With any luck, this wouldn't make the news and give Bridget's any bad press.

After she ushered him out the door and loaded up the animals, she drove Luke to the emergency room.

She never once looked at his hand.

She might seem calm and in control, but it was the elephant in the room. He'd lost any ground he'd gained with her.

And to top it off, in all the excitement, the closing plea for money hadn't happened.

Sitting on the edge of the emergency room bed, Luke could only shake his head. "Why was there a German shepherd in the restaurant?"

She sat on a hard orange chair that had seen better days. Both her feet were on the floor, and her hands were folded in her lap.

Gripped in her lap was a better word.

She was pale, and as he watched her hands, he realized she was clutching them tightly together to try to stop them from shaking. Her voice was a little uneven when she said, "It was a service dog, probably a little spoiled by his teenage owner."

"Meredith is going to rib me on this. Yoda's never bitten anyone, ever."

"Instinct always wins." Katie stood, abruptly, the orange chair scooting back and almost falling. "You allowed yourself to be in a situation. The moment Yoda got scared—"

"Yoda wasn't scared. He was itching for a fight."

"Whatever. Yoda was being territorial."

"His territory is back at Bridget's."

"Which is where I told you you should have left him. If I were in charge—"

Luke gave a wry smile. "If you were in charge, the animals would be behind electric fences so no one would be able to get close to them. Yoda was just making sure he was recognized as alpha."

"A good alpha," Katie said, "knows when to fight and when to retreat. He also knows when to be grateful that his three stitches weren't thirty."

Seeing Katie, the way she was now—mad, worried about him and with her heart showing plainly in her eyes—Luke was glad she was only staying two weeks. If she stayed any longer, it might be his heart that needed stitches.

Because she would rip it in two when she left.

CHAPTER TEN

RUTH WAS AWAKE, waiting and worried when Katie finally came through the door. She glared pointedly at the clock and was about to say something. Then she really looked at Katie.

"What happened?" she said, leaning forward in alarm. "Did one of the animals get hurt? Why wasn't I called?"

Katie glanced down at her Bridget's shirt and saw a few streaks of blood. "No animals were hurt. Yoda bit Luke, but really, they're both fine."

Katie filled Ruth in, repeating her advice about leaving Yoda behind from now on.

"Luke's still learning," Ruth said. "He wasn't raised with wild or exotic animals, but he has the willingness and the spunk. Combine that with his business savvy and he'll do Bridget's proud. Someday."

Ruth didn't allow Katie to respond; she just gave Katie a sly look and continued. "I just hope we have enough time to let 'someday' happen. Now, go upstairs, shower and change clothes.

I'm going to make you some hot tea. You'll feel better, and it will help you sleep."

Katie wouldn't have any trouble sleeping. The evening had zapped her. But Ruth was being kind, and she'd waited up. She'd waited up for Katie last night, too. Ruth would never admit it, but Katie figured she liked having company.

Twenty minutes later, they sat at the dining room table, one of Ruth's favorite places. The tea was good. The cookies that accompanied it were even better.

"I'm very impressed with you," Ruth said. "You knew what to do with Scoot. And you were a pro tonight, too."

Katie hesitated. She didn't want to say it came naturally. That's exactly what they were all waiting for. She should remind them that such situations wouldn't happen if people thought of the dangers first.

Her hostess, however, had a pet lion who actually allowed his teeth to be brushed.

"I did what had to be done," Katie finally said.

Ruth stirred her tea. "So, how do you like it here?"

"Your house is beautiful."

"I mean at Bridget's," Ruth persisted. "How does it compare to your father's place?"

"It doesn't compare at all. I grew up on an

animal compound. We didn't have acres and acres of land. The animals were treated well, but they were working animals."

"Which do you like better?"

"That's easy. I like Bridget's. I like that George only does one show a day and the rest of the time he gets to play in a huge enclosure. I like that Ollie pretty much has Jasper to himself. I think Kobie's in love with Cheeky."

"And Aquila?"

Katie hesitated, a little guilty that she'd given no attention to Aquila.

Today, during a brief break, she'd walked by Aquila's enclosure, but she hadn't been able to stop.

"Aquila will be fine," Katie said. "Meredith will eventually convince Aquila that she's his best friend. Then I can quit worrying."

"You think?" Ruth queried. "When I donated Terrance to Bridget's, I meant for it to be permanent, and I'd just visit once in a while. But every time I went to visit, there was something that needed to be done and I was the best qualified to do it. No one takes care of him like I do. Don't you feel like that with Aquila?"

Katie swallowed.

In her heart, maybe, but her feet still refused to go near Aquila.

"It's been more than a decade since I felt that

way," Katie said. "I've got my sister to worry about instead. She's avoiding my calls and texts."

"Is she your only worry?" Ruth asked.

"Yes."

"For many years, Terrance was my only worry. That wasn't good for me and it wasn't good for him." With that, Ruth picked up her plate and headed for the kitchen.

TUESDAY, JUST after five in the morning, Luke found Jasper at a breakfast café just down the road from Bridget's. To outsiders, it looked like a hole in the wall. To the neighborhood, it was an oasis. Jasper went there every morning. They usually had his breakfast waiting for him, as he never changed what he ordered.

"Aren't we a pair?" Jasper said, pointing to his black eye when Luke sat across from him. "I heard about your hand."

"Who told you?"

"Ruth."

"Then you know Katie came to the rescue."

Jasper nodded. "I'm not surprised. She's always been one to take care of people."

"Well," Luke said after he gave the waitress his order, "I was surprised. Yoda sank his teeth in, the blood dripped and I looked over to where she'd been standing and she was gone. I as-

sumed she was either on the floor or halfway
to Dallas. But next thing I know, she's taking
over the presentation and had the audience eating out of her hand."

"She hasn't forgotten anything," Jasper said
proudly.

"It's a shame she's so dead set against working with wild animals. If she'd overcome her
fears, she'd be an excellent addition to our staff."
The words were out of Luke's mouth before he
could stop them.

"You couldn't afford her," Jasper said. "If she
wanted a job with animals, her résumé would
be a who's who and then some."

"She amazed me last night, and I'm not easily amazed."

Jasper nodded sagely.

"She had Yoda on the leash and restrained in
moments. She made sure the other animals were
out of harm's way. She gave the kid a free pass
to our animal park and then got me out the door
and drove to the emergency room."

"Katie's never been afraid of taking charge.
And when I knew her, she wasn't afraid of a
little blood."

"Then why is she so afraid of Aquila? Why is
she so resistant to working with animals? Both
you and Katie claim it's because of what hap-

pened to Janie and how Katie blames herself for it, but surely there's more."

Jasper took a long sip of coffee before finally musing, "For half her life, I watched over her. I was there when she took her first step. I drove her to her first day of kindergarten. Did you know that? Her mom was pregnant with Janie, due any day, and Bob had a shoot. Now here at Bridget's, watching over her again, I've had some time to really think on the past."

Luke was amazed by how much Jasper was talking. It was as if having Katie here had opened some door to Jasper's heart, and now everything that was inside could come pouring out. Luke just had to ask the right questions.

Luke needed to know everything he could about Katie.

So she'd be able to help Aquila.

And maybe stay. With him.

Jasper frowned at his breakfast, pushing it away. "I've changed a few of my opinions in the last few days. I wonder if I, let alone Katie, was aware of all the reasons she was sent away."

"You told us," Luke responded. "Her father was scared that something else would happen to his girls. He had to choose."

"That was part of it," Jasper agreed. "And for years, I believed that was all of it. But now, watching her…" Jasper shook his head. "When the papers came to cover the story of the attack, which Bob made sure they did, it was Katie's name they mentioned first, it was her photo they showed on the news."

"I'm surprised he wanted the story on the news. His daughter was hurt." Luke's breakfast arrived then.

"Bob believed any press was good press."

But Jasper wasn't done. "Katie took care of everything right after the attack, efficiently, and the few of us who witnessed it were impressed. I'm no longer completely sure Bob sent Katie away because he feared for her safety."

Luke had a sense of what was coming next and wasn't sure he wanted to hear the words. He couldn't fathom a father so selfish.

Jasper finished his coffee with a grimace. "I took her and Janie to the bus. I can still see Katie climbing on board, tears rolling down her cheeks, staring back at me. She couldn't believe she was being sent away. She stopped crying when the bus pulled away. I thought it was for the best then, but now…"

Staring into his empty coffee mug, Jasper added, "More and more I wonder if Bob sent Katie away because she had the potential to be his competition, and he couldn't handle it."

"Even when he found out his sister wasn't

treating his daughters well." Luke whispered the question but it came out a statement.

"There was some justice to be had," Jasper said. "Bob knew for the rest of his life that animals worked for him, not with him. And he was lonely. The animals didn't replace his family."

Luke had met Katie all of three days ago. And already she'd made such an imprint that if she left, he'd be lonely.

But, unlike her father, he'd never send her away. He'd do almost anything to keep her.

YOLANDA KNOCKED AT Katie's door, cracked it open a bit when Katie answered and asked, "Pancakes?"

"That would be great."

At six-fifteen, Katie met her in the kitchen and settled down at the small table. Out the nearby window, Katie could see the mountains and desert…and two men busy doing something to one of the bushes past Ruth's pool.

"How many people work for Ruth?" Katie asked. Until now, she had only seen Yolanda.

"Just me and the lawn guys, but they only come twice a week and they never come in."

"How long have you been with Ruth?"

"Forever. My mother used to work here. Back when Mr. Moore was alive. They had a full staff then. Five people. My mother was the cook."

"Where's your mother now?"

"Retired."

"And you're here because…"

That's all it took. Soon, Yolanda and Katie were comparing their lives. They were the same age, but opposites in appearance. Yolanda was thin and dark with short hair, while Katie was curvy and blond with long hair.

"I'm working my way through college here. And I make my own hours, really."

Yolanda also remembered when Terrance had lived on the grounds. "I think he's happier at the zoo," she confided.

Katie took that knowledge with her as she helped Yolanda with the few dishes, then headed out the door to Bridget's.

Life was funny. Ruth had a heart the size of Arizona, yet she'd never had children to care for. Katie's aunt Betsy had a heart the size of a shriveled raisin and she'd been given two girls to care for.

Katie considered the twist of fate that had brought her here. The longer Katie stayed the more she liked Scorpion Ridge, Arizona.

And it scared her…because what she liked best about Scorpion Ridge was Bridget's. And Luke.

Both had the potential to cause her pain. And that was a risk Katie didn't dare take.

Mornings were special at Bridget's. The cooler temperature put both man and animal in a good mood. As an early riser, Katie fit in with those who were the heart and soul of the park.

Like Adam, already at his station when Katie arrived.

"Go on in," he said.

Katie admired the portion of wall Adam had just finished. He was a strange bird, all right. He didn't mind people watching him but had a sign posted that instructed them to please not ask questions because it broke his concentration.

She moved on to the entrance where new signs had been posted near the pay booths. On Tuesdays, senior citizens got in for half price, children under ten were free and anyone who brought in canned goods—for charity—got a free hot dog.

Good marketing, and probably Luke's doing. For a moment, Katie considered going to find him. Instead, she headed exactly where she didn't want to go.

But needed to go.

To Aquila.

She took the long way, thinking there was something peaceful about a zoo before the morning visitors came with their strollers, cell phones and conversations. Still, she was well aware that her little detour was just one more attempt to put off the inevitable.

Jasper drove by on a cart and offered her a ride.

She refused.

Ruth was giving a personal tour and stopped to introduce Katie.

One of the college volunteers waved.

It was almost impossible for Katie to feel out of place, but she did. As if she'd taken a wrong turn in a neighborhood she knew well and found a corner she'd not seen before: similar but different.

Hers but not.

The closer she got to Aquila's enclosure, the more lost she felt. Maybe it was all the open space. At Bob's Animal Kingdom, her dad had housed his animals in cages, so Aquila, Tyre, George and Ollie were always visible. Here at Bridget's, they were often a good distance away.

She stopped at Ollie's exhibit first. The orangutan was walking toward an outcropping of rock near the back of his enclosure. There, a tiny waterfall cascaded into a small pool. Unaware of her presence, he sat and picked up his right foot, bent it at an angle Katie wouldn't be able to mimic and stared at his toenail. From a distance, Katie thought she recognized contentment on his face. Even if it was only her imagination, it made her happy.

Funny, she'd wanted her father's animals to have a good home. Now that she was here, though, walking through Bridget's, she felt guilty she'd sold them to such a great place more or less by accident.

Before she'd signed the bill of sale, she should have visited Bridget's, toured the facilities and interviewed Luke to discover if he was the best of keepers.

She'd lucked into a perfect place where George, of all animals, frolicked with a coconut in his pen, as only an old bear can do.

Clearly, Ollie and George didn't need her.

Aquila did.

When she arrived at his enclosure, he was spread out across a rock, bigger than she remembered and just as beautiful. No, not beautiful, handsome, handsome as only a black panther can be. His fur so black it rippled dark blue…and it was hanging on him.

"I knew you'd come here."

Katie ignored Luke and kept her eyes on Aquila. She'd forgotten the joy of watching an animal that she'd cared for, hugged, played with.

Loved.

Finally, she said, "Then you know more than me. I can't begin to tell you how lost I feel."

"Because of what happened last night?"

She shrugged.

"You were a pro. I'm glad you were there." He glanced at his hand. "It could have been so much worse."

She didn't answer, didn't want to. He looked at Aquila and then back at her, his eyes full of expectations she couldn't fill. Expectations that weren't entirely about the animals. This man made her long for something she couldn't have, and she wished she hadn't realized she even *halfway* wanted it.

"You need to get a better handle on how the animals are treated here, or there's going to be an accident. An animal will get loose and possibly hurt someone. There are not enough safeguards in place."

"Yes, there are. You're just too blind to see them." He sounded annoyed.

"I'm not blind, I'm practical. I know when to draw the line between heart and logic."

He looked across the fence at Aquila. "No heart, huh? Why are you still here, then?"

"You threatening to give back the animals you purchased even though I have no place to keep them?"

He nodded and said, "That's a problem we still have to resolve."

It wasn't exactly the response she *wanted* to

hear. And if she admitted the truth, it wasn't what she *expected* to hear, either.

We?

A problem *we* need to solve?

Surely he realized he asked the impossible.

"Help me help him," Luke pleaded.

"Have you tried putting Terrance in here? Maybe they'd be friends?" Katie suggested. "They've both been raised by hand. They're both used to being around other animals."

Luke shot her a look she deserved, one of disbelief. "Ruth won't go for it and neither will I. We won't put Terrance in danger. Aquila's unpredictable." In a softer voice, he added, "Plus, Terrance would be no company. He's old and sleeps a lot."

"All cats sleep a lot."

"Terrance once fell asleep while eating fresh game. He actually licked it and then simply rolled to his side and flopped his tail once before closing his eyes."

"I don't believe you."

Luke's expression was sheepish, and it somehow made him look incredibly cute. "Maybe I exaggerated a little bit."

"A lot," she countered.

"Animals are not so different than people. We've tried all the tricks with Aquila. There's only one thing Aquila wants. He wants things the way they used to be."

"You're right," Katie said softly. "Animals mourn, just like people. He's been torn away from all he knows. His home, my father."

She choked back the words, surprised by the wash of emotion. When her father had sent her and Janie to live with Betsy, Katie had done much the same as Aquila. She'd mourned. She'd lost weight. What had kept her from giving up was taking care of Janie.

Of course, right now, based on how Janie was avoiding all her calls and texts, Janie didn't want to be taken care of. She didn't want Katie asking about school, homework, responsibility.

"I wonder why Jasper can't reach him."

"Jasper says he never worked with the cats much."

"If I can get Aquila eating and alert, what are you going to do when I leave? What if he just goes back to this?"

"I hate to even consider that scenario," Luke admitted. "I might have to send Aquila somewhere else and eat the cost of acquiring another big cat. I've got a lead in New Mexico. But right now I've got to believe you can accomplish a miracle. Maybe if Meredith is around while you work with him, he'll respond to her when you're gone. That's all we can hope for."

Katie gazed into the enclosure. A bright red ball lay near the base of a tree. "Aquila's not a typical panther."

"I know that."

"I fed him when he weighed just a pound. Every two hours. I cleaned up after him, played with him, made him my top priority. I was eleven and I fell in love. As for your miracle, eighty percent of cubs born in captivity die. My father and I saved not one but two panthers."

"Ah, that's what I needed to hear." He caught her gaze with an intense look. "Do it again," Luke said. "Keep him alive."

"I'm a different person."

"Jasper doesn't think so."

"Jasper's a bit partial. He believes I'll get involved with Bridget's, take on more and more and then one day walk up to Aquila and everything will be fine."

"Jasper's a smart man," Luke says.

"He is, about some things," Katie agreed, turning to walk away.

Luke didn't follow.

Katie made sure, however, that he heard her next words. "He didn't marry, didn't have children and made sure he could devote his whole life to animals without hurting anyone but himself."

She might have been talking about Jasper, but she wasn't thinking about Jasper. She was thinking about her father.

KATIE'S JOB, all Tuesday, was to help Luke, because of his hand. Luckily, his main area was the burros and mules, and she was already a pro there. She was less enthused about the snakes. Luckily, none of them needed feeding, and the lizards were easy.

Louie even nodded at her.

Luke made it a point to stop by the infirmary often with her. Scoot was a bit more active, if moving his head and mewing counted. Mostly he looked pathetic in the cast that covered more than half his body.

From there, Luke almost always took a detour to Aquila's enclosure.

Aquila didn't nod at her.

They did the snake show at ten. Rexette gave the exact same performance as before. But as Katie peered down into the snake's opaque eyes, nope, there was not a single blink or movement of recognition.

Jasper was helping to lift her this time while Luke assured the audience that, no, Rexette had not mistaken his hand for a midnight snack.

After lunch, which they ate at two because they were busy making sure the staff got breaks,

Katie left Luke muttering in his office, typing with one hand, and went to check on Jasper, as the spit-wad line drive he'd received from Cheeky had turned into quite a shiner. He was with Ollie.

"Not my first black eye," Jasper said, "not my last."

"Ollie's still your favorite, isn't he?" Katie asked.

"Pretty much. He's got a personality, he does." Jasper busied himself filling a round Tupperware bowl with ripe fruit. "Some fool visitors were here yesterday. I caught them feeding him popcorn even though the signs say 'Don't Feed the Animals.' I went over and scolded them. There was Ollie, hand out for more popcorn. You know what he did?" Jasper chuckled but didn't wait for Katie to answer. "He blew a raspberry at me. Then he blew kisses at the people who'd been feeding him popcorn."

Jasper shook his head, a big smile on his face. "Kobie doesn't need me. George doesn't care. But old Ollie here perks up whenever I come near. Like Aquila does when you come near him."

"I don't think Aquila notices."

"Yes, he does. Ruth says he's eating a bit more. Plus, he's gotten his ass off the stone bench and paced."

"An aggravated pace," Katie reminded him.

With a grin, Jasper secured the lid and opened Ollie's gate. With a toss any eighty-year-old would be proud of, he let the container soar through the air, over Ollie's head, to land against a tree trunk. "Women do aggravate, that's for sure."

"How would you know?" Katie teased, watching Ollie make his way to the bowl. "You're married to your job."

Jasper didn't flinch, didn't even blink, but Katie remembered the expression he wore when something bothered him. It hadn't happened often, usually when her dad treated an animal in a way Jasper didn't approve of, or when somebody said something hateful to someone he cared about, or when he was worried about something he couldn't control.

It was a look in his eye, a mental retreat.

He had that look now.

Did he regret never marrying, or was he aware his job was threatened?

Katie was familiar with jobs being threatened. Just that morning she'd had a call from her employer wanting to confirm her return in a week and a half. She'd assured them that she'd be back. But the words had sounded hollow.

Ollie had the bowl and was tossing it in the air, joy on his face. It didn't escape her notice that both Jasper and Ollie were graying around the ears.

"Aquila's coming alive again," Jasper said. "Aggravation is akin to hate, and you can only hate what you want to love."

Ten minutes later, Katie stood in front of Aquila's enclosure. She watched as he paced back and forth, tossing her dirty looks whenever he neared the wall she leaned against.

"Quit being a baby," she told Aquila. "You're in a great place, and Jasper's here. If you behave, do what you're supposed to do, both of you can stay."

Aquila ignored her.

"This isn't my life anymore. I'm in Dallas, taking care of Janie and making a new life."

If anything, Aquila slowed his pace and the dirty look lasted a bit longer.

"You have a good life here."

His tail flicked, just for a moment. When she'd worked with him, he'd always used his tail to communicate his state of mind. The flick meant he didn't care for what she was doing.

"I can't help you," she finally said.

"You already have," said a voice behind her. The deep rich tone made her shiver, as only his could.

It was Luke Rittenhouse.

It never failed. Whenever she let down her defenses, either Meredith or Luke managed to be nearby. Meredith, though, would have scoffed at Katie "talking" to Aquila instead of "doing" something. Luke considered "talking" progress.

Meredith made Katie want to go home; Luke made Katie question where home was.

CHAPTER ELEVEN

"DON'T YOU HAVE things to do?" Katie asked Luke.

"Aquila is one of my top priorities." Luke moved away from her and started motioning.

Behind them, a truck pulled up. It was only then that Katie noticed a small crowd was gathering. Most were watching Aquila, but some were watching both her and the cat.

"Feeding time?" she asked.

"Think you can hoist a fifty-pound piece of horse meat over the wall?" Luke asked.

"No, and neither can you," she said, nodding at his hand.

Two of the college student volunteers walked over to Terrance's enclosure. Katie felt a little guilty suddenly. She'd come to visit Aquila every day, but she'd never once glanced at Terrance. Her budding friendship with Ruth should have warranted Terrance more than a passing glance.

The crowd followed the two college students. Both were physically fit, obviously not afraid to get dirty and willing to joke with the crowd about serving horseflesh.

Terrance waited for his meal. When the meat landed just to the left of him, he gave an aloof glare—clearly critical of the volunteer's aim—and walked over. Instead of carrying it off, though, he lay on the ground and promptly bit down. Luke told the crowd, "A decade ago, he'd have taken this off to a private area and start tearing into it, but in lion years he's about one hundred and thirty-five."

The college boys came to Aquila's enclosure next. One sauntered over and introduced himself to Katie before saying, "We're glad you're here. Aquila's a great guy. We're all looking forward to seeing him gain weight."

The crowd gathered closer, mesmerized by what was about to happen. Most were families, but a few couples rounded out the group. The meat sailed over the top of the fence, landing exactly where Aquila was pacing toward. When it landed, it rolled.

"Come on, guy," Katie whispered.

"He's never attacked his food," Luke said. "Not once."

"And it doesn't look like it will happen today," said the college student.

It was Ruth who snapped Katie out of her silence. "Girl, say something, yell at that fool panther. Even if you won't go inside his area, you can open your mouth."

Before she could think, or even breathe, Katie yelled, "Aquila, go for it!"

Aquila's ears went up. Slowly, one paw went in front of the other. It couldn't be deemed a run, but was definitely movement. When Aquila got to the meat, he picked it up firmly. Then, carrying it, he turned and walked away from the crowd.

"Good," Luke breathed.

Katie took one step in his direction.

But a familiar sound threading through the noise of the crowd stilled Katie's steps: someone talking, but not. Katie retreated to watch a young girl who was speaking as she signed to a woman who was probably her mother. "Will eat? Seem sick."

The woman signed back. "Think yes."

Katie smiled at the wistful glimmer in the girl's eyes.

Most of the crowd followed behind the truck as the volunteers moved on to feed other animals. The young girl remained, staring at where Aquila had stood. Katie stepped over to the girl and signed: "My cat. He eat now. Sick yes. Getting well."

The teenage girl brightened and identified herself as Amanda. Her signs came fast and furious, asking about Katie and Aquila, about the zoo. Next thing Katie knew, she was giving the girl and her mother a private tour, ending at the infirmary with Scoot.

It felt good to squire Amanda and her mother around Bridget's, talking about the animals and their routines. There was a joyous light in Amanda's eyes, a light that Katie had put there.

By the time the pair left, Bridget's had been closed for thirty minutes. Meredith was annoyed that Katie hadn't helped with the burros. Jasper tsked and said, "They were just fine before Katie got here. You're just searching for something to fuss about."

Not letting either of them ruin her jubilant mood, Katie washed up and went to find Luke.

"I just made a friend," she said when she finally found him in his office.

But he didn't look up, he just kept staring at what appeared to be a spreadsheet filled with numbers on his computer screen. "I saw you with the girl, and I was impressed. You must be very good at your job. You were quite a teacher, a natural, in your element."

"I am good. Not at teaching, but I'm an excellent interpreter and…" Katie's words tapered off. She was particularly good when what she was signing excited her. It had been a long time since she'd been so engaged. Signing a lecture during a statistics class practically put her to sleep.

Katie continued, trying to get back a little of the jubilance she'd experienced earlier, a little surprised by Luke's somewhat serious mood. "Her mom signs great, but Amanda was curious about the behind-the-scenes details. She's a junior high school student and—"

His phone rang.

She could only hear one side of the conversation, but by his tone, something had him on edge. "Yes, we welcome ideas that promote Bridget's. Uh-huh. Yes, I enjoyed talking to the Rotary Club last night. Yes, you did hear me say that Ruth brushes Terrance's teeth. We've talked about filming it and making a YouTube video to help promote Bridget's. What? Well, I'm not surprised your mother is a Red Hat Lady. Ruth loves that organization." Next came a long pause followed by "I agree, Katie is quite good with animals."

Katie sat up. Whoever was on the phone was pushing an idea that had to do with her.

Whether she liked it or not.

"Yes, her father was Bob Vincent, but no," Luke was saying, "Katie's not the one who brushes Terrance's teeth. Ruth does that. No, Terrance does not know Katie. She can't brush his teeth. Here at Bridget's, Katie works with the burros, mules and snakes." Luke listened for a moment, then glanced up and asked her, "Anything special you can do with a snake, Katie?"

She shook her head, but he was already saying, "We might be able to come up with something involving Rexette, the anaconda. No, Katie doesn't work with the cats. Not yet. She is, however, caring for a very ill baby bear that was dropped off here a few days ago."

Katie shook her head. She could tell where this conversation was heading and wanted no part in it.

Luke held up his hand, signaling for her to wait. Another long pause, and then he said, "I'll talk to her. We can always use free publicity."

"What was that about?" she asked when he hung up. "And why did you tell him about Scoot?"

"One of the men at the Rotary Club meeting was impressed by you last night. He teaches film at the community college, and after watching us, he decided to assign a project to his sophomore class about animal welfare. He thinks Bridget's will be the perfect place for them to film it. He was amazed by the threat of snakes like Rexette being let loose in the canals. And who wouldn't be touched by Scoot's story? I guess he said something about doing his own film to his mother, who happens to be friends with Ruth."

"One of her Red Hats."

"Yes. He said brushing a lion's teeth would be a funny human interest story and a good draw, but he needed something more. Apparently he looked you up on Google, found the connection to your father and got interested in doing something with big cats. I think he was going for a theme. The baby bear also appealed to him."

"How would his film and school assignment help with marketing?"

"You never know where these short films will show up. A YouTube video that goes viral could bring in out-of-towners. A video of that baby bear and all he's been through could bring in donations." He glanced at the screen on his computer. "We need the money."

"I'm not the best choice. Remember the fainting?"

Annoyance boiled under the surface of her skin. Every time she turned around, this man was asking her to do the impossible. Work with Aquila. Save Scoot. Toss out logic and change her mind about animals in captivity.

"Scoot's just a baby," came Luke's final argument. "Without you and people like you, he'd be dead."

Luke was right, and she admitted part of her

wanted to pitch in. She could do it. Aquila's care, as a newborn, was vivid in her mind. She remembered exactly how much formula she'd given him, and how many heating pads she'd gone through to get him warm.

"You should let me help with Scoot because I'm good at caring for animals, not because it's a promotional opportunity."

He looked her right in the eye. "I wish I could think that way." He dropped his eyes to the spreadsheet again. "But I need you to help with Scoot because you're good at caring for animals *and* because it's good for Bridget's. If we're going to save Scoot, we have to raise money. It's no secret that we're struggling. But I haven't let on how much we're struggling. We need this. Or we're finished."

LUKE'S WORDS STAYED with Katie the next morning. He was losing patience with her.

It shouldn't matter. He'd forced her here, after all.

She'd been honest with him, told him she didn't work with animals.

Yet here she was, working with animals—and doing a good job.

It just wasn't the job Luke had brought her here to do.

She fumed as she helped him ready the burros. "I realize I was played," Katie said to him. "You *know* how uncomfortable I am with certain animals, and you *know* I don't want to be linked to my father's name."

Luke, bandage off and using his wounded hand hesitantly, responded, "And you know how much Aquila and Scoot need you. How desperate Bridget's is for exposure. Your father spent his life building a reputation with animals. By association, you generate the same interest."

"That sounds so cold."

She didn't like this Luke, yet she understood him. Concern for his animals warred with his concern for his people.

She was one of his people now, and although she'd only be here for a little over a week longer, she could tell she mattered to him.

It was how much she mattered to him that unsettled her.

"Caring for a cub is a far cry from stepping into an enclosure with a full-grown panther."

"You tell me when you're ready," Luke said.

"I may never be."

He didn't respond; there was nothing left to say. So they continued on their rounds.

Eventually she asked, "Your hand hurting?"

"It is. Meredith already called me a wimp."

"Meredith didn't see the size of the other dog."

Luke chuckled. "I'm starting to really like you."

This time, it was Katie who didn't respond.

At ten she helped with the snake show, her fear all but gone.

At eleven, Luke took a phone call from Jake at Game and Fish. They'd been checking emergency rooms between Phoenix and Tucson to see if anyone had shown up last Saturday night with scratches severe enough to come from a bear.

"It's hard to imagine Scoot putting up much of a fight, not in his condition," Luke confided when he hung up, "but I appreciate that they're doing something."

"What else are they doing?"

"They're visiting veterinarians who've had their licenses revoked, hoping someone will slip up and mention the declawing."

At noon, the college film class showed up. It turned out to be five students and their teacher. The guys were tall, gangly and tattooed. The girls were tall, thin and tattooed.

Fred frowned at the intrusion, Jasper frowned, but Ruth said, "Come on in."

Ever since the professor's phone call, the one Ruth claimed would make Terrance a star, Ruth had been dancing with happiness. She hadn't, however, expected the group to show up so soon. She'd wanted Terrance bathed, groomed and on display when they arrived.

But to everyone who worked at Bridget's amazement, Terrance happened to be awake.

"I'm Coty Clark," the college instructor introduced himself. He fell in step with Katie and Ruth, leaving Luke and Jasper a couple of steps behind with the students.

"I was quite impressed with you Monday night," Coty said to Katie. "You made me both want a wolf and glad I don't have one."

Katie laughed. He was so nice she could almost forget that he was betting her last name would get his film noticed.

"I didn't even know you guys were here," one kid said. "Strange place for a zoo, out in the middle of nowhere. I thought this was just a golf community."

"We're not really a zoo," Luke said. "We're an inspiring habitat. Most of our animals are native to Arizona and—"

"But we're here to film a lion. That's not native to Arizona."

"Terrance has called Arizona home for more than twenty years. That makes him practically a native," Ruth said. "Before he came to Bridget's, he belonged to me as a pet."

"Lions can't be pets," one of the young men pointed out. Of the five, he appeared to be the youngest, yet also the most mature. His tennis shoes were frayed, but not because that was cool, more because they were old. His steps were purposeful. He checked his cell phone for the time even as he made the statement.

"Terrance is," Ruth said. They arrived at Terrance's enclosure. Katie stepped back to watch, Luke right at her side. Ruth, however, was at the front, standing by the serious guy.

"Terrance is only two years short of making the *Guinness Book of World Records* for being the oldest documented lion in captivity."

"Cool."

That was all the encouragement Ruth required. She went right into her Terrance-is-the-best-lion-on-earth spiel.

"It won't bite?" one of the guy asked.

"Not enough teeth," Jasper assured him, "but he's got strong jaws."

"Not an it," Ruth argued, "Terrance is a he."

"I'm more worried about the claws," said one of the girls. "My sister has a cat and she's forever getting scratched. His claws could take off an arm."

Ruth opened the security door to Terrance's enclosure, disappeared and, after a moment, stepped from the exit door into Terrance's territory. "Come," she shouted.

Slowly, as if he had nothing else planned

that day, the lion sauntered over and sat by her. His tail thumped once and Ruth's hand went to stroke his mane. She turned to the students. "I've been Terrance's mother for twenty-one years."

Terrance rubbed his head against Ruth's hand, and it reminded Katie of Aquila. As a baby, he'd followed her, not just with his body but with his eyes. Those eyes had always told her he considered her his mother.

Babies were trusting, sometimes too trusting.

People were, too, sometimes.

Ruth, standing next to her lion, was too trusting. Katie imagined Terrance, feeling threatened by the film students, lashing out, his claws tearing through Ruth's skin.

If Katie were in charge, there'd be no treating lions as if they were pets. They weren't! Why didn't Luke realize this?

But the visit with Terrance was uneventful, and an hour later, they arrived at the infirmary.

"I'm relieved you're here," Fred said to Katie as if the film crew didn't exist. "I'd love some downtime. Ruth's already done what she can, and quite frankly Meredith doesn't have a moment to spare."

Katie peered into the small carrier where Scoot nestled on a blanket. At least now the cub was awake and off the tube. A bowl of black-berries lay untouched beside him.

"He should want to eat," Fred said, handing Katie a bottle. "Try coaxing him with this. Then bathe him and see if you can convince him to play—even if he just swats at your finger. We need some show of life from him."

Katie picked up the bear and, out of habit, arranged Scoot so his claws wouldn't get her. But then she noticed the bandages and remembered, *he doesn't have claws. An idiot cut them out.*

Nestled in her arms, Scoot merely rested against her chest, uninterested in what was happening to him. Katie held him close, rocking him as she offered him the bottle, hoping he'd strain for it.

He whimpered but didn't move. "I still believe," she said, "he should have been put down."

Fred was filling out some form. "I'm not sure I disagree. It may still happen."

Luke, of course, offered his two cents. "If there's a chance he could live, I want to take it."

The same thing he'd said before.

The students acted as if they'd entered a funeral home. Finally, one managed to say, "He looks scruffy."

"That comes from malnutrition," Fred said. "We're offering him food. He's just not taking it. Thus the missing fur around his face and stomach."

He took no interest in the bottle, a Pedialyte and applesauce mix Fred had prepared. And he barely moved when she next tried bathing him.

"Got any ideas?" Fred asked, peering at her over his glasses. "What would your dad have done?"

"My dad would have gotten rid of him because he'd never be a show bear." As she said the words, Katie scratched behind Scoot's ear. A tiny rumble came from his stomach. It probably just meant the bear was hungry, but part of her wanted to believe it was a response to her touch.

Luke looked at Katie, his expression daring her to admit what was in her heart.

"It's too bad," Katie said, "that we don't have another baby bear. Siblings make a difference. Aquila and Tyre had a special bond. My dad noticed it, too."

"A buddy might help," Luke said. "Maybe I should have let him go to a bear rescue. Moving him now, though… And would the little guy's immune system even be up to being around a friend?"

"He wouldn't even notice another animal right now," Fred observed. "My ultimate goal is for him to gain a pound a day. When he starts doing that, introducing a friend is an option. Too bad there isn't a sibling."

Siblings definitely made an impact, Katie thought, suddenly missing Janie.

She'd fought for Janie.

Luke had fought for Bridget.

Who would fight for Scoot?

She scratched Scoot behind the ear again and bent down with the bottle. "Come on, little man."

THE NEXT DAY, the students came back. As their spokesperson for Bridget's, Katie was put in charge of seeing to their every need.

This time Ruth was ready for them. Terrance was groomed to near feline perfection and eager to be filmed.

In the end, only one of the students was willing to go into the enclosure with Ruth: the female who didn't have a sister with cats. The filming took all afternoon. Luke stayed away, leaving Katie in charge.

Throughout the day, all the employees of Bridget's had their chance to put on a show. Jasper and Ollie had their turn in the spotlight, both of them reading the newspaper. Then Luke went on with Rexette, who didn't primp at all. Fred insisted his hedgehogs get some attention.

An hour before Bridget's closed, the professor

turned to Katie. "Today we're focusing on bond-
ing. I remember you're working with Scoot the
bear, but besides him, which animal is yours?"

Katie had hovered over Scoot off and on for
the past twenty-four hours, staying late into the
evening and coming in early. She liked Scoot.

She missed Aquila.

CHAPTER TWELVE

THE FILM CLASS stayed until closing, promising they'd be back after the weekend. They were indignant at Scoot's situation and passionate as only college-age kids could be about injustice.

Their passion was oddly contagious, tempting Katie to care. And, ridiculous as it might be, she wasn't sure if it was Scoot she wanted to care for, or Luke.

She really had to get that man off her mind before he took over and she couldn't make a rational decision.

After spending time with Scoot—petting him, rubbing his stomach, cleaning him up— she walked around Bridget's, trying to figure out why she was still at Bridget's as the sun set over the park. She could be at her favorite sub shop, she could be at Ruth's all curled up in a chair watching television or she could be glaring at her phone as she received a one-word response to the heartfelt Where R U? I miss you text she'd sent to Janie.

She searched for Jasper, but he was nowhere

to be found. Ruth most likely was at home resting or updating her calendar. Meredith had proved her worth before leaving and prepped all the animals for bed.

Tonight was Luke's turn to pull the evening shift.

Already, Katie knew Bridget's backward and forward, knew which animals anticipated Luke stopping by their enclosure and which animals couldn't care less.

"Is it just us?" she asked when she found him.

"Yes, and some of the cleaning crew. Usually we'd have Adam, too, but he had some kind of appointment. How many times did you try today?"

Luke always took it back to Aquila.

Great. Even when she thought no one was watching, someone was. "Twice."

"Did you get any closer?"

"I can get to the door of his enclosure. Perhaps if there was no other place to go, I'd walk in. But it's too easy to turn around and decide to try again later. He is moving around. Maybe," she said hopefully, "he no longer needs me."

Luke just harrumphed. "Will you stick around with me tonight?"

Katie was surprised by the question and then a little apprehensive—a good kind of apprehensive. Since her arrival, her days had begun and ended with this man, seeking his approval, his direction.

"Ah, do you need me?"

"No, I don't need you," he said. "But it's nice to have your company." He looked down at his sore, bandaged hand. "And it never hurts to have a ride to the emergency room."

"Funny. So, what are you doing tonight?"

"The animals have been put to bed. Occasionally on the night shift, I walk the zoo to make sure everything's all right and to strategize. I get some of my best ideas when I'm here alone." He held up a hand before she could say anything. "Don't worry. I consider you inspiration. My ultimate goal tonight is to come up with something spectacular for this year's Halloween season. We string up lights and have different animal trick-or-treat stations. But if you've done that once, you've done it enough. It's not much of a draw. Last year I brought in jump houses. I'll do that again, but I want something new to advertise."

"Will the film students be done by then? Will we be allowed to use any of their footage for advertising?"

"Not sure they filmed anything that ties in to Halloween."

"Maybe we could entice one of them to come back."

"And film what? It can't be Scoot."

He ran a hand through his hair and she suddenly noticed the fatigue in his eyes.

"How worried are you?" she asked.

For a moment, she wasn't sure he'd answer. Then he said, "Worried enough that I'm wondering which keeper to cut, which animal to sell and how to save on our food bill."

Wow, that serious.

"Do your employees know what you're considering?"

"They're aware we might have to sell a high-maintenance animal, and they're aware that may be only the first step. I already mentioned we have to rethink our monthly food bill."

"Who would you let go?"

If possible, Luke's fatigue deepened. "Which one would you let go?"

"I'd get rid of the animal first and watch my budget for three months," she responded quickly.

"Really?" He had that expression on his face, the one that dared her to be honest. He had her and he knew it. "Then?"

"Then I'd do everything in my power to bring more money in."

"Ruth's working on that. She's got a Facebook page going for Scoot, and believe me, I'm impressed. She got the film students here. She's arranged two more conservation talks for me, one at a community college—the same community college our film students attend, by the way—and another at a library."

"I wouldn't think college students or library patrons come to such events expecting to give money."

"They don't, but you never know who might be in the audience, what connection you might make. Ruth's brought more money to Bridget's than anyone else. She's *donated* more money to Bridget's than anyone else."

Katie understood what he was saying. If he had to let go of a keeper, it wouldn't be Ruth. That meant either Meredith or Jasper.

Jasper was well past retirement, but probably made less.

Meredith aspired for Luke's job and, from what Katie had seen, was worth her weight in gold when it came to working with the animals.

She took their discussion in a slightly different direction. "We have to make money. From my perspective—and this is just from working Sunday at the gift shop—the way to get people to spend is ensure kids say, *'Can I have...'* So, what do kids like to do?"

He answered without hesitation, "Hands-on activities." Then he stepped closer to her, bending his head so he was just inches away. Her whole body tingled from his warmth.

Katie swallowed and her hands grew sweaty. She tilted her face up, wanting the touch of his lips.

And he didn't disappoint.

His lips came down on hers even as his arms wrapped around her, pulling her close. For a moment, the worries of the day fell away.

Tentatively she reached her hand up, her fingers tangling in his hair and locking into a gentle grip as she clutched him—impossibly—closer. Her eyes closed as she melted into the moment.

A peacock screamed.

Her eyes opened and locked with his. His gaze was dark, hooded, unreadable, but he didn't let go.

The peacock screamed again and Katie stepped away. Nervously she said, "Um, that was unexpected."

He didn't appear nervous. "I like it when you say *we*."

"When did I say we?"

"You said *we* have to make money. There's a whole lot of things *we* could get right if we did them together."

Red heat hit her cheeks. She had to change the direction of this conversation before he realized she'd already given some thought—and just now had some proof—to how well they could get along. But ultimately they were doomed.

He was Arizona; she was Texas.

He was into animals; she was *not*.

There could be no "we."

"So," she said brightly, "on Halloween what do you do with the burro carts?"

He looked surprised by how quickly she'd changed gears. "Well, they're made up so they resemble little horse-drawn hearses."

"What about the playground?"

"Nothing planned. Kids just go there and play."

"What about having a kids' haunted house there?"

"Some kids get scared. I want Bridget's to be a place kids feel safe."

She realized that somewhere in the past, the real Bridget had gotten scared. "How about the cabin, then? And make the haunted house for twelve and over."

"That would cost money and we don't have it. Besides, there's no guarantee that enough people would come. Haunted houses are a dime a dozen around here."

"Then we have to make ours different."

"Again, that costs money."

"What do you do with the camels?"

"Decorate them in black, and whoever is working that area leads the camels around dressed as a skeleton."

"Do the kids get to ride?"

"Only if I have someone skilled enough to lead the camels and watch the riders."

"And that would be…"

"Meredith."

"Meredith's pretty valuable, too, eh?"

"She knows animals, more than Ruth and more than me."

"Not more than Jasper."

"He's eighty-plus," Luke said gently. "I'm very careful with what and where I assign him."

"He'd probably work here for free."

She didn't like the shadow that suddenly fell across Luke's face.

"Not fair to him."

"Is this why you asked me to stay, so you could tell me Jasper's job is in jeopardy? So you could once again remind me how important it is that I get Aquila to perform?"

"No," Luke admitted, a bit sheepish. "It just keeps coming back to that. And right now it's the last thing I want to think about."

The sheepish look disappeared. He stepped close again. His eyes asked a question. If Katie so much as tilted her head, she'd be saying yes. She turned away. "I should get back to Ruth's."

IT HADN'T TAKEN Katie and Ruth long to realize they enjoyed each other's company, especially at dinner. Tonight Katie wasn't much company. But if Ruth noticed that Katie merely moved her food around on her plate, she didn't mention it. Instead, she made it easy for Katie and simply stuck to small talk, such as what was happening with Scoot, with the film students and with the upcoming Halloween venture Bridget's was undertaking.

Ruth had even found a hearse to use.

She didn't mention Luke, and Katie wondered just what Ruth was thinking.

Katie was thinking entirely too much.

She was thinking that she was starting to like Luke—the way he got along with his staff, the way he got along with the animals…the way his lips curled in a half smile whenever he looked at her.

Katie was daydreaming so much about Luke that she missed part of the conversation, only returning to it when she caught the tail end of Ruth's question. "What if Meredith is let go?"

"Huh?" Katie choked, but managed to recover. "Meredith won't be let go."

"No?" Ruth queried.

Suddenly, Katie realized she wasn't the only one simply moving her food around the plate. Ruth's appetite must be waning, too.

"Both Meredith and Luke have been hired within the last five years—Jasper, too," Ruth said. "Before that, it was just me and a man named Thomas."

"What happened to him?"

"He disappeared."

Katie considered Bridget's. How everyone worked together and enjoyed their job. It was hard to imagine a two-man operation.

"What happened?"

"One night Thomas counted the day's receipts, took what was in the safe and disappeared."

"I'm surprised you didn't quit. Donate the animals to other rescue centers or zoos, maybe sell them. You could have brought Terrance back here."

Ruth shook her head. "Never crossed my mind. When I moved Terrance to the animal park, I meant for it to be permanent, and I decided I'd help out there until somebody came along who loved it as much as I did. And someone did—Luke."

Ruth wasn't finished. Sounding as serious as Luke had earlier in the day, she asked, "So, who would you let go?"

"If I were Luke?"

Ruth nodded.

"If you were Luke."

"A high-maintenance animal," Katie finally said.

"Like Aquila?" Without waiting for an answer, Ruth picked up her plate and headed for the kitchen. She always seemed to know when to exit, leaving Katie to ponder at some hidden meaning, some trick, in Ruth's words.

She'd made her point, though. It had only been a week and already Katie knew if the choice were up to her, Aquila would be in no danger of leaving.

Meaning Katie was as softhearted—weak?— as Luke.

WHEN KATIE SHOWED up at Bridget's on Friday, she headed for Scoot first. He gave her a faint *Grrrr* and tried to wiggle a greeting.

"I call that progress," Ruth said. "He's alert and eating a bit."

Katie didn't comment on Ruth's definition of alert, or the fact that what Ruth called "eating a bit" wasn't really eating at all. Her heart sank. Which was silly, because she'd said from the beginning that it was inhumane to let him suffer.

After that, Katie headed for Luke's office. A stack of papers—and Tinker—lay on Luke's desk, and another stack rested on the table next to Katie's favorite couch. Postal boxes were arranged next to the door. Luke Rittenhouse personified the word *busy.*

The pictures on the wall told the tale of Bridget's, starting with the one showing the real Bridget standing next to Cheeky the camel. Behind her was open space and sky. Bridget's the animal park hadn't blossomed yet. Katie walked the perimeter of the room, aware all the while that Luke was watching her. She admired a photo of Rexette doing a show by the oddly pink-colored snake house.

Adam really had done a superb job.

The photo of kids riding the burros revealed the burro enclosure looked much the same as it did today, except there were no mules in the background. She hesitated at the photo of Aquila's enclosure midconstruction.

"One of my favorite pictures," Luke said, coming up behind her. "To me, it proved we were making progress."

And she, Katie, was hindering that progress.

Luke stayed where he was, so close she could feel him, even though they weren't touching. She savored the closeness for a moment then said, "Scoot should be put down."

"I said no."

"Why not?"

"There's still a chance."

"Have you been over there this morning? Have you spoken with Fred?"

"I will. It won't change my mind."

She dropped it. "So, where are you assigning me today?"

He took a deep breath, and his words made her wonder if she'd pushed him too hard. "Why don't you take the day off? You've been here every day, sometimes twelve to fourteen hours."

"I don't have anything else to do, not really," she protested. "I could read all day, or leave twenty text messages for my sister that she'll either ignore or send one-word responses to."

"Go to Tucson. There are some great places to explore."

Katie considered it. Growing up, if Janie hadn't been with her, she'd happily gone places alone. She'd never minded. But now, honestly, she'd rather be here.

Bridget's made her feel needed and alive. Maybe that was why she *should* get away, clear her head. "I could go into Tucson and start buying some stuff for the haunted house—second hand or at discount stores, of course. That would be fun."

"We haven't sat down with Ruth to discuss a budget."

"You talking about me?" Ruth walked into the room—without knocking—and put her hands on her hips, just waiting for an argument. "Katie explained the haunted house idea this morning. Sounds great to me."

"You guys are ganging up on me."

"So," Ruth accused, "you're giving Katie a day off and leaving her unattended."

"I'm a grown woman."

"And he's an overworked man who will have a heart attack before he's forty if he doesn't start relaxing and having fun."

"I have fun." Now it was Luke who was protesting. But the twinkle in his eye said he enjoyed it.

"In case you haven't figured it out," Ruth told Katie, "he gives two hundred percent of himself to the people and things he loves. For example, he loves his family and he loves this animal park."

She gave him a despairing look. "So much so that he hasn't taken a day off in months."

"I'll take a vacation when Bridget's gets back on her feet."

"And if that never happens?"

He stared at her as if she'd suddenly sprouted two heads.

Ruth ignored him. "And when was the last time you took out a pretty girl? Go with Katie. Have fun. We're a good crew and can handle the load."

"But Rexette's show—"

"Fred will do the handling and Jasper will do the talking."

"We don't have enough—"

"Instead of three audience volunteers, we'll get five."

"Do we have any school field trips scheduled today?"

"Only one."

Tinker had been leaning against Luke, and the cat seemed offended when Luke stood and left him. Tinker wasn't offended long, though, he simply curled up right on top of the papers Luke had been working on and went to sleep.

Luke walked to the main window of his office, the one that overlooked the whole zoo. They weren't open yet, so the dirt walkways that snaked across Bridget's were mostly empty except for the occasional bird or prairie dog. Katie came and stood next to him. Meredith was off in the distance, driving the cart and already taking care of feedings.

"Jasper's out there, too," Luke said. "Probably with Ollie. I'll go find him and tell him I'll be off property for a while."

Katie wasn't sure what to think. She'd not get to clear her head if Luke was with her. No... more likely her head would be more muddled than ever.

He walked from the office, and Ruth joined her by the window. At the front gate, two young people came in.

"The first of our student volunteers. They're on time," Ruth noted. To Katie, she added, "That's one of the best programs Luke started. He went to the colleges and talked to any department that had to do with animals. The first year we only had three volunteers. This year we had over two hundred applications and chose ten."

"And you don't pay them."

"No, they get a letter of recommendation for working with the animals. However, a few, to make ends meet, work the concession stands on the weekends or on holidays, our busy time."

"And none of the volunteers have ever gotten hurt?"

"Two years ago Louie about took the finger off a junior. I think the kid changed his major to journalism soon after."

Katie laughed.

"I enjoy being around young people," Ruth confided as she watched two more student volunteers arrive. "The ones who work in the morning seem to be the ones more geared to the educational programs. They help with the shows." She frowned, thinking, "Well, some of the shows."

Katie understood that Terrance would be off-limits to students, except for throwing food over his fence. Ollie and George, too. They probably helped Meredith. Katie really should make time to go to one of Meredith's shows. She'd caught part of one the other day. Meredith had been demonstrating a bird, some sort of hawk.

"Others," Ruth continued, "show up at three or four. They're the animal lovers. They don't need a human audience."

"What about the ones that are both?" Katie asked.

"They're the ones we want to hire when we expand. Someone like you."

Katie was saved from responding by Luke's return.

Not that she'd been rescued. The expression *out of the frying pan and into the fire, came to mind....*

BRIDGET'S WAS JUST opening when they drove out of the parking lot. Ruth had provided, thanks to a few quick phone calls, a budget for their venture. In exchange for the donation, some of the local businesses would expect signs reading This Haunted House is Sponsored by Wendy's Sub Shop or Sponsored by Bristol Dental Stop.

"I'm just glad," Luke confided, "that she didn't call the local funeral home."

"Hmmm," Katie said. "Maybe I'll suggest it to her."

This trip, they didn't take the animal park's truck. Instead, Luke squired her to a dark blue Ford half-ton pickup. It was cleaner than Ruth's car.

"You don't have any pets at home?" Katie queried.

"I take Tinker back and forth if I'm going to miss a day of work."

"And the last time you missed work was…?"

He paused, thinking, and said, "Today."

"Before that!"

"My sister's wedding. I *had* to miss a day. I was in the wedding party."

"How long ago was that?"

"Two years."

"You haven't had a day off in two years?"

"I have," he protested. "I just don't remember."

Instead of Tucson, he drove her into Phoenix. "Otherwise, you might never see it before you go home," he said.

It was a reminder that in just seven days she'd be heading back to Dallas and the duties she had there.

It seemed a lifetime away.

"THE BEST DAY to do this," Katie said to him as they walked around the discount store, "would have been last November first. The day after a holiday is when you get the best prices on everything. I know about pinching pennies."

"How old were you, again, when you got custody of Janie?"

"Eighteen."

At eighteen, Luke had been starting college. His life had been school and squiring Bridget around when necessary, but otherwise it was video games, movies, sports and, every once in a while, he'd studied. He'd worked part-time for his dad at the car dealership.

He'd had no worries except for a math class that had kicked his butt until he'd dropped it and taken it a few semesters later.

"I'll bet you could teach me a thing or two about saving money," Luke said. He gazed around the discount store. Halloween had definitely taken over. Maybe Katie was right. Halloween brought out kids. And kids and animals went hand in hand.

"The big zoo in Phoenix does a Zoo Lights display," Luke said. "It's a big event. We discussed trying something similar, Ruth and I, but the cost to purchase that many lights, hire a crew to put them up and then pay for the electricity is out of our league. We don't for a minute think we can compete with them. Plus, we'd be small time while the Phoenix Zoo is big-time. Why drive out to see us?"

"Which is why we're doing something different—the haunted house."

"I hope you're right. Bridget's just seems, well, it seems too friendly to have a haunted house."

Katie put ten bags of white spider-web material in her shopping cart. "That's the beauty of where the cabin is. It's far enough away that parents with small children can avoid it. And those who are brave enough will love the fact that they can be driven to the haunted house in a real horse-drawn hearse from 1850."

"Which they'll pay dearly for." Luke smiled. "Ruth never ceases to amaze me. She has contacts with everyone. Of course, the ancient hearse she's borrowing only has room for the corpse and the driver plus one passenger, so most haunted house attendees will travel by hayride."

"Still, I'm sure you'll make money this year," Katie said, "even though we're only doing it for the week of Halloween. Next year will be better. You can do it for the entire month of October. You'll make even more money."

Luke noticed that she'd said *you'll make* and not *we'll make*. It shouldn't bother him, but it did. He'd liked the *we* she'd said after the kiss.

He'd gotten used to having her around. So much so that he found it difficult to picture the place without her.

She, however, never let go of her belief that he was too lax with the animals, or that she had to get back to Janie.

Never mind that she'd still not managed to get close to Aquila.

A couple of hours later, they each pushed a shopping cart filled to overflowing to the check-out. They'd spent five hundred and thirty-three dollars. Ruth had given them five hundred; Luke kicked in the thirty-three when he noticed Katie starting to put things back.

It was another side of her he admired. He knew she was independent; he knew she was gutsy; he'd just not realized how strong she'd had to be.

Suddenly everything Jasper'd told him made sense.

"Who are we going to get to play the ghouls?" Luke asked as they pushed the carts to his truck.

"Oh, didn't I tell you? I've gotten quite friendly with the five film students. They realize the animal park's in trouble, and they want to help. I suggested four of them could be in costume while the fifth films it. They're also putting together a scary display outside the cabin where, for another twenty dollars, attendees can get their picture taken. Adam's already agreed to help build it."

"I'm the marketing guru," Luke said, opening the door to the extended cab and helping Katie unload her basket. "But it sounds like you've come up with the best idea and plan ever."

"I've always been lucky that way," Katie confided. "I don't usually have many friends, but the ones I do make are lasting."

Luke thought of Jasper who believed, even after a decade apart, that Katie Vincent hung the moon.

Luke was starting to feel the same way.

"I might not have been so lucky with my aunt," Katie continued, "but we were blessed that the family next door was so generous. They not only donated used clothes for Janie and me, but two or three times a week we ate at their house. I lived for those meals."

More and more Luke disliked this aunt who hadn't let go of her addictions to realize she had two scared girls to take care of.

There was that feeling again. The desire to pull her close, touch her, take care of her.

"Hey," Katie finally said, her basket almost empty. "Earth to Luke?"

Smiling, she nudged him with the witch's broom she'd just pulled from the cart. He moved to grab it away from her. But when he tugged on the broom, she came with it and he pulled her directly into his arms. She felt good: warm, alive, tempting. Best of all, she didn't break away when his arms tightened.

Maybe she was just surprised by the contact.

Or maybe, right now, she needed his touch as much as he needed hers.

She backed away. Maybe not.

"We've got things to do," she said.

"Kissing's a thing," he said.

"You're my boss."

"Only for one more week."

It was the wrong thing to say. It reminded them both she'd be leaving soon.

"Yes," she echoed, "only for one more week, and then I go home to my real job and my sister."

"Does Janie realize how lucky she is to have you?"

"No, though quite frankly, I was luckier to have her. She gave me purpose, direction."

"You've never come right out and said it—what exactly was your aunt addicted to?"

"Alcohol and prescription drugs. The drugs helped her sleep all day, and the neighborhood bar was her home at night. The apartment, when we came to live with her, pretty much had a bed and a television. There was a kitchen table but no chairs. It was the same story in all the apartments we lived in, and we moved a lot. The only thing that made them seem like a home was Janie's drawings. She colored all over the walls."

Luke couldn't imagine living that way. "And your aunt never worked?"

"She must have worked at some point. She'd been married and then divorced. They had no children."

Luke started loading their purchases into the back. "Jasper told me he wishes he'd found you, brought you home and made your dad do his job as a father."

"That first year," Katie whispered, "I kept Janie's and my suitcase packed because I expected Jasper to show up. He never did. I always believed it would be Jasper who came for us. Not my father, but Jasper. Isn't that odd?"

"Not at all, because Jasper wanted to come." Luke tugged a witch's hat from her fingers, tossed it in the backseat of the cab and then took both her hands in his. "Your father made a very poor choice. One, I believe, he regretted the rest of his life."

"Why do you say that?"

"I visited Bob's Backyard Kingdom when I was considering purchasing the animals. There was nothing in his house that was personal. It was sterile, empty."

She believed it. She'd noticed it herself after her mother died, the beginning of emptiness. "I tried to fill the void," she admitted. "I just couldn't do enough. There wasn't time. If only Jasper had—"

"Your father threatened to charge Jasper with kidnapping if he went after you." The October wind strengthened and Katie shivered. He wasn't sure, though, if he could really blame the wind.

Katie pulled her hand from his. Her chin jutted out, strong, proud.

"I understand now why you didn't go to his funeral," he said.

She looked thoughtful. "If I had it to do over again, I'd go."

"I shouldn't have judged you for not being there. I only knew your dad through television and magazine articles."

"Dad made sure there were plenty of those. If we'd been doing a haunted house to promote his Animal Kingdom, he'd have been the star."

"Hmm," Luke said, trying to lighten the mood, "you mean I'm not the star of Bridget's haunted house?"

That worked. Her resulting smile didn't quite reach her eyes, but the strong, proud tilt of her head assured him she'd be okay.

More than okay.

"I need to talk to Jasper," she mused. "I didn't know Dad had threatened to accuse him of kidnapping. Since I've come to Bridget's, I've thought about it a lot, about why he didn't come to get us. I figured it had something to do with deportation."

"Jasper's a legalized citizen," Luke said. "I've seen his papers. But it would have been easy to threaten him. He's only learned to read well in the last few years."

Katie's eyes went wide.

"When your dad's kingdom went down to just a few animals, Jasper had time on his hands. He found a literacy group, and for four years he studied their program. When we hired him, Ruth took him under her wing and made him read the newspaper to her. Then he'd go and read it to Ollie, who actually appeared to listen and even enjoy it."

"I thought Ruth and Jasper were at odds."

"Ruth is a little too impressed with his skills. She sees him as more head honcho than she is. She couldn't be more wrong. It's a love-hate kind of thing. A couple of times she rubbed him the wrong way and so he kinda played her."

"The way you sometimes play me?"

He laughed. "Exactly."

"You know what's most interesting about this conversation?" she asked.

"What?"

"You have no idea who's really doing the playing."

He put a finger on her chin and traced it up to her lips, his eyes so focused on her lips she wondered if he would kiss her again. He leaned close, but before he touched his lips to hers, he whispered, "Maybe I want to be played."

"Good," she said. And then she tugged on his shirt and kissed him.

Unfortunately it was a quick and easy kiss, more teasing than anything else. Nothing to suggest more was to come.

"Thank you," she said. "You've given Jasper back to me."

Jasper? The last thing Luke wanted Katie to be thinking about when she kissed him was another man, even if the other man was over eighty!

Even if Katie was playing him.

With that realization came one more.

Luke no longer thought of Katie as being there at Bridget's for Aquila. He thought of her as being there for him.

CHAPTER THIRTEEN

"I PROMISE," Luke said, half an hour later, "you won't be pressured to go into an enclosure, or to hold a snake, or to help a child onto a ride. We'll just walk around and enjoy something we both love—animals."

"You're kidding." Katie couldn't decide whether to laugh or cry. "We're going to visit a zoo on your only day off?"

"I just want to see what they're doing."

She shook her head. He had it bad.

The Phoenix Zoo's parking lot was almost full. Luke's expression of awe increased as he counted one, two, three, four, five school buses in line to pick up students. He parked his truck a whole city block from the entrance. Around them fathers were pulling strollers from car trunks, mothers were lathering protection onto little bodies and a few couples were making this their day's adventure, too.

She felt herself being sucked in, but in a different way than usual. She'd not visited a zoo since she'd left her father. Even when she was a student, if the school had planned a field trip to a zoo, she made an excuse to be absent. It wasn't as if Betsy cared about her education.

"Our parking lot's only been full once," he lamented to Katie as they made their way to the entrance. "When was that?"

"Two years ago. Some actor from a reality show tweeted that he'd be in Scorpion Ridge playing golf and taking his kids to the zoo."

"Well, at least it got people there."

"Yes, but most of them went away disgruntled because he didn't show."

"That's one problem we didn't have with my father's menagerie."

They walked across a bridge and dutifully stopped to admire the turtles.

"It wasn't open to the public," Luke said for her.

"No, but I was talking more about the actors. If one of my father's animals was being used in a movie, the actors would often come out to become familiar with the animal. George, especially, had many famous visitors. Some of them were very nice."

It had been years since Katie had remembered Bob's Animal Kingdom that way, not thinking about how she'd left it, but rather how she'd lived it.

A good memory.

She and Luke said goodbye to the turtles, paid an admission price that made Katie raise her eyebrow—Luke didn't even ask the price—and entered a world very different from Bridget's.

Here, just inside the entrance, the roar of humans competed with animal sounds. The gift shop dwarfed the one at Bridget's. A food concession haven in front of her offered not just run-of-the-mill popcorn but all kinds of delights. To her left she could choose to rent a stroller, pet a stingray or enter one of the animal enclosures.

Lots of choices that Bridget's could never compete with.

She had to drag him away from the carousel after he'd ridden it three times. Then Luke took a dozen photos of it with his phone. He was seeing more than the brightly colored animals on the side.

"Spill," she ordered.

"When I was twelve, we all went to the fair. The only thing Bridget wanted to ride was the carousel, but the music was so loud that she held her ears and started crying. We wound up going home. From then on, she collected carousels even though she never rode one."

"You could have asked them to turn the music off."

"I was twelve. It didn't occur to me."

They left the carousel and rode a tram around the exhibits, listening as the driver explained the history of each animal, whether it was endangered or not and the human interest stories. Katie hung on to every word the driver shared.

She shuddered when he talked about the populations dwindling and how breeding possibilities were decreasing because of bloodlines and kinship ranking.

"Ruth can't bear this part of the tour," Luke said. "She feels so guilty about domesticating Terrance. When she decided to make Bridget's her life work, it was because she couldn't do the one thing she really wanted to do, release him back into the wild."

"He'd never survive," Katie agreed.

"So she makes sure that there's a place for animals like him, a place where they're understood and appreciated."

"Like you want to make sure there's a place for people like the real Bridget."

He blinked, surprised. "I've never quite considered it that way. But you're right. Sometimes I feel like I'm so busy keeping Bridget's afloat, that I don't get to do what I really want, such as have a day dedicated to Down Syndrome."

"It will happen," Katie assured him.

He nodded but didn't appear completely convinced. "Yes. I need to learn Ruth's secret. If I hear about an animal that is hurt and discarded, I open Bridget's door. And somehow she finds the money to make room for him. I have to work harder to make money, find money."

"I'm liking Ruth more and more each day."

"Just Ruth?" He sounded offended.

She pretended to hit him, this time without the help of a broom, and when she settled deeper into the seat, somehow his arm had stretched across the back of the tram's chair.

"But I don't want to talk about money," he said. "Not today."

"Okay. So, tell me, are most of the animals at Bridget's because they've been hurt?"

"I wouldn't say most, but quite a few. The rest, like the burros, just wound up homeless, or they'd gotten too old for most zoos to consider taking them," Luke said. "You weren't aware of that?"

"Nooo," she said slowly. But, as she thought about it, it made sense. The first day, Luke had talked about a burro rescue around the Grand Canyon and a misguided camel venture the military had. She knew Rexette was a displaced pet. Yoda had a limp that would keep him from surviving in the wild, and he was too wild to be a pet. Her father's animals were too used to humans. "You've made a difference in all of their lives."

"You made a difference in the lives of Aquila and Tyre," Luke said as they left the big cat area.

She nodded, hearing the driver inform the riders of diminishing numbers of wild animals, loss of habitat and man's encroachment.

"It says something that your dad gave you responsibility of Aquila while he took care of Tyre."

"My father recognized a marketable animal when he saw one. Tyre was this beautiful golden color, and he had black markings that looked like another animal had walked all over him with muddy paws. The fur at his stomach was white, all fluffy, like angel wings. I'd never seen a leopard so beautiful, felt one so soft. Aquila was soft, but he was all male, played in the dirt. When I rubbed his fur I often felt dirt resin. Tyre's paws were oversize and floppy, like an overgrown house cat. My father knew he could make Tyre into a star."

"I'd imagined Aquila and Tyre had similar features."

"No. And apart from their physical differences, Aquila was gentle from the moment I held him in my arms to feed him." She relaxed, breathing in the zoo, waiting to glimpse the next animal on the tour, and enjoying Luke's company.

"This is a great zoo," she finally said, breaking the comfortable silence.

"But?"

"But Bridget's is better."

She was so surprised when he didn't agree right away she nudged him.

"This place has it all," he said. "It has three orangutans, three elephants and a carousel!"

"But at Bridget's, we have a three-cheeked camel, one orangutan that reads the newspaper and a black panther who enjoys Cindy Lauper music," Katie said. Slipping her hand in his, she added, "Come on, let's go home."

They exited the tram at the next stop. On the way to the exit, she dawdled at the lion's enclosure until he took her by the hand and tugged her toward him. She let him, enjoying the camaraderie, and enjoying that he wanted to take care of her as he guided her from the enclosure to the walkway.

She didn't let go of his hand. Instead, she stepped closer to him, seeking his comfort.

"What's wrong?"

She glanced behind her for another peek at the lion. "Being here, it brings back all the memories of Aquila and Tyre."

"That's probably good."

She kept staring at the regal cat, his head cocked, in the distance.

Luke checked his watch. "If we're going to

make it to Ruth's in time for dinner, we have to go."

At that she nodded, taking one last mental picture of the lion, and then letting Luke hurry her to the exit.

Settled in Luke's vehicle again, Katie watched as the zoo grew smaller behind her.

Just as Bridget's would grow smaller in exactly one week.

When she left it.

Funny, at one time, leaving was all she could think of. Getting the two weeks over and done with, and going home.

But Bridget's, or more accurately Luke, made her question exactly where home was.

"IT'S BEEN A WHILE since I've come for dinner," said Luke, bending down to give Ruth a kiss on the cheek.

"We're always working. We should remember to have some fun outside the park, too," Ruth responded. "I'm so glad you're the kind of man who walks a girl to the door. Yolanda's got the enchiladas in. They'll only take twenty minutes or so. Tell me, did you have a good time today?"

"We spent all your money and then some."

"Well done. I think the haunted house is a great idea."

Katie ran up to her room, dropped off her purse and used the restroom to freshen up.

Back downstairs, Yolanda was setting the table. It almost looked too pretty to eat off. At home, she and Janie were hot dog, pizza and peanut butter and jelly kind of girls. Janie, however, went on plenty of dates, so her leftovers were often the meals of choice.

Even though he claimed it had been a while, Luke was very much at home at Ruth's. After Ruth finished filling Luke in about her day with Scoot and Terrance, she headed off, saying she was needed in the kitchen. She suggested to Luke that he take Katie outside and show her where Terrance used to roam.

They strolled the impeccably manicured grounds in companionable silence for a while, before he led her into what looked like a barn.

Inside, Katie stopped to admire some of the pictures that had been tacked to the walls. One thing about animal enthusiasts, they took pictures. Lots of pictures. The photos weren't just of Terrance, though. In a few shots, an old man in old-fashioned coveralls and a straw hat was shown, always with an animal at his heels or crooked in his arms.

"That's Uncle Albert."

"Why does Ruth have photos of him?"

"They were neighbors for a long time and

shared a love of animals. I think he and his animals gave her a place to go and something more to do when she needed a retreat. In return," he continued, "she kept her husband off Albert's back. He called my uncle an embarrassment and a squatter."

"Your uncle was a squatter?"

"Yes."

"Then who owns the land Bridget's is on?"

"For many years, Ruth did. Now's it's owned by a private nonprofit society. So far, since I've taken over, they've been hands-off."

"Does that worry you?"

He smiled. "Not a bit."

Before Katie could ask anything else, Yolanda called them in to eat.

It was almost eleven before Yolanda and Luke left Ruth's. Katie glanced at the clock, momentarily guilty that she hadn't checked on Janie even once that day, and fell into bed.

She couldn't remember the last time she'd had this much fun.

Or felt this needed.

SATURDAY WAS THE first morning that Katie didn't go searching for Luke. She knew her schedule and didn't need him to tell her where to go.

First she went to the infirmary and got the

update on Scoot from Fred—the bear was no better.

"Hey, little fellow," Katie greeted him. "I see Ruth was here."

Ruth had started trying to feed Scoot marshmallows. Three tiny ones lay on his blanket. Scoot pulled himself toward Katie, doing a disjointed combat slide maneuver. He whimpered while he did it. Watching his awkward attempts to move, Katie could only shake her head. If he'd been left with his mother, he'd be a robust bundle of energy.

Human contact had reduced him to this.

She settled Scoot onto the scale, confirming that he hadn't gained any weight since they'd taken him in. She opened the infirmary door and carried Scoot to the back, where a gated rehabilitation pen waited.

And so did Luke, arms crossed, leaning against the gate. "How's he doing?"

"Fred's worried about his bones," Katie said, placing the little bear on the ground and walking over to where Luke stood. "He says they're the thinnest he's ever seen, so thin he can't insert plates or pins to help with the healing."

"He's a lot more active," Luke observed.

"You're comparing Scoot now to Scoot three days ago. The real comparison would be to a bear his same age and breed."

"It's okay to measure Scoot differently," Luke said cheerily.

"Luke, he's not eating well, and he's not moving well. If his condition doesn't improve, and soon, he should be put down."

"Katie's right." Fred joined the conversation as he entered the pen.

"Let's give it a few more days."

She tucked Scoot into his makeshift nest and rubbed his head, letting it drop for now. "I can't imagine the kind of people who would be *this* cruel to animals."

"Your father never had to deal with people dropping off unwanted wildlife?"

"Never."

Fred bent to check Scoot's paws. "Why they didn't just file his nails down is beyond me. It would have been easier."

"They weren't the best kind of people, that's for sure." Katie sat cross-legged in front of Scoot, took a towel and rubbed his face with it, letting him grab it with his teeth and pull. "Has Jake gotten back to you again? Any chance they'll find out who did this?"

Luke watched her, a contemplative expression on his face. She was fairly sure he wasn't thinking about the bear or about Jake, but about her. And her stance on putting the little bear down.

Without taking his eyes off her, he said, "I

don't really expect them to. They've got a lot on their plate."

Scoot was clearly in good hands with Fred, so Katie stood, brushing leaves and whatever Scoot had on his paws from her pants. "I'll spend a few hours with the burros. If we're slow, I'm heading to the cabin. I'll start taking our Halloween decorations over, get an idea of what should be done and if we've forgotten anything."

Luke pushed away from the wall and made his way toward her. "And you're sure Ruth wants to take over at the cabin when you go back to Dallas?"

"She says she's always wanted to do a haunted house, remember?"

"What I remember," Luke said slowly, "is that she said she once peed her pants at a haunted house when a man with a chain saw chased her."

"I promised her no chain saws."

"What you should have promised her," Luke advised with a smile, "was that if a man were to chase her, it would be Jasper."

Katie laughed. "You're right."

Fred looked aghast.

"Oh, come on," Luke said, "they're perfect for each other. Just imagine how efficient they'd be as a team."

Fred didn't seem convinced. "She's got a doctorate from the University of Arizona. He can barely read."

"They both love animals," said Katie.

"He rents a small house. She has a mansion."

Katie lost her smile. "The man who bought her that mansion only gave her four walls. He didn't fill them with what she needed most."

"You're going to get all girly on me, aren't you?" Luke asked.

She raised an eyebrow. "What do you mean?"

"You're going to tell me, 'better one room filled with love than a mansion filled with emptiness.'"

"I was going to say, 'better than a mansion missing love.' I'm not sure you can fill a mansion with emptiness."

She stared at him, her eyes big and clear. "On second thought, you can fill rooms with emptiness," she said. "But when you do, that emptiness is called despair."

CHAPTER FOURTEEN

"YOU'LL BE HELPING with the cameras in about an hour," Luke radioed.

"The college kids are actually giving up a Saturday to be here at Bridget's?" Katie couldn't believe it, not this last-minute, this quick.

"No, it's not our film school kids. Apparently one of the Tucson channels heard about Scoot via Ruth's Facebook page. They think it will be a great human interest story. They'll be here in an hour to interview you."

"Why not Meredith?"

"She's on an errand for me off-site. Never fear, Fred and I will be there. He'll answer any questions. Don't let him redirect them to his hedgehogs. I'll be there, too, but I'll be dealing with the camera, and I need someone dealing with Scoot."

"How about Jasper—"

"You seen his eye today?"

"Ruth?"

"Ruth is the one who suggested you."

"That makes no sense."

"If advertising made sense, America's top advertising spokesperson wouldn't be a little green gecko with an Aussie accent. For what it's worth, I think she's right. You're photogenic. Plus, Ruth would be directing them over to Terrance. She just can't help herself."

"No," Katie muttered as she left his office, "it's me who can't help herself." After all, she'd agreed to get in front of the camera again and be the point man for Scoot.

Luke ended the conversation by warning her, "Just don't mention that you advocate putting him down."

Katie went to work with Scoot, trying to get a sense for what might appeal to the camera. The little bear was awake and starting to move more, although most of the time he just lay there, looking up at whoever was nearby as if wanting an explanation for the atrocity.

"I wish I spoke bear," Katie told him.

Saturday at Bridget's was unlike any other day in terms of crowds. The line for the burros was twenty deep. There was a birthday party at the playground area. And there was even a busload of tourists making their way through the park.

Katie radioed Luke. "Hear anything about the cameras yet?"

"No. Ruth's convinced they got lost on their way to Scorpion Ridge."

"It's possible. There's nothing more I can do with Scoot until they get here. Where do you want me now?"

There was a pause. Luke finally said, "Go spend some time with Aquila. Just stare at him if that's all you can do. We know just seeing you has made a slight difference in his condition. Let's see if we can get him to play with his log, or climb up one of the branches."

"I've made a difference?" Katie said the words before she'd fully thought them through. "And that's what you wanted from me."

Maybe he was telling her she'd fulfilled her purpose. She'd gotten Aquila back on course.

She could leave.

On the other hand, maybe he was telling her she'd made a difference with Aquila and now they expected more.

She could stay.

"Ruth says he's beginning to eat—not enough, but a little," Luke said lightly, as if he had no idea the effect his words were having on her.

"So now you want me to get him to eat more and act like a normal panther."

"Yes," Luke agreed. "He's not like Scoot. Aquila hasn't been abused. *He* can get better."

Yesterday's shopping trip and visit to the

Phoenix Zoo seemed a distant memory. Then she'd believed Luke understood. She'd started to hope he was different. But in the end, it was the animals that mattered most to him.

More than she did.

Katie made it to Aquila's enclosure. No one stood in front of it. Aquila, as usual, lay next to the wall, so hidden by bushes that only the tip of his tail could be seen.

Luke expected too much of her. He feared nothing, nothing except Bridget's closing, while Katie feared almost everything. She feared being out of work, feared losing control of Janie.

And one way or another, she feared all these animals.

Katie leaned against the wall, noting the spiderwebs laced through the bushes, the flies that called this enclosure home and the condition of the playthings in Aquila's enclosure. They all still looked new, unused.

"You can't get in there from here," came a voice behind her. Jasper got off the cart he was driving and stepped beside her.

"I didn't even hear you," she admitted.

"Lost in thought. I know how that goes."

Together they stared into the enclosure. After a moment, when Jasper didn't make any suggestions like "Go ahead, try to go in," or "You can do it," or "We're really depending on you," Katie relaxed.

"Luke told me that my father threatened to charge you with kidnapping if you came after Janie and me."

"Luke shouldn't have told you that."

"I'm glad he did."

Jasper shook his head, his gaze still focused on Aquila's enclosure. "Why, so you could forgive me?"

Katie started. "Is that what you thought, that I was mad and unforgiving?"

"I'm not sure, maybe. Since you've gotten here, you've barely said a word to me, unless it's about Bridget's or the care of animals."

"That's all we ever talked about when I was growing up," she pointed out.

"No, it wasn't."

Surprised, she looked him full in the face. "What did we talk about?"

"You'd tell me about school, about the songs you liked, about how you missed your mom and worried about Janie."

She didn't remember that.

"That last year, you didn't like school because you'd have rather been with Aquila or with the red fox your dad had picked up who'd taken a shine to you. You loved some kitchen-sounding singing group. And you were upset because Janie kept wetting the bed."

"You remember all that?"

"You were the only kid I'd ever been around, really. I guess you made an impression."

"Tremor was the fox's name. I'd forgotten him until now. The group I liked was the Spice Girls."

"You had a pretty good childhood up until age twelve," Jasper reminded her.

"Tell me one good thing after that."

Jasper didn't have an answer.

"Tell me one thing my father did after that because he loved me."

"He got rid of Tyre and kept Aquila."

Jasper's radio crackled. He jumped a little and said, "Oh, gosh, I forgot. The news crew is here. I'm supposed to take you over there."

Under her breath, Katie muttered, "I'd rather he'd gotten rid of Tyre and kept Janie and me."

IN THE FIVE years Luke had called Bridget's home, he'd never had a major news channel visit. Now with their van parked, their gear unpacked and their reporter all freshly made up and ready to go, Bridget's was about to get her fifteen minutes of fame.

He was impressed by their crew. Besides the reporter, there were two cameramen plus a producer- or director-type person. Copies of Scoot's photos were handed over and releases were signed. Fred led the group through his too-small infirmary, pointing out the peacock who was suffering an infection brought on by too much human food.

"This one's a bit of a pig," Fred said. "We've posted signs about not feeding them, but Mr. Piggy here hangs around the trash cans just waiting for scraps to fall."

The peacock dutifully cocked its head to one side as if saying, "Me?" It was enough to snag some camera time. Yoda was a patient today, too. The wolfdog had managed to step on a thorn and Fred still wasn't sure he'd gotten the whole thing out. But he didn't quite get the attention Meredith would have encouraged for him. Then they were out the door and with the bear.

"Where's Ruth?" Katie asked, rubbing her palms against her jeans nervously. "I thought she'd be here."

Luke wasn't sure why he felt so strongly that Katie needed to be here, needed to do this.

He radioed Ruth who said she was on her way. Katie didn't relax at all.

Neither Meredith nor Jasper was anywhere in sight. Luke checked his watch. "Meredith is in the middle of the kestrel show. Jasper's probably with Ollie."

"So, Katie," said the beautiful dark-haired reporter, "tell us about Scoot."

Katie looked at Luke. He smiled, and she did what he'd asked of her.

First she enticed the bear to pull himself nearer the film crew. The maneuver took a while, thanks to Scoot's extensive cast. Fred stepped in, carefully manipulating Scoot's paws so the repair could be seen. He spoke about the cub's recovery and why Scoot couldn't be released back into the wild. He talked about a bear's diet and why bears should never be pets. Katie talked about what they were doing to help Scoot the best they could. Ruth showed up at the last minute and they filmed her tossing marshmallows to Scoot. Then Luke took the crew to George's enclosure, and they filmed George juggling hats with the news station's logo on them.

"It's humbling," one of the cameramen said. "This is what Scoot should grow up to be. But will he?"

"No," Katie and Fred said in unison.

"Is there a chance," the reporter said, "that he'll be put down?"

Katie started to nod, but Luke cut in, shooting her a warning glare. "We're determined to give him a fighting chance."

Done filming, the team stood around a moment longer and the reporter asked, "How did you get George?"

Luke waited for Katie to answer. When she didn't jump in, he explained how he'd acquired Bob's Animal Kingdom...and Jasper. Next thing Luke knew, Jasper was getting his picture taken with George and then reading the paper with Ollie.

Luke gave Katie more than one opportunity to mention Aquila, but whenever he looked at her, she looked away.

How could she not make Aquila a priority, especially since she believed Scoot didn't have a chance?

Didn't she realize what a difference she could make?

And not just in Aquila's life, but in Luke's.

THE EARLY EVENING sunset painted orange-and-red streaks across a sky that was already fading to a husky glow. The front gate was closed and locked and Adam long gone. The concessions were empty but littered with the evidence of a good day. Across the animal park, a loud cry—maybe Ollie—echoed a welcome to the raw power of the coming night. Peacocks screamed in frustration, or maybe they just wanted to make noise.

Katie and Luke had just put the burros to bed and were walking down one of the main thoroughfares. They worked well together, a team, but there was a distance between them now that hadn't been there yesterday.

Katie knew what he wanted. He wanted her to start thinking more about Aquila. And she wanted him to be more understanding about Scoot, about what Scoot's future looked like. In short, they were at an impasse.

"You going to check on him now?" Luke wasn't one to miss an opportunity.

When she didn't answer, he said, "I've got paperwork to do. Before you leave, stop in and update me on whatever you decide to do." And with that, he stalked off toward his office.

In some ways, his leaving the decision up to her only made it worse because he had expectations. By not giving her an order, he was showing her that he trusted her to do the right thing.

Whatever that was.

Something pulled her in Aquila's direction. It would be nice to work with an animal that had a chance. It would do her heart good.

But, of all the animals, big cats had not only given Katie the most, they'd always taken away the most.

Today, like every other day, she might make it to Aquila's cage door only to turn away at the last minute, experiencing a hunger she wasn't sure how to fill.

One that left her frustrated and angry.

Without realizing she was headed there, she stood in front of Aquila. He was awake, alert but unmoving.

"Go ahead," Katie urged him, her voice echoing when the rest of the wildlife decided to take a moment of silence.

Aquila put his nose to the ground, and when he raised it again, he looked as if he'd found something worth keeping. He walked to the wall where he'd settled down so many times, right out of her view. On this occasion, though, he coughed, deep in his throat, as if he were about to get rid of a giant fur ball.

"You're okay," Katie said, wanting to stroke the fur on his head. It had been a decade since she'd done so.

In the stillness of evening, Katie made it right to the door that opened into his pen. He sauntered her way, doing his part. She could hear a rumbling coming from deep in his chest.

She took a step. Put her hand on the lock. And froze.

Every reason why she couldn't work with Aquila swirled through her mind.

I might hurt him. I might enable him to escape. He might hurt me. After all, it's been months since someone's worked with Aquila. Years since I've worked with her. Cats aren't bicycles; you don't just pick up where you left off. Realistically, it might be months before it's safe for me to enter his enclosure—if ever.

She looked at the sky, so beautiful, so unlike any she'd ever seen. Just over a week ago, she'd been exiting Dallas, irritated as all get out that this man had disrupted her life.

Now she felt as if she'd known Luke forever, even though he frustrated her as much as Aquila did.

He expected what she couldn't give.

Aquila, apparently tired of waiting at the door, turned and slowly walked away.

After a moment, Katie did the same.

LUKE WAS STILL in his office, so Katie flopped on the couch and pulled her cell phone out and hit the number one contact. Her sister, of course, did not answer.

"I'll fly you to Dallas if you want to check up on her," Luke offered.

Everyone knew that Janie wasn't returning Katie's calls.

"No, she's texting me. She's let me know that she's fine. If she's to be believed, she's had a week of movies and going out. Not one mention of school."

He angled away from his paperwork to type something into his computer, dislodging Tinker. The cat stretched and then jumped down, stopping to sit on Katie.

"Smart cat," Luke remarked. He picked up a pencil, tapped it against the desktop a few times then tossed it down before standing and coming her way.

"I made it through college." He plopped down next to her on the couch, close enough so she knew he wanted more but far enough away to give both of them space. "But," he continued, "both my sisters dropped out. Suzy wants to go back, and she probably will after her wedding. She's considering special ed."

"Because of Bridget?"

He chuckled. "Suzy was a second mother to Bridget. No doubt that was an influence. The school system's come a long way in dealing with children with Down Syndrome. But it will be people like Suzy who make sure it stays good."

"What about your other sister?"

"Jennifer is quite happily anticipating the birth of her first child. She hated school and likes her job."

"What does she do?"

"She works for my dad at the car dealership."

"That makes her happy?" Katie said.

"It does. She's family-oriented. She also wants to take over his dealership someday. She says on-the-job training is more important than a degree for that. Don't quote me on this, especially to my parents, but I agree."

"Your parents own a car dealership?"

"My great-grandfather started it in the nineteen fifties. It's one of the few family-run dealerships still around."

"I'd like to see it."

"If you're free tomorrow night, you can join the family. We go to church as a family on Sunday evenings, and then head out for dinner. My sisters, especially, want to meet you."

"Because they've been hearing updates on how I'm *not* helping Aquila?"

"They'll probably be more fascinated by how quickly you've won over Tinker. She doesn't go to anyone, and look at her now. But, also, I've been filling them in on how you're helping Scoot. Plus, they're impressed you've actually touched Rexette, even though you're scared of her."

"I'm not scared of her."

He leaned back, legs resting on top of the coffee table, an arm finding its way behind her shoulders. He seemed ready to fall asleep. She couldn't help herself. She leaned back into his arms, enjoying the intimacy, amazed by how much she enjoyed his company.

"You were afraid, at first," he said. "Then things changed."

She started to protest, but he interrupted. "If you got over your fear of Rexette, you'll get over your fear of Aquila. I have a whole week to watch it happen."

"Or a whole week to realize that just because you want something to happen doesn't mean it will."

"You're underestimating yourself."

He untangled his arm from her shoulders, smiling while he did it. Then he held out his hand to her and helped her up.

"I want to move my office to the ground level. A few visitors have stopped by, and it was a hardship for them to get up the stairs."

"Is that all you want?" Katie asked.

"No, there are a few other things I want."

Even in the semidarkness, she could see into his eyes.

"I want you to st—"

She knew exactly what he was going to say, and it wasn't about Aquila.

"I always wanted to go to college," Katie interrupted. She walked to the window, staring out at the view she now knew like the back of her hand. It felt as though it should be hers.

Maybe that's why she wanted to run.

But where to?

Who to?

"To me," she continued, "going to college meant I'd done something, or perhaps it was more like I'd refused to let things be done to me. There were plenty of people who looked down on Janie and me. We didn't have the right clothes, didn't get to go many places, didn't have the gadgets of teenage-hood."

"I like that word, teenage-hood."

He came to stand next to her, still giving her space, but letting her know that given the opportunity, he'd still say the words she'd prevented him from speaking.

He checked his watch. "I need to head over to the wolf area. Meredith says something's upsetting Yoda. I want to check it out before we go. If you're free, how about we do something tonight?"

She should say no. Come next Saturday, she was out of here. Instead, she gave in. "Sure, and we can check on Scoot, too."

Yoda and his pack mates seemed plenty active to Katie. Luke took out his notebook and wrote something down.

"Where does Yoda fall in the pack's ranking?" Katie asked.

"He's about in the middle. That guy over

there—" Luke pointed to one of the few wolves lying down, the rest pacing "—is the lowest-ranking wolf. Meredith is right. The wolves are restless."

"What will you do?"

"Feed them more and try more whole foods."

His words were typical Luke: solve the problem. But after a week of seeing this man every day and, yes, thinking about him just about every hour, she recognized something was off.

"Are you worried about the cost?"

"Yes." In some ways, he resembled the wolves, so tense, ready to pounce.

"The special event at Halloween will bring in some extra money."

"Nothing extra about it," Luke said. "It's already earmarked and spent. And there probably still won't be enough to go around."

Katie didn't say anything else as they walked toward the infirmary. Scoot was another expense Luke hadn't budgeted for.

She was an expense Luke hadn't budgeted for.

Just one more reason why she couldn't allow him to ask her to stay.

Ruth was just ahead of them. She turned, a smile on her face. It faded when she saw Katie.

"That's odd," Ruth said.

"What?"

"I just saw you with Aquila."

"How long ago?"

"No more than three minutes."

Beside her, Luke tensed. "Couldn't be. Katie's been with me for the last hour. Are you sure it wasn't Meredith or one of the maintenance workers?"

Ruth stared at Katie. "She sure looked like Katie."

CHAPTER FIFTEEN

"JANIE VINCENT, what are you doing here?" All the worry and anxiety Katie had been feeling for her sister over the past week swelled up and threatened to erupt.

Janie managed to seem indignant and innocent at the same time, no easy feat. "You can't be mad."

"What do you mean I can't be mad? I am mad. I leave you alone for two weeks. No, not two weeks. It's only been *one* week, and you leave your classes and come here. I tried a dozen times to call you and—"

"And I didn't answer because I knew exactly what you'd say."

"That doesn't matter."

"Sure it does," Janie said reasonably. "You'd ask about school, if I was doing my homework, if I was keeping the apartment halfway clean."

"Of course I would. Those things are important."

Janie crossed her arms, no longer going for

an indignant and innocent air. Her words were openly defiant. "Important to *you*."

"They should be important to you, too! These days, a college education is mandatory. Did you miss a day of classes to come here? How did you get here, anyway?"

Janie didn't answer. Instead, her eyes grew big and she pushed by Katie. "Jasper! Do you remember me?"

Jasper hurried around the corner of Aquila's enclosure. He smiled and opened his arms; Janie went into them, easily and without hesitation.

"How you doing, little girl?" Jasper held her by the shoulders, stepped back and then smoothed an errant strand of hair from her cheek. He paused, his finger tracing the faint scar etched from her cheek to under her hair. He lifted her blond strands and then he smiled.

"You can hardly tell."

Janie patted his hand away and lifted her hair. "It doesn't bother me a bit. It makes a rather good conversation piece when I go out with a guy for the first time."

"Your father said he'd find the best surgeon. I guess he did."

"And," Janie added, "I'm not so little any-more."

"Neither of you is," Jasper agreed, bringing Katie into the conversation. "Both of you've grown into fine young ladies. Your mother would be proud."

That statement took some of the wind out of Katie's anger.

"I'm doing fine." Janie gave Katie a pointed glare. "I'm not sick, I'm not on the police's most wanted list and I gave blood last week in order to help my fellow man."

Ruth and Luke, who'd already stepped aside to let Jasper draw close, now moved even farther away from the two sisters. Clearly they were smart enough to recognize a domestic argument was about to erupt. They were steering clear.

Behind them, Aquila paced, every once in a while pausing to step on a log, but he never pushed it or leaped onto it.

Speaking as calmly as she knew how, Katie said, "I'm not sick, either. I'm not on the police's most wanted list and I attended a Rotary Club meeting last Monday night to educate my fellow man. And I did all of that around my work schedule. I've sacrificed and saved so you could go focus on school. *That's* your work."

"And I gave it my best shot. Here's the truth. I'm failing both math and English, mostly because I don't want to be there. My art teacher says I'm a natural. I want to go to graphic design school. Why won't you listen?"

"Because more people are graduating from

graphic design schools than there are jobs. You have to try a different approach."

"I'm good. I'm really good."

Where else had Katie heard that line? Oh, yes. Luke had said it about Adam. Adam was a twenty-five-year-old high school dropout. Adam, at twenty-five, was still a kid.

Katie could only assume Adam must have a caring family stashed somewhere with their arms open to catch him if he fell.

Janie only had Katie; Katie couldn't fail at the job.

She took a breath. They'd had this same conversation a dozen times, and she didn't want the thirteenth, the unlucky thirteenth, to take place here. "We'll talk later. Perhaps missing a class or two won't put you behind."

Janie stood next to Jasper, as if she was sure he'd be on her side. Katie wasn't sure if he was or not. She only knew that it seemed as if no one was on *her* side.

"I've withdrawn from all my classes," Janie said. "It's final. I'm not going back."

"Yes, you are. You have to. I paid for those classes. We have the apartment and a lease. We're putting our lives on track."

Luke moved to stand beside Katie.

Janie's gaze went from Luke to Katie and back to Luke.

"I want to be here," Janie said. "Even if it's only for a week. I never got to say goodbye to George or Ollie or Jasper. I couldn't stand that you were here and I wasn't. I've missed being around animals."

"You never said you liked animals," Katie protested.

"Because you never asked and you obviously didn't want to know. I draw them all the time."

"You didn't help back with them when we lived with—"

"Because nobody asked me to."

Ruth spoke up then. "Girls, you're tired, and it's getting late. Let's head over to my place. We'll get Janie settled in and figure out a plan."

"I already have a plan," Janie said proudly. "Adam told me all about his projects and he offered me a paintbrush. Tomorrow morning, I'm taking it."

Katie opened her mouth, but no words came out. Ruth quickly aimed Janie for the exit. Jasper, with a quick guilty look at Katie, followed.

Luke touched her shoulder and whispered, "Ruth's right. Let's get you to her place and you and Janie can talk in private. I'll take you to dinner tomorrow night. Janie can come, too."

"She'll have school on Monday, I'll…" She saw it in Luke's eyes. He didn't believe she'd be able to convince Janie to return to Dallas, return to school.

Katie spun away from Luke, hurrying to catch up to Janie. "How'd you get here?"

"Greyhound bus."

"Very brave," Ruth said. "You came a long way by yourself."

"How'd you get from the bus to Bridget's?"

"I called the animal park and Adam answered. When I told him who I was and where I was, he came to get me. He's very nice."

"Why didn't you call me on my cell?" Katie demanded.

"Then I'd be stuck in the car with you, and you'd scold me the whole way. It was a long bus ride, and I was tired and dirty. I just wanted to get to Bridget's and face you out in the open, not confined in a car."

Jasper shot Janie a look of sympathy. It didn't escape Katie's attention that no one was shooting *her* understanding looks. That was no surprise—neither Luke, Ruth nor Jasper had ever raised a human child. They'd only raised animals.

Animals were easier.

Ten minutes later, she'd hustled Janie into her car. Luke leaned down to peer through Katie's car window. He patted her on the shoulder, letting his fingers tighten for just a minute, and said, "Everything's going to work out. You'll see."

When he walked away, Janie said from the passenger seat, "Who's he, really? He can't be the director you were so upset at. He's too young."

"He's the director, the one who purchased Dad's animals, the one who made me come all the way here. And, yes, he's younger than I expected."

"You're certainly friendly with him."

"For the next week, he's my boss." Katie neglected to mention that tonight he'd almost been her date—until Janie showed up.

Now, instead, he'd invited her out on Sunday night. Dinner with his family, of all things.

Janie yawned. "Then I guess he's my boss, too. If I help Adam with the painting."

"Janie, they can't pay you. You've got other things to do. You can't stay."

"I'm not worried about money, not for just a week. This is what I want to do. I've got no place to go."

"You can go home."

"You call that apartment home? It's just a place to crash. I want to be here and visit with the animals. Maybe have some fun. When was the last time we had fun?"

It was on the tip of Katie's tongue to say *You*

always have fun, every weekend. Instead, she said, "We could come back, say over Christmas or during the summer."

Janie tossed her blond hair, a response Katie had seen many times, and it always meant she didn't believe a word Katie was saying.

"If I thought in a million years that you'd offer that suggestion on the phone, I'd have answered."

"You have to go home," Katie protested weakly. "Someone has to be in the apartment."

"Billy's there." Janie yawned again and started to lean back.

"Billy?"

"A guy from my art class. We've been working on the wall in my bedroom. I was painting a black panther when I realized that I didn't want to just *paint* a panther, I wanted to *see* one. Billy's sticking around to finish it. And he needed a place to crash."

Great, another wall for a landlord to have to paint over, another cost Katie'd be charged for.

Ten minutes later, Janie was unloading her duffel bag and stashing it in yet another of Ruth's spare bedrooms.

"Been a long while since I had this much company." Ruth turned down the bed and straightened an imaginary wrinkle from the sheet.

"Janie won't be staying long."

"Just a week," Janie said brightly.

When Ruth discovered that the last thing Janie had eaten was a stale bag of chips at the New Mexico/Arizona border, she led Janie to the kitchen.

Katie followed. She wanted this Billy's phone number. She got it and punched in the number, only to hear it ring and ring.

"We'll make something easy," Ruth said. "Do you like spaghetti?"

Katie turned from the phone and glimpsed something she'd been longing to see in Dallas. Janie Vincent standing at the stove, helping prepare dinner and laughing.

Looking as though she was home.

LUKE'S PHONE RANG an hour after he got to his apartment. He grabbed it quickly, annoyed at himself that he wanted it to be Katie. It was a restricted number, though, and he debated whether or not to answer.

But it was his job to answer. The caller was Jake Farraday; he needed help with a rescue.

"Sorry, Luke," Jake said an hour later as Luke parked in a remote area and hopped out of his truck.

"I realize it's Saturday night," Jake apologized, "but I've tried everyone. The Scorpion

Ridge Wildlife Rescue is already helping with a call out in the Santa Catalina Mountains. Then I thought of you."

"Scraping the bottom of the barrel, huh?"

Jake laughed. "Guess you came to mind because of Scoot. But I would have called you eventually. Look."

Luke crouched down by a wrought-iron fence in front of an old, dilapidated mobile home. A bear, only three or four months old, by the size, had its head stuck in the bars of the fence.

Luke pointed not to the bear's head but to his paws.

This bear had been luckier than Scoot. While the toes were deformed, they weren't butchered as Scoot's had been.

"You've searched for the mother?" Luke asked.

"Everywhere," Jake said. "But there's a place behind the trailer that looks like a pen for bears. The owners—" he nodded his head in the direction of a tall man with long blond hair and a dark-haired woman "—say they've never seen the bear before, and have no idea why we'd accuse them of keeping bears in their yard. They have dogs."

His skeptical expression said it all. They might have dogs, but they didn't keep them in a pen in the yard.

The couple stood in front of their house. "You got no right to be here," muttered the man. The woman just clutched her hands together.

"I showed them my badge, but I have no real proof of a crime. Right now," Jake said, "our job is getting this little fellow free."

Luke hunkered down. The little guy didn't shy away—he was obviously exhausted and used to humans. Not that he could move, thanks to the bars holding him prisoner.

"How long has he been stuck?"

"Not sure. We got the call four hours ago. A kid on his bike noticed the bear stuck in the fence. He went home to tell his mother. She didn't believe him at first, but he pestered her enough that she finally got in her car and came to investigate. She called us. The trailer's owners say they didn't know the bear was out here, but it's clear by the state of the fence that someone tried to free this little guy."

"Couldn't do it and walked away?" Luke asked.

"Maybe they were going to try again later, but we arrived. Like I said, there's a pen in the back."

The cub's fur was matted with what looked like grease.

"It's Crisco oil. I made the lady there fetch me some and tried to slick his head," Jake explained. "I didn't work, though. They're not willing to help any further, say they're scared. I've called the sheriff. He'll be here soon, but I didn't want the bear to wait any longer. Now that you're here, we can get him out. Keep the cub calm while I push his head. Or," Jake said hopefully, "you can push his head and I'll calm him?"

Luke scanned the ground then called to the couple, "Bring me a towel."

They didn't move.

"Arizona has a Good Samaritan law," Jake added. "Chances are you'll get in more trouble for not helping than you will for having a bear on your property."

The man started muttering again and the woman fetched a towel.

Luke covered the bear's face and spoke in a low tone while scratching behind one of his ears. Jake pushed.

"This isn't working," Jake exclaimed a few minutes later, out of breath and irritated.

Luke had to laugh. "Maybe you're just out of shape." Jake often called him to assist with a rescue, and the two men had become friends.

"We could cut the bars," suggested Luke. Then, louder, to the couple, he shouted, "Hey, we're going to cut the bars!"

"We're renters," the woman called back.

"You have the authority to do this?" Luke asked Jake.

"I'd say yes. The attorney general might say otherwise, though. Maybe I'd better take a few more pictures."

While Jake took out his camera, Luke said to the couple, "Call your landlord."

"Already told them to do that," Jake said. "They claim they don't have his number. We're not leaving this cub trapped all night."

"What tools do you have?" Luke asked.

"None that would break through this type of fence."

Luke tested one of the bars a few spaces down from the bear. It was solid, about an inch thick, and didn't budge, even when he used all his strength. "It's not new. This was made when they made things to last."

The bear whined a bit, and Jake went to get it some more water.

"You sure are stuck, little fellow." Ignoring the goo spread across the bear's fur, Luke rubbed the top of his head. The bear let out a big whoosh of air and whimpered even louder.

"Don't worry," Luke said. "We'll get you out."

The bear shook its head slightly and slumped.

Settling back, Luke took out his cell phone and dialed Fred's number. It went straight to voice mail. It was Saturday night; Fred was probably at the movies with his wife.

Next, Luke tried Katie. She answered. He quickly brought her up to speed. "I'll be right there," she promised. Then she reconsidered and said, "Give Ruth the directions, and we'll be right there."

He'd just hung up when a police car, a fire engine and a Tucson news van pulled up.

"Looks like you'll get more exposure," Jake said.

"We're going to need it if this bear is as undernourished as Scoot."

Two things soon became apparent. Sheriff Rafael Salazar was well acquainted with the occupants of the mobile home. Acquainted enough to be sure that they were, in fact, the owners. The Good Samaritan law was brought up again, this time by someone with a badge, and permission to cut the bars was granted.

"Pretty nice fence for out here," one of the fireman remarked.

"Used to be a hundred-year-old farmhouse," Sheriff Salazar said. "The house burned down about two years ago."

Ruth, Katie and Janie pulled up just as the firemen were positioning the hydraulic spreading pliers to nudge the bars apart and release the bear.

It took all of five minutes.

The bear was too tired to lift itself up enough to escape. Without Fred, Luke was hesitant to move the creature, but Jake had a tranquilizer gun.

Twenty minutes later, Katie was next to him in his truck, the bear cub in her lap. Ruth and Janie were following them back to Bridget's.

It was quiet in the truck. Luke glanced at Katie. She was idly stroking the top of the bear's head and gazing out the window.

She looked at peace.

Funny, he *felt* at peace.

They finally arrived at Bridget's. In the darkness of darkness, Luke and Katie carried the baby bear to the infirmary and placed it in one of the holding pens. She arranged a blanket for him and turned on the heating lamp.

"We should feed him," she said.

"You get a hold of Fred yet?" Ruth asked.

"I've left three messages. Way I figure, the movie started at seven. He should be calling back just after nine."

"I can stay," Ruth volunteered.

"No." Luke bent down and studied the bear. "I'm high on adrenaline after all that. I'll stay."

"So, you think these are the same people who had Scoot?" Katie asked. She was in the refrigerator getting out the special milk Fred was using.

"I'm almost sure of it. Jake thinks so, too."

He watched as Katie expertly made up a bottle and put in the refrigerator for when the cub woke up. She then checked Scoot's chart to see what he needed next.

"This cub should be off milk by now," Ruth said, frowning at the bear.

"Human interference," Katie responded.

"What will happen to those people?" Janie asked.

"I imagine they'll be asked to produce their license to own wildlife in Arizona. Then there will be an investigation into whether they were taking care of their animals."

"Did you see that place?" Ruth asked. "Trash everywhere. Not a chance they were taking care of their animals."

"And they have the audacity to claim the trash is what drew the bear into their yard."

"With no mama in sight," Ruth practically spat. "Right."

"All we can do," Luke said reasonably, "is work on this little guy and get him back to good health."

Janie glanced around the infirmary. "No other animals here beside the bears. That's good."

"Very good," Luke agreed. "Fred usually has

the weekends off, so we work hard to get inoculations and such done during the week."

"We've all been pitching in to help with Scoot," Katie explained to Janie. "But he likes Ruth the most."

"I'm easy to like," Ruth agreed. "Scoot hums when I try to feed him. I could start to love him as much as I do Terrance."

"Terrance?" Janie asked.

"My lion."

Janie laughed. "I knew it would be fun here."

With the cub asleep, there was nothing else to do but wait for Fred.

"I'll stick around with you," Katie said to Luke. "Will you take me home later? After Fred gets here?"

"Sure."

Luke and Katie followed Ruth and Janie to the exit and said their goodbyes.

Walking back to the infirmary, Luke reached out and took Katie's hand. She didn't move away. He liked the way her fingers twined with his. He liked how she didn't mind that he was covered in dirt and smelled of Crisco.

Well, she smelled of Crisco, too.

The zoo had a deserted yet calm feeling to it as they strolled. The gift shop was dark. Aquila was playing with his log. The wolves were running, even Yoda.

"You love it here, don't you?" Katie asked.

"More than I ever imagined possible."

She was quiet, and he wondered what she was thinking. Finally, he said, "Your sister looks just like you."

"Everyone says that."

"I thought you said she hated animals."

"I was wrong."

"You might be wrong about a lot of things."

"I'm understanding that more and more."

He thought he felt the slightest bit of pressure, as if she were clutching his fingers tighter, bringing him closer to her.

"You know what you're most wrong about?"

"What?"

"You're wrong about you being afraid of animals. Tonight, again, you were a seasoned professional. You were part of Bridget's. I want you to stay."

She let go of his fingers.

CHAPTER SIXTEEN

FRED SHOWED UP soon after that and went to work on Crisco—the name they'd given to the new cub. Katie was amazed at the man's dedication. Back at her father's place, the veterinarian had come around once a week, or for emergencies. Fred was at Bridget's every day. He was vet, nutritionist and educator.

If he noticed anything amiss between Katie and Luke when he arrived, he didn't say. Katie, for her part, stayed near the cub. Luke paced, every once in a while running his fingers through his hair.

"This cub will be fine," Fred assured him.

Relieved, Luke drove Katie home just after ten.

The drive to Ruth's house was silent. Katie stared out the window and Luke studied the road.

At Ruth's, she waved goodbye but hurried up the steps before he could say anything.

Sunday morning, bright and early, Katie

pulled into Bridget's parking lot. It had three cars: Fred's, Luke's and Meredith's.

She knew where Luke would be, with the burros. Fred would be with Ollie. Meredith would be with the birds.

Since Ollie was on her way, she went there first.

Both Ollie and Jasper were cleaning. Jasper was sweeping the area where Ollie slept. Ollie was pretending to sweep a spot under a tree.

Jasper looked up. "Morning! After last night, I figured you'd sleep in."

"I didn't sleep well."

"Worried about the new cub, eh?"

More like worried about the big director.

"Jasper, you said something yesterday that surprised me. You said my father got the best plastic surgeon for Janie. I don't remember that, I only remember him not visiting Janie in the hospital and you driving me back and forth."

"It was the same hospital your mother died in," Jasper said quietly. "He couldn't force himself to go in. But he came once or twice. And he flew Janie to San Diego to the best plastic surgeon he could find. He sold Tyre to pay for it."

"I had no idea," she whispered.

"It was a hard couple of months. He was worried about money, he was worried about you and he probably overreacted when he decided to send you girls away."

Overreacted was putting it nicely. Getting rid of Tyre might have paid to heal Janie's physical scars, but getting rid of his children had made a different kind of scar.

Could it heal?

Especially in this setting?

Katie wasn't sure, but for the first time, she was willing to try.

Walking away from Jasper, she headed for Aquila. He was awake and in good spirits.

"Hey, boy," Katie called, and because there was no one around to hear, she promised, "Maybe today."

Finally, she walked into the infirmary. Fred was already working, the new bear tucked between his legs on the floor. He shook his head, more in bewilderment than anger. "This one's not as bad as Scoot."

"What do you mean?"

"Crisco was probably given the right kind of milk, just not enough of it. His bones are a bit weak, but they'll be strong enough for plates if I have to do more than change his diet."

"He'll be fine?"

"As fine as a declawed bear taken away from his mama too early can be."

Scoot, however, wasn't fine. He lay in the corner of his holding pen, not moving.

"Is Scoot excited that another bear is here?"

"Not so's you can tell. Now that I can compare the two, I'm even more worried about Scoot. He's got a fever. Wouldn't surprise me if we're dealing with some kind of infection."

"He's not strong enough to fight it."

Katie did a few things for Fred and then headed for Luke's office. He wasn't there. Tinker was alone on top of a book. Before Katie could back out, Tinker stood, stretched and jumped off the desk—knocking over a coffee mug in the process.

"Oh, you," Katie scolded. She headed for the desk and righted the cup.

Beside the book was a single piece of paper with a bunch of doodles, mostly of bears and a list of five things right in the middle.

Katie read the first item. It matched the first item on the dry-erase board on the wall: EMPLOYEE SALARIES AND BENEFITS. After that, though, the paper list was different. Instead of GENERAL OPERATIONS for number two, it read BUY CAROUSEL.

Rather than FACILITIES MAINTENANCE, the third item read PAY OFF AQUILA'S ENCLOSURE.

She'd never really tallied the cost of such an

enclosure. Jasper would know. Instead of CAP-ITAL RENEWAL, the fourth line on the list read BECOME A WILDLIFE REHABILITOR.

This one stumped her. They were already taking in injured animals. Bridget's was full of them. Every animal had a story.

Suddenly Katie experienced a bit of guilt. She was reading something personal. These were Luke's dreams, his *personal* dreams. He put his employees first. He wanted more than fair pay and benefits. But he also wanted a carousel, a new exhibit and for Bridget's to be a place where animals came to be cared for and then released into their natural environment.

Katie examined the list on the dry-erase board. The fifth item there was ACQUIRE AN EXOTIC BIG CAT. It was the only one with a checkmark beside it, at least on the wall. Number five on his personal list was BUY AN-OTHER BIG CAT.

The words were underlined three times, and next to it was a phone number.

There was also a sixth item on his paper list: KATIE.

"I saw you on the news last night," Katie said when she found Luke and Jasper getting the burro rides ready. "You looked pretty good except for a very shiny face."

"That was the Crisco." Luke smiled, but Katie noticed it didn't quite make it to his eyes. "I had to shower twice last night to get it all off."

"Speaking of Crisco, Fred says he's in better shape than Scoot, although he thinks the milk they were using wasn't fatty enough for either bear. For Scoot, the milk wasn't fatty at all. That's what Fred says." She was rambling, wishing the smile went to his eyes, wishing she hadn't seen the list.

"Fred's the expert," Jasper said. He checked his watch.

Luke was nice to her; he was cordial. He was also holding back, and she knew why. Last night, she'd rejected Bridget's. Rejected him.

He should erase her name from his list.

Katie should get back to Dallas.

Even though being here at Bridget's made Katie come alive. So what did she want to do? What was she capable of? Going or staying?

Janie certainly wanted to stay.

As if reading her thoughts, Jasper said, "Where's Janie?"

"She's at some Red Hat breakfast with Ruth."

"Fool woman invited me to some Red Hat event next week," Jasper said.

"You going?" Luke asked.

Jasper's lack of a reply implied *yes*.

Katie's phone rang, and Luke motioned for her to sit on a nearby bench.

"This is Billy," a male voice announced with pure Texan twang.

"And this is the woman who signed the lease on the apartment you're staying in."

But after a few minutes, Katie was somewhat convinced that Billy wasn't the sort to throw wild parties and destroy things.

"You know," Luke said when she hung up, "you can fly back to Dallas and check up on things if you want."

"It's crossed my mind," Katie admitted.

"I can call the airlines."

"No, that's all right. It's just a week."

"A lot of things can happen in a week," Luke said.

Katie silently agreed. If she were that kind of girl, she'd even believe love could happen in a week.

"There's really not much there I need," Katie admitted. "If our place caught on fire, there's nothing I'd save."

Luke glanced up from putting chains between the swingles. "Really?"

"Really."

"What about pictures, mementoes, trophies, your family Bible?"

"There's a few of those, but really, nothing that can't be replaced."

Luke's radio went off, saving Katie from having to answer any more questions. On the other end, Meredith sounded excited about something.

"I'll finish here," Jasper offered Luke. "You go see what Meredith wants. That girl rarely gets excited." Jasper checked his watch again. "I'm heading for morning service in about twenty minutes. Katie, you want to come with me?"

Luke had walked away without looking her way, without inviting Katie to come along.

"Yeah, I'll come with you."

If Janie had stayed in school because of Katie's pushing and praying, maybe praying would get a few other things accomplished.

JASPER ATTENDED THE church closest to Bridget's. The service had already started when they arrived—they missed Sunday school—and Jasper slipped into the last pew on the right. The place was full.

After a song or two, the sermon began and Jasper leaned forward, intent on the message, nodding every once in a while. Katie remembered her father getting angry when they were on shoots and Jasper took off on Sunday morning. He'd work before service and after service, but every Sunday—no matter where they were—Jasper went to church.

Next to him, Katie could smell a hint of the burros he'd been dealing with only an hour ago. Maybe she smelled the same. Well, it wouldn't be the first time, or the last.

Or the last?

"You praying that Janie goes home?" he whispered.

Katie shook her head. She'd prayed all night about that. Besides, Janie was at a Red Hat event with Ruth. It was the first time in years Janie had a mother figure. She deserved that time.

Katie sat somewhat listening to the sermon but mostly watching Jasper. When the pastor spoke the closing prayer, Katie bowed her head. But instead of asking for something, she said thank you.

A thank you for letting her get to know Jasper again.

When the service ended, Jasper reached out a hand to help her up. "Nice to have company," he said. "You used to come with me when you were little."

"Before my father put me to work."

Jasper smiled. "It wasn't quite like that."

A few people stopped to say hi to Jasper. They all welcomed Katie. A few said they'd stop by Bridget's later. They wanted to see the bears.

Walking from the building, Katie couldn't help admiring the Arizona afternoon. The wind was blowing and the temperature had dropped ten degrees from last week. Mountains, brown and orange, rose to the sky on her left. And on her right. She was surrounded by beauty.

"Jasper, what should I do?" Katie asked when they got to the Bridget's truck they'd driven to the service. In all the years she'd known him, he'd never had his own vehicle. Animals were his life's work. He used a work truck.

"Only you can decide that, Katie."

"I've spent the last decade trying to protect Janie. Only she doesn't want protecting anymore."

"Your protection is what has made her brave enough to take risks now. Did you ever think of that?"

"Only fools take risks. Wise people plan."

"Then I'm not very wise. Most of my life has been one risk after another."

"That's not what I mean."

"Getting out of bed in the morning is a risk. Getting behind the wheel of a car is a risk."

"You know what I mean! I was sending her to college."

"She's an adult. She should be sending herself to college."

"It's not that easy. If I'd had help, maybe—"

"Janie's not you. You always take on the weight of the world. It's time to shrug it off and take your own risk."

"By working with Aquila."

"By doing something that makes you happy."

"What makes me happy is having a clean apartment in a safe neighborhood. It's being sure Janie and I have enough food to eat."

Jasper winced a little. "Your father made plenty of mistakes, but I honestly don't believe he realized just how bad it was with his sister."

"That's in the past. I'm in control of now."

"If you were in control, you'd be happy. Your father was the same way."

"But—"

"We have an hour or so. I want to show you something."

He drove just a block from the church to his home. He lived in a small boxlike house with a tidy yard. In the back, she could hear chickens. He'd always kept chickens.

"I thought of this when you were talking about not having anything worth saving in your apartment. I wish now I'd insisted you come in person to sell your dad's things. You needed to say goodbye, and you needed to pick up the pieces."

"I did pick up the pieces. I sold everything. I found..." She stopped. It had really been Jasper who'd found a buyer for her father's remaining animals. She'd simply signed the paperwork. "Did my father leave you anything?" Katie asked.

"He made me the executor and told me to take what you didn't want."

"What did you take?"

"Nothing. Once I had a job here, with Ollie and George, I had everything I needed."

Great, something else for Katie to be guilty about. She hadn't even considered Jasper, who'd been her father's right-hand man for three decades.

"I'm sorry."

"Don't be. Having both you and Janie and the animals here is the only thing I would have asked for. But that's not why I invited you over. Give me just a moment."

He disappeared into a room that must have been his bedroom. The house was so small that only two doors opened off the combination living room and kitchen. The other had to be the bathroom.

Katie slowly looked around. On the wall above a simple green couch was a photo of three people. One was a little red-headed child with an impish grin. He couldn't have been more than five or six. Behind him were two people with very serious expressions.

The rest of the living room held framed circus advertisements, some from the forties. There were newspaper articles. There were also pictures of Jasper with…Katie bent closer to the pictures…a president.

These were Jasper's treasures.

"My parents died when I was ten," Jasper said, coming back into the room with an old brown suitcase.

"Car accident?"

"Hitler."

"Hitler?" she whispered. She was so surprised she sat down on the couch.

"I grew up in Czechoslovakia. We were actually quite well off. I remember my father saying that anyone who had power would lose it all during the German occupation. He was right. One night we were called out into the streets and loaded into buses."

"You lived in a concentration camp?"

"No. My father pushed me down behind some trash cans and told me not to move, not even to breathe, until morning, and then to go to his friend Tomas's house. I did. I stayed with Tomas and his family for just over a year."

"And your parents?"

"We never found out. Tomas was afraid to ask too many questions. Tomas never said it, but he believed they'd been executed. Finally, they sent me to stay with some of their friends in Austria. But I didn't fit in. I was young, angry and itching for a fight. As soon as I was old enough, I ran away and wound up joining the Circus Medrano."

"Is that who you were with before Ringling Brothers?"

"No, that was a circus in Moscow. But that's ancient history and a story for another day." He glanced at her. "Like you, I only got to be young for a short while. I was angry for many years. Once I stopped being angry, I started to live."

She put her hand on his, noting the thick fingers, the hard skin, the warm touch.

"America did that for me," he added. "Once I got here, I learned to laugh again. I started working with animals on my terms, and the circus became my family in ways I couldn't imagine."

She twined her fingers in his. All these years, she'd thought only of how she'd suffered when her father sent her away, and blamed Jasper for not rescuing her.

He unsnapped the latches on the suitcase. "When I retired from Ringling Brothers, I needed a job. One of the bear handlers said I should go see your father. He hired me, and the rest is yet another history."

"I don't remember a time when you weren't a part of Bob's Animal Kingdom."

He opened the suitcase and positioned it between them on the couch. "I packed this up when I went through the house after Bob died. I figured you'd be coming, and he'd want you to have it. When you didn't come, I added a few things to it and threw it in the truck when I moved here."

"I was angry," she whispered.

"It's okay to be angry sometimes," Jasper said. "Anger can often keep your feet moving. Anger served me well once or twice.

"But if anger is holding you back, it's time to let it go." He took the first item out of the box and showed it to her. "Most everything was in this suitcase already. Your mother started it the day you were born."

Katie took the family photo from his hand. She didn't remember seeing it before. Bob stood in the back. Katie's mother was seated on a chair. Katie, probably a month old, was in her mother's lap. Bob was gazing down at both of them, smiling.

It was not the smile he'd given the cameras. It was real.

The photos were interspersed with a few odds and ends of baby clothing, and even a few school papers. There were toys. Katie recognized the old purple-maned plastic horse wrapped in a soft green blanket. It had been her favorite.

It was the photos, though, that Katie lingered over. "While Mom was alive, she took lots of photos of the family."

"Yes," Jasper agreed.

"After Mom died, there's just a few."

Jasper nodded. "Since you've been here, all I can think about is the week Bob sent you away, and why he did it. Whenever you or Luke asks questions—"

"Luke's been asking questions?"

"Even more than you," Jasper answered. "You've hooked that boy, though he's not sure whether he wants you to reel him in or release him. Right now he's taking the bait."

Trust Jasper to come up with an animal analogy.

"Anyway," he continued, "whenever you or Luke asks questions, the answers I've been giving don't always match the great man I worked with. How could I respect a man who could do such a thing? I finally realized I respected him because he always moved forward and he was good with animals."

"He was that," Katie agreed.

"Look at this picture," Jasper said. It showed Katie, probably about seven, holding a tiny Janie in her arms while riding a camel. Bob was be-

hind Katie, holding on to her. Leading the camel
was Katie's mom.

Bob's right arm was protectively holding on
to both Katie and Janie. His smile, however, was
aimed at her mother.

Then came the handful of photos, taken later,
of Bob and Katie. One was of her—about two
years old—atop a Clydesdale, Katie's feet sticking straight out. Her father was leading the
horse. There were only two photos that included
Janie. After studying them, Katie finally realized what Jasper was trying to show her.

"Dad's smile changed after my mother died."

"It did. I think his anger at her death kept him
moving forward. But it held him back with you
girls. If he'd let go of his anger, he might have
been a great father again."

It was a lot for Katie to take in. She didn't
even remember the day they'd taken the photo
with the camel. Her memories of her mother
were of a woman who'd played with her one
day and who was in bed the next.

"Take these home with you, Katie." Jasper
took the photo from her hand and returned it to
the suitcase. "Display them in your apartment.
Then the place will feel more like a home."

"Is that why you have all these memories displayed?"

He gazed around his living room, barely pausing at anything until he stood, turned around and studied the painting behind the couch.

"Tomas's oldest son sent me this when I was at Ringling Brothers. He'd found it in an estate sale. He'd been to our house enough times to recognize it. I had it in storage until I bought this house. It's all I have left of my family's history. You're lucky you have Janie."

Katie stood, put her arm around his waist and said, "I'm lucky I have you."

THE GIFT SHOP was jammed with customers from the moment it opened its door, so Luke sent Katie to help out. Within the first half hour, they'd sold every tiny stuffed bear they had on display. Katie went in the back room and found the box labeled "stuffed bears."

She'd stored the brown suitcase there for the moment, as well. Tonight she and Janie would go through it, divide up the photos and laugh at the old clothes and toys.

She restocked the stuffed bears again, and over the next couple of hours again, and again. Gloria made a notation to order more ASAP.

At two, Luke sauntered in. "Can you get by for an hour without her, Gloria?"

The line at the cash register was five deep, but the store was only half-full. Gloria frowned.

"Never mind," Luke said. Katie watched him

leave. He pulled out a cell phone and made a call before hopping into his cart. He looked tired, he acted distant and Katie wished she were in the cart with him.

She wished she hadn't let go of his hand.

"You still going with him to dinner at his family's house?" Gloria asked.

"I'm not sure. He only mentioned it once. Maybe he's forgotten."

"Not a chance," said Gloria. "I can handle closing the store by myself. That way you can run on to Ruth's and get all cleaned up."

Katie glanced down. Working in the gift shop was a far cry from working with the animals. But the shop had been so busy she hadn't even left to help with Rexette's show.

Strange that she'd wanted to.

At four, Luke showed up and whisked her away. He didn't even ask, he simply held open the gift shop door and nodded toward the cart with a smile.

"What's happening?"

"You'll see."

"Where are we going?"

"You'll see."

She'd been away from the animal park all day. She relaxed a little as they drove by Ollie's. Jasper was inside spreading greens. First Jasper waved and then Ollie.

Meredith met them by Aquila's wall.

"He ate the whole meal," she announced proudly. "Quickly, happily and exactly the way he's supposed to."

"What did you do?" Katie asked, peering in at Aquila, who was licking his front left paw contentedly.

"Me? Nothing. Well, nothing that I haven't been doing for the last six months. I gave him an extra portion and threw a ball at him."

Katie looked for the ball and noticed it lying unloved and neglected in the corner of the enclosure.

Meredith shook her head. "I don't care about the ball. I care about the cat. And to think, I'm the keeper who didn't believe sending for you would do him any good. Guess I was wrong."

"I didn't do anything. I haven't gone in there, touched Aquila or even really issued a command except for a couple of days ago."

"I've never put much stock in commands for big cats," Meredith said. "They behave certain ways because they want to. Just seeing you has made Aquila want to." Katie was acutely aware that both Meredith and Luke were watching as she took the keys Meredith offered and made her way to the entry marked "for employees." This time Katie wouldn't be standing at the door alone with no one, save Aquila, to witness when she failed.

She'd been here a week and a day.

She'd helped a snake, a wolf and two bears.

It was Aquila's turn.

A peacock screamed, and then all the birds fell silent. The key opened first one door, then a second and finally a third. The smell of big cat increased with each step. Katie's heart pounded and her palms started to sweat. Unbidden came advice from her father: "Don't show fear. They'll smell it and won't respect you."

She wiped her palms on her pant leg and stepped through the last door.

She was in Aquila's enclosure.

She turned to see Jasper watching with an expression of pride on his face. Ruth appeared worried. Katie couldn't find Luke. For some reason, his absence stilled her steps. The air whooshed out of her lungs and she suddenly couldn't breathe.

The door behind her slowly shut. Out of instinct, she checked to make sure it was secure. She picked up the pole leaning against the wall and forced herself to breathe. Taking two steps, she made it to the first log she came to and sat down, leaning the pole next to her where Aquila wouldn't notice it but where she could reach it if she needed it.

The wind whipped around and the hairs on her arms stood up.

But not out of fear.

From the corner of her eye, she saw Janie and Adam walk up. Both had paint on the front of their shirts. They were laughing right up until they stopped next to Ruth. Then they quieted.

Aquila was lying by his favorite wall. No one outside the enclosure could glimpse more than a square inch of him. All Katie could see was the top of his back and the start of his tail.

Which began to twitch.

She forced herself to stay still.

Slowly Aquila stood, managing to appear both bored and calculating. He didn't look at Katie. First he paced the front of his enclosure, stopping short of the crowd, as if denying them the chance to view him in all his glory. There were more people clustered outside now, including a whole family Katie didn't recognize. Why were they here if Bridget's was closed?

Putting the crowd out of her mind, Katie stood but didn't move toward Aquila. She was so close she could see the regal set of his nose, the intelligence in his eyes and the power behind each footfall. He angled toward her, as if he'd been aware of her presence all along. He stalked nearer to her until he was right in front of her. She touched him, first on the right side of his neck and then on the left. He moved forward, until the top of his head was under her hand.

Tears came, unbidden and healing. They slipped from her eyes Aquila smelled her, rubbed against her, but seemed to understand that he was keeping her from falling.

"Good boy," she whispered.

Then she heard a sound as welcome as the feel of Aquila's fur under her hand.

There in the doorway to Aquila's enclosure was Luke, once again close enough to save her if she needed it. And when he realized she didn't require saving, he made the moment even better by switching on the speakers.

Not loud, not soft, but at just the right volume came the opening lyrics of "Girls Just Want to Have Fun."

And Katie and Aquila danced.

CHAPTER SEVENTEEN

SHE WAS IN THE pen for thirty minutes, walking beside Aquila and dancing, albeit hesitantly, alongside him. But it seemed like only ten. And when she exited the enclosure, she slipped through the door and into Luke's arms.

They closed around her, strong and sure and protective. And when he bent down to kiss her, she met him halfway.

Aquila growled.

"Great," Luke whispered in her ear, "now I have a second animal who considers me a threat."

"Live with it," Katie advised.

"I'd rather live with you."

She didn't answer. *I'd rather live with you* was even stronger than *I want you to stay*. This man was a risk taker. She'd always played it safe, and—

Aquila hit the door, hard, jarring both of them. Luke pulled away. "Rexette knows how to share" was his only comment.

Together they passed through the short walkway behind Terrance's and Aquila's enclosures and out to the path where Ruth and the others waited.

Meredith got to them first. She shook Katie's hand and said, "You're just what he needed." Since she was looking at Luke, Katie wasn't sure if Meredith was referring to Luke or Aquila.

Ruth was crying. Jasper was next to her, gingerly patting her on the shoulder.

Janie was to the point. "Awesome, sis. And I could tell you had a thing for your boss."

Adam had been about to say something, but Janie's comment obviously caught him by surprise. He stared at Luke and said, "Dude."

That's when the family Katie didn't recognize moved forward. She belatedly noticed they were all solidly built, had dark hair and the same piercing black eyes as Luke.

"Katie, these are my parents, my sisters and their families. When it became obvious that we weren't going to make it to Tucson, I called to cancel and—"

"And we decided," said one of the women, "to come down and see who was responsible for disrupting our little brother's routine."

"We got here at the perfect moment." This came from Luke's dad. "He's been so worried about Aquila, and then last night it was obvious he was even more worried about you."

It had been a long time since someone had worried about Katie. Usually she did all the worrying.

"I made a reservation at Taco Tavern by the Green," Luke said.

"That's a real restaurant?" Janie asked.

Luke's whole family as well as Ruth, Jasper and Meredith nodded.

"Jasper and I will stay and patrol the grounds. Right, Jasper?"

"Wrong," came Fred's voice. "Tonight Gloria and I will help out. It will be easy. The animals are all put to bed. Jasper, you go with them. I know how much the girls mean to you. And, Meredith, unless I'm not remembering correctly, you've got someplace to go tomorrow bright and early."

The reservation was for ten people, but the Taco Tavern easily made it twelve. Katie wound up next to Luke—no surprise—and across from his sisters, who had enough questions to fill the whole evening.

By the time the meal ended, Katie had promised to come to Tucson one evening to visit the family without the jokes from Adam, the animal talk from Jasper and the biased compliments from Ruth.

"Wow," Janie said as they made their way to Luke's truck, "you mean you really contemplated leaving all this to return to Dallas?"

Katie didn't want to answer.

She'd only known all this for a week and one day.

She didn't believe in love at first sight.

She *really* didn't believe in throwing away a good job or a college diploma on an animal park that was barely making it.

Did she?

MONDAY MORNING, Katie headed for breakfast and met Yolanda.

Yolanda was grinning.

"Don't tell me," Katie said. "Ruth has already given you all the details about dinner last night and my budding romance with Luke."

"The only thing she left out was the wedding date," Yolanda said.

"Things aren't moving quite that fast."

"My parents knew each other for nine weeks before they got married. I was born nine months later."

"You're not helping, and I haven't even raised Janie all the way."

"Please," said Janie, coming into the kitchen, "leave me out of this."

Katie checked her watch. It was seven. Janie had never gotten out of bed this early on her own.

"Adam said to meet him at eight," Janie explained when Katie asked. "We're almost done with the south wall. Now that I'm here, he has lots of ideas."

"Has he said he's going to pay you?" Katie asked. She desperately needed to regain control. She hadn't experienced this much change in such a short period since they'd first arrived at Aunt Betsy's.

It hadn't been good then, and she was afraid to trust it now.

"He doesn't get paid," Janie admitted.

"He makes money on the weekends doing face drawings," Katie pointed out. "His art has also gotten the notice of quite a few businesses who've hired him. You talk money with him. If you work, you should get paid."

Janie made a face and sat down at the kitchen table. "You're not getting paid."

Katie was aware of that, but Luke had mentioned intending to pay her more than once. Now that she'd been at Bridget's, though, she knew she couldn't take the money. "My pay came six months ago when Luke purchased the animals. My pay comes when he keeps them."

"As if he won't," Janie said a bit smartly, as

only a younger sister could do. "He wants to keep you."

In a way, their new relationship made Katie feel much the same as she had when she'd been trying to get up the courage to work with Aquila. There was fear—something could go wrong and someone could get hurt. And there was exhilaration. This was where she belonged, where she was needed.

Where she was loved.

Yolanda made pancakes for everyone. Then she rushed out the door to make it to an early class. Janie left quickly, too, probably worried that Katie would mention how smart Yolanda was for actually attending her morning class and not dropping it.

Alone for the first time in a long while, Katie stepped out on the back porch and stared out at the land spreading toward the distant mountain.

She could breathe here.

No wonder she'd not been the perfect interpreter, letting little things like cell phone rules and awkward language bother her. The classroom was wonderful, but not as her full-time job. She needed air, freedom and something to love.

There was that word again.

If it was eight in the morning in Arizona, that

meant in Texas it was nine or possibly ten. She could never keep the time difference straight, especially now that she was in Arizona where the time never changed.

It took all of two minutes to give her notice. They weren't surprised.

Hanging up the phone, Katie waited for the fear to grip her. She'd just quit her job! She had no plan, no money and no home. Instead, she was elated. She'd use the money she'd earmarked to pay for Janie's college and live off it for the next few months while she helped at Bridget's and made some tough decisions.

"What did they say?" Ruth joined her on the patio, still in her robe and carrying a cup of coffee. She sat at the table and waited until Katie had pocketed her phone.

Katie sat beside her, tucking her hands in the pockets of her sweater for warmth. "I thought you were already at Bridget's."

"Going out for dinner with all you young people last night kept me from getting my beauty sleep. When my alarm went off, I ignored it."

"When do you have to be at work?"

"I make my own hours."

Katie started to say *must be nice* until she remembered how many hours Ruth put in. Except for the few hours she was with the Red Hats or in church, Ruth was at Bridget's.

"So," Ruth prompted, "you just gave notice. What did they say?"

Katie smiled. "That they've already replaced me."

"And what are you going to do?"

"I'm going to see about either attending school here, or working at one of the zoos in Tucson or Phoenix."

Ruth took a long sip of coffee before asking, "Why not work at Bridget's? We just might be able to make you an offer you can't refuse."

"Luke needs to let someone go, not hire another person. Don't worry, though. I'll come on my days off to spend time with Aquila, Scoot, Jasper and everyone else."

"Everyone else including Luke?"

"We have to talk, just him and me. I do like him, but this week we've been thrown together a lot. Our relationship will change when he's not my boss."

"What if he wasn't your boss?" Ruth asked.

"I can't imagine him not being in charge of Bridget's. He loves it. He has such dreams for the place."

Ruth was nodding.

"He does," Ruth agreed. "He's turned Bridget's

around in so many ways. But he's not your boss. The park is owned by a private nonprofit society. Which is really a society of one."

Katie, somehow, wasn't surprised by what came next.

"Me."

"You own Bridget's?"

"Yes."

Katie fell silent.

"I never wanted Luke to know," Ruth said. "He needed to be the one in charge. And I needed to see what he could do, especially with the budget. With the animals and staff, he's far exceeded my expectations. But his every decision is driven by his heart. I learned from my husband that when you run a business, logic has to be an equal part of the equation. That's where you would come in. Together, you two would ensure Bridget's a long and healthy future."

It scared Katie to realize Bridget's was funded by one person. Because if something happened to Ruth, Bridget's would go under, the animals would be homeless and the staff would be out of jobs.

It was more than Katie wanted to think about.

Be responsible for.

If Ruth was spelling this out because she wanted to appeal to Katie's logic, then she'd made an error in judgment. Nothing Katie had done in the week she'd been here had been logical.

Unfortunately the phone rang before she could tell Ruth how very wrong she was to put her trust in Katie.

LUKE WAS TIRED. Last night his parents—well, his mother—had called just five minutes after he'd fallen asleep. She wanted all the details about Katie.

"She's not someone you'll need to support?" Carla Rittenhouse asked. "You tend to be an enabler."

His mother had all kinds of clinical words left over from caring for Bridget. She also blamed herself for Luke taking on too much of the burden when it had come to his sister.

"You were just such a natural," she'd say, and then apologize.

"No, I won't need to support Katie. She'll do just fine on her own. And, Mom, we haven't even had a real date yet. There are too many people and too many animals who interfere."

It took another fifteen minutes to get her off the phone, and he'd failed to convince his mother that Katie wasn't future daughter-in-law material.

Carla was expecting her first grandchild, thanks to Jennifer, and already wanting more.

Last night even Suzy had been a little frightened at their mother's enthusiasm.

It had probably sent Katie running back to Texas.

After a sleepless night, Luke was unprepared to face the kind of day Monday morning promised. He walked the zoo, checking every animal and their enclosures. A maintenance man was in the snake house working on the heating lights. Luke assured Louie the Iguana that all would be made right. Then Luke went to check on a bald eagle Meredith had been nursing to health since it had been brought in last month. This one, they hoped, would be released into the wild very soon. Jasper was with Ollie, cleaning up his night house.

Neither Ruth nor Katie was anywhere to be found.

Terrance and Aquila both growled their displeasure.

"They'll be here," Luke assured them.

He was about to take off on Pixie for an early-morning ride when his radio went off.

"Hey," Fred said, his normally booming voice subdued. "You close to the infirmary?"

"Close enough."

"Come on over. Scoot's not doing too good."

Luke slumped and nudged Pixie through Bridget's and down the main path.

Even among wild animals, news seemed to spread on an unseen wave. A chorus of peacock screams followed Pixie as she delivered Luke to the infirmary. Even a screech from Ollie could be heard. Ruth came around the corner.

"I already called Jasper and Ruth."

By the time Luke entered the infirmary, Katie was already standing next to Fred. Her hand was on Scoot's head. The little bear didn't move, just stared blankly at the wall.

"His bones aren't healing. And now there's an infection. I've pumped the little guy full of antibiotics, but all we're doing is temporary. It's over. We need to put him down."

"No," Luke said. "We can call in a specialist. I don't care what we spend."

"Luke," Katie said gently. "You can't save them all, and the money would be best spent somewhere else, saving an animal that can be saved."

Luke looked at Ruth. She shook her head. Jasper didn't say anything. Luke's gaze returned to Katie.

She was no longer the temporary help for Aquila. She was, instead, Bob Vincent's daughter, a woman sure of who she was and what was best for an animal in her care.

"We can't give him quality of life, Luke. He's in pain. We should put him down," Katie said.

Behind them, Crisco whimpered.

"No," Luke ordered, his voice hoarse.

Ruth spun away, knuckles in her mouth. Jasper patted her back and led her to the door.

"It's the right thing to do," Katie insisted.

Luke stomped from the room.

He hadn't given the order and Fred wouldn't act without his blessing, not yet.

The burros and mules didn't catch on to his bad mood, and Katie was careful with her words when she joined him a few minutes later. "Am I working here today?"

In truth, he needed her everywhere. He needed her here with the burros, he needed her with Fred in case the media called, he needed her with Aquila.

He needed her by his side because he couldn't give the order to put down a helpless bear, even though it was the right thing to do. It went against his nature to allow harm to anything, anyone, who was different.

Katie understood that.

He fished his iPad out of his backpack and searched to see who was scheduled to be in the burro pen. "No, we're fine here. Spend your day either with Aquila or with Fred."

She nodded and he strode away, wishing she were walking beside him, reminding him of why he had to do it.

Throughout the day, he sought her out. She'd made Crisco a priority, and was often in the infirmary. On one visit, she huddled with Luke in the corner away from prying eyes and said, "Every time Ruth comes here to try to help, she starts crying."

He touched Katie's hand, understanding that sometimes it was harder not to cry, harder to do the work that needed to be done. She reached up and put her hand on his cheek, cradling it.

Her eyes asked a question he wasn't ready to answer.

More than one, really.

Fred cleared his throat. "Ah, you're getting a bit more attention than the bear."

They were, too. Two elderly couples standing at the door were smiling.

For once, it seemed, the infirmary was on Bridget's map. After the news special, there'd been a steady stream of people who wanted to talk to either Fred or Katie about Scoot. Often, depending on the size of the crowd, they'd lead them around back so they could watch Crisco in his pen.

"Will he be released into the wild again?" a few people asked.

Fred would say no and explain about the bear's claws, why they were important and how criminal it had been to remove them.

Every time Luke heard the story, he got mad all over again.

Today, though, it was easy to get mad. But no matter how angry he got, he couldn't bring himself to give the order to put the bear down.

What kind of director could he be if he couldn't make the tough decisions?

When Katie wasn't with Fred and the bears, Luke found her with Aquila. She usually sat still on the same log as yesterday, just letting Aquila get used to her presence. No rush, no risks, doing everything the way she'd been brought up to do.

It didn't seem to matter to Katie what Aquila was doing, whether he roamed, nuzzled her hand or snoozed. She just enjoyed his company.

Luke hoped that someday they would have the same kind of easy relationship. Maybe he'd be out working in the yard of their home while she read a book, or he'd curl up next to her on the couch, or they'd snooze together.

No matter what they did, though, they'd enjoy each other's company.

This was only her second week and he couldn't imagine Bridget's without her, couldn't remember Bridget's without her.

At ten, without his prompting, she showed up to help with Rexette's show.

He'd wanted to eat lunch with her afterward,

but she disappeared while he returned Rexette to her pond.

"Where's your sister?" he asked, joining Janie and Adam at the concession stand by the gift shop. He needed to tell Katie that he knew she was right, knew what he had to do about Scoot, and that he'd already put things in motion, including calling the film crew. Scoot's story needed to be documented to decrease the odds of it happening again.

"She took off with Ruth in the cart."

"Everything's a bit off for a Monday," Adam added, as if Luke didn't already know. He realized he'd spent the whole day following Katie around instead of doing his job. It was time to be the director.

KATIE WAS HELPING Fred in the infirmary when Amanda, her mother and a van full of girls arrived. Katie signed how happy she was to see them. For the next two hours, Katie toured them around Bridget's, introducing them to both animals and people.

It was around closing when Katie made their last stop the big cat area. She wanted to show the group, but especially Amanda, how much better Aquila was. Although they wouldn't be able to hear the music, she planned to turn on

"Girls Just Want to Have Fun" and dance with Aquila.

But when she turned the corner, she halted abruptly. Holding out her hand, she gestured for the girls to stop and not get any closer.

Just a few feet in front of Katie stood Terrance. Not in his enclosure but on the path. Free. And he was facing Janie.

Ruth was beside Janie saying, "He's a little cranky from having his tooth pulled. He won't hurt you. You're not in danger."

"Is he hungry?" Janie asked.

Katie moved to the side so she could figure out what was going on.

"He'd rather have raw meat," Ruth said.

Katie swallowed and her hands immediately went damp. She opened her mouth to say something, but words didn't come.

Katie took one step, going up on the toe of her left foot and positioning her right. She could run, stand in front of Janie.

"What are you doing, Katie?" Ruth said.

"Trying to get to Janie, keep her safe."

"Terrance is more afraid of her than she is of him," Ruth insisted. "He doesn't know you. Keep back."

Katie doubted that. "Can we give him a toy?" she asked. "Something he'd rather play with than Janie?"

She hadn't been with the big lion much during the week she'd been here. Her help hadn't been necessary. Ruth took care of his every need. Now Katie took in his huge black mane, his size, the shape of his jaw, the twitch in his tail, the anger in his eyes.

She might not be familiar with the lion, but she could tell he was ready to attack.

"Terrance, you big baby," Ruth said. "Sit."

Katie took a step toward Ruth.

"Don't," Ruth advised. "Just stand still. He's a bit confused. I want to give him a moment to get his bearings."

"I have to get to Janie."

"I know my cat. He won't hurt her."

Standing still had never been Katie's policy. She'd always been the one to go into the cage, take charge of the situation, make sure everyone around her was safe.

Whether the enemy was animal or human.

"There's always a first time," Katie argued, "and it's not going to be Janie."

Behind her, the deaf girls were slowly moving away. Their eyes were wide with fear. Their hands were going a mile a minute. Katie finally focused on one word: man.

Katie finally took her eyes off Janie. Luke stood off to the side. He had a rifle, but he wasn't aiming.

Why wasn't he aiming!

Fred came from behind the deaf girls. "Get them out of the way," he ordered Katie calmly.

It was the last thing she wanted to do. She needed to get Janie out of harm's way first. The deaf girls weren't in Terrance's path. Her sister was.

Terrance roared.

Fred shot her a look that said *Do what I say.*

Katie moved to her charges, urging them back, all the while keeping her eyes on her sister.

Terrance went up on his hind legs, standing a good ten feet tall in that stance. His front paws stroked the air in front of him.

"What?" Ruth sounded impressed. "Terrance, you never stand. What's gotten into you? Sit!"

As if realizing he was on his hind legs, Terrance went down quickly and took two long, rambling steps toward Janie.

Janie pursed her lips, the way she always did when she was about to disagree with Katie. She took a step to the left, amazingly confident, and then she parroted Ruth, shouting, "Sit! Terrance, sit!"

Terrance halted, looking a bit surprised, and sat down.

"I told you there was no danger," Ruth said, moving to Terrance.

Katie wasn't sure if Ruth was talking to Janie or Terrance. She didn't care.

No one moved, especially not Janie.

Fred got to Terrance first and slipped the leading ring around his muzzle. Ruth immediately rushed to Terrance, brushing his side with her hands, checking to make sure he was okay. Then she took him by the mane and led him back into his enclosure.

Katie finally found the strength to make her way to Janie, who had slipped to the ground on her knees.

She knelt beside her sister. "Are you all right?"

"Of course," Janie said. "Wow, I've never been so afraid in my life. How'd I do?"

"How'd you do? What do you mean?"

"Adam says when you work at an animal park, you should expect to get war wounds. I showed him that I already had one. He was quite impressed. This time, I didn't even get a scratch." She looked quite smug.

"Janie, this isn't funny."

Luke bent down, helping Janie to her feet. "What exactly happened?"

"I was searching for Katie. I figured she'd be with Aquila. I came around the corner and Terrance was sitting in the middle of the path. I remember being grateful I'd found him instead of a guest."

"Did you back away, call for help?"

Janie shook her head. "I went to get my cell from my pocket, but the movement got his attention. I looked around for something I could grab to put between him and me, but I didn't think I had the strength to hoist one of the trash cans, so I stayed perfectly still and kept my eyes down." She gazed at Katie. "Like you always told me to do. I didn't want to surprise him or make him feel cornered."

"You did exactly right," Katie said.

"See," Luke said to Katie, "I told you, you are a natural teacher. She remembers exactly what you taught her."

"If she remembered everything I taught her, she wouldn't be here. She wouldn't be anywhere near an exotic animal whose gut instinct is to kill. I told you wild animals and people don't mix." It all came out in a rush of anger, fear and adrenaline.

Luke reached out, but Katie backed away.

"Katie," Janie said gently. "You can't hide from life. There's a greater chance I'll get hit by a car than be attacked by another cat."

"Oh, really?" Katie was shaking. "Because a cat almost attacked you just now."

"We'd have stopped him," Luke promised. "Both Fred and I were ready."

"But what if you weren't here?"

Luke just shook his head. "We're careful."

"You're not careful enough! A lion escaped today. What more proof do you need?"

Ruth came up then, half walking, half skipping in her haste. Jasper by her side. "I'm so sorry." She took Janie's hand between hers and stroked. "My mind was on Scoot and I must have forgotten to close the doors. Terrance obviously wanted to follow me and got into the service hallway without me noticing. I can't imagine how I could make so many mistakes."

"You didn't make many." Jasper obviously wanted to make her feel better.

"This is a place, though," Katie said softly, "where one mistake can take a life."

"This is a place," Ruth said, sniffing, "where every day you make a difference in a life. Like we're doing with Terrance, Aquila and Crisco." She glanced over to the group of girls waiting for Katie. "Like you're doing for them. Life isn't meant to be safe. It's meant to be lived."

Katie brought her eyes to Luke's, her tears threatening to spill down her cheeks.

"What we do now," Luke said, "is make sure this never happens again."

"Not possible," Katie stated. "Mistakes happen."

"And life goes on. This *business* goes on. You have about five teenage girls and a mom who think they've got the story of a lifetime. Offer them free passes to the haunted house and a personal tour that night."

"But I won't be here."

He looked her right in the eye. His were all piercing blackness and sweet promises.

She bit her bottom lip.

"You're too strong. You love animals too much. How can you even consider leaving?" Luke's voice sounded different than she remembered. He sounded sure. He sounded as if he was the only one who could see into her heart and tell her what was there.

"Janie's here now," he continued. "Ruth said you gave notice at your job, that you'd started to make plans here."

"Things have changed. I need to think."

"You can have all the time you want," Ruth said.

"Halloween's just a few weeks away," Luke said. "Stay that long. This Thursday, remember, we're going to start decorating the cabin, as you suggested."

"I can't do this."

Luke rubbed the back of Katie's neck. "You

don't have to do anything you don't want to do. Heck, we'll post you in the gift shop forever if you want."

Against her will, her body relaxed under his touch and she leaned toward him like a ship to port.

"Ah," Jasper said, "I'll take the girls to the exit and tell them about the haunted house offer." He didn't wait for an answer.

"I'm going to check on Terrance," Ruth muttered.

"Just wait until Adam hears how I tamed Terrance," Janie said, hurrying off.

When they were gone, Luke asked quietly, "So, really, how bad a setback is this?"

"When Janie was attacked last time, no one was around but Dad and me. Here, everyone came running. And you were willing to shoot Terrance, weren't you?"

"If I had to, yes."

"I'm—" She choked on the word. "I'm going to keep working with Aquila. I'm here to stay."

The fingers caressing the nape of her neck stilled. Then they tightened, bringing her even closer to him. His lips settled on hers, warm and strong and demanding. The sounds of the park merged into white noise and she gave herself up to his kiss.

"Oh, dear."

Katie heard Ruth's words from far away, but they finally penetrated. Katie pushed at Luke, a little disorientated as she struggled to find out what Ruth wanted.

She glanced up and saw the college kids. Filming them.

CHAPTER EIGHTEEN

JASPER HAD APPARENTLY let the college film crew into the park as he'd escorted the teenagers and their mother to the exit.

"We were expecting to find a somber group," the teacher explained, "because of what's happening to Scoot. We made sure to be quiet as we hunted you down."

"You were certainly quiet," Luke agreed, glancing at Katie and liking the red blush that graced her cheeks.

Two of the kids held Panasonic Varicams and still had them aimed at him and Katie. "Just doing what we do best," they said.

"Did you try to call?" Luke asked. He took Katie's hand and moved toward the college students and their teacher. It was enough to convince the cameramen to quit teasing.

"No, we really should have, but when we heard about Scoot, we had to come. We all felt bad. Then we all decided we wanted to help."

Ruth and Luke exchanged looks. On one hand, more coverage about the plight of the baby cubs would increase Jake at Fish and Game's chance of catching whoever had declawed them. On the other hand, what Bridget's didn't need was a segment about an escaped lion who'd almost attacked a nineteen-year-old girl.

"We'll take you to the infirmary."

Luke hoped the film crew would assume Katie was crying because of Scoot, and not dwell on the incident with Terrance.

But he was also aware he was taking Katie from one incident that had nearly shredded her tenuous confidence to deliver her to yet another gut-wrenching experience.

Putting Scoot down.

He met Katie's gaze. "We have to do the right thing."

He said the words, but part of him still didn't believe them.

He'd failed.

Taking out his cell phone, Luke called ahead and informed Fred they were on their way.

Fred, ever the professional, didn't so much as raise an eyebrow when six people crowded in to watch.

"In vet school, they tell you you'll get used to this. You do get used to it, but you never enjoy it, not when you're using a euthanasia solution to put down an animal this young."

No one spoke, asked questions or moved.

Fred gently picked Scoot up from his cage and carried him to the table. Scoot just lay there. Except for an occasional ripple, maybe a shiver, he acted dead already.

"This little guy should be out following his mother, climbing trees, getting ready to hibernate in a few weeks."

Luke put his hand on Katie's shoulder, leaned down and whispered, "I should have turned him over to a bear rescue. They might have—"

"—put him down sooner," she whispered back. "You gave him a fighting chance. More than anyone else would have done. Like you always do."

"Typically," Fred said, drawing out a syringe, "he'd live to twenty or so."

"What exactly caused so much damage?" the teacher asked. "Was it any one thing?"

"I'd blame the milk they fed him," Fred said. "Because it wasn't right, his bones didn't mature. The declawing didn't help. Now there's a fever."

"So much wrong," Luke added.

Deftly, Fred administered the shot. "This will be delivered quickly into his bloodstream. Soon, the anesthesia will reach his heart and brain, causing them to stop working. He'll go to sleep. Then his heart will stop beating."

"So," Luke said, "we'll go full circle from

man causing pain to man relieving pain. I only wish we could find the man who caused his suffering."

"You're too busy," Katie stated, "righting the circle of life."

He was still surprised at how convinced she was that he'd made the best choices. Luke tightened the hand he had on her shoulder. He could learn from her, learn a lot.

She leaned into him. "There's nothing else we could have done. You've stopped his pain."

It was enough to give Luke hope.

Katie put a hand on Scoot's chest. It didn't rise.

IT WAS ALMOST like a wake. After the film crew left and the animals were put to bed, Janie, Adam, Luke and Katie had headed over to Ruth's.

She was now in the kitchen setting out chips and salsa. Adam and Janie were at the kitchen table with long sheets of white paper spread out. They were making pencil drawings. Soon a picture of Scoot would appear on the front wall with his name and a description of his plight.

"Look, Katie," Janie said, "I've got you and Luke penciled in playing with Scoot."

Luke winced at his image. "I'm glad you're a painter and not a sculptor." To Katie, he said,

"Those two will create a masterpiece that will cost too much money to even consider erecting."

"Bridget's is growing," Adam called. "We have to show people we're a force to be reckoned with."

Katie stood behind Janie and watched her draw for a while. She'd been wrong to ignore such talent. Janie was good. Janie was doing what she loved.

Still, Janie needed a degree, needed something to fall back on if Katie wasn't around. But maybe she could stop worrying. Janie would be fine.

If only Katie could be as sure about herself.

When Janie started doodling a black panther in the corner of the paper, Katie remembered something she'd meant to do. Running up to her room, she dragged out the brown suitcase she'd intended to share with Janie last night. Tonight would be better, just about everyone was here.

"I've got some things to show you, Janie. Luke, too." Katie settled down next to Luke on the couch.

Janie came over, Adam behind her, and settled cross-legged on the floor. "What is it?"

"Jasper gave this to me, really us, yesterday. It has pictures in it. Pictures I was too angry to realize I should pack up after Dad died."

"Wow, let me see."

After the second picture, Katie realized Janie had no memory of these events. She'd been too little. But she was desperate for them. Janie clutched the photos of her, Katie and both parents.

"The only picture I have of Mom is the one taken right before she died. I was two." Janie raised her eyes to Katie. "It's back in Dallas."

"We need to go get our stuff," Katie said.

"What few pictures we have." Janie returned her gaze to the picture. "Life would have been so cool if she'd lived."

Katie nodded, once again staring at the picture of her father sitting behind them on the camel, making sure they didn't fall off.

"Jasper said Dad had a one-owner heart. That after Mom died, he didn't know how to go on. That's why he buried himself in his work."

Ruth set the chips and salsa on the coffee table. "Let me see."

Janie handed the photo over.

"You were a beautiful family," Ruth said before handing it back. "You won't make the same mistake as Bob."

Janie looked surprised. "What mistake?"

"Of having one-owner hearts. Here at Bridget's, there are too many of us demanding your love and attention. Now," she said, dragging Janie into the dining room, "show me the drawing you two have been working on. Explain why it's necessary and where it would go."

That left only Katie and Luke in the living room.

"So," Luke said, nuzzling her ear, "you are definitely staying?"

"I'll stay here until Halloween, until I decide what I want to do."

"Does what *I* want you to do matter at all?" he teased.

"Of course you matter, but—"

She couldn't say anything else; his lips were in the way.

LUKE NOTICED RUTH in the kitchen talking on her cell. After a moment she came into the living room and said, "That was Jasper. He says everything is all right at Bridget's. He also said that Amanda and her friends talked the old coot into letting them help decorate the cabin for Halloween. They'll be up there all day Thursday. Apparently there's no school. It's a teacher in-service day or something."

"I'm not surprised they're starting to feel involved. That's unavoidable at Bridget's. So where's Meredith? Isn't it her turn at night watch?"

"She drove up to New Mexico this morning."

Katie gave him a puzzled glance.

"I didn't think anything would come of it, and in all the excitement, I almost forgot. We got a call a few months ago. There was a man up in Lordsburg, New Mexico. He was getting older and starting to worry about what would happen to his leopard once he died."

"So," Katie prompted, "this is another owner pleading with you to take an animal off his hands."

"At the time, yes, but we couldn't afford the cost. This man's had an exotic or two for more than forty years. From everything I could find out, he was well trained to care for them. When he first called back in July, I told him we'd just acquired a panther, and while we might want another big cat later on, we weren't in the market just now to purchase Frisky."

"Frisky's a leopard?"

"Yes, he's spotted and apparently in excellent health."

"So you've kept in contact with this guy."

"Off and on. He called again in September, offering to come down on the price. He just wanted a good home for his animal, and was trying to handpick where Frisky wound up. But we didn't have the money. But by August, Aquila wasn't eating and I was starting to wonder if I should reconsider purchasing Frisky."

"But you didn't."

"You agreed to come down, so I put him off again."

"What's changed now?"

"I got another call the day your friend Amanda first came to Bridget's. I'd watched you walk around with her, signing and being the perfect teacher. I thought you were doing what you loved. I figured I had to accept that you weren't going to stay here, and that you couldn't help Aquila. This time, however, the caller wasn't the leopard's owner, it was his son."

"Oh, no."

"Right, the old man had died. The son found my name in some correspondence and wanted to honor his father's last wish. He doesn't even want money, just a good home for Frisky. I hesitated at first, but the guy sounded desperate. I decided to at least take a look."

"But you didn't go. You sent Meredith. Why? And why didn't you mention any of this to me?"

"I didn't mention it because I truly didn't think anything would come of it." The way he looked at her suddenly changed, darkened, deepened. "And I sent Meredith because I didn't really want to go."

"Why?"

"Quite honestly, I wasn't sure I could go a day without you. And Meredith wanted to go," he continued. "She keeps reminding me she's head keeper and should be involved with everything. She may be feeling a little threatened."

"Like Ruth was with Jasper?"

"Maybe a little."

Katie scooted closer. "So you didn't want to be away from me for even a day?"

He put his hands behind his neck, stretched, gazed at the ceiling and then sheepishly admitted, "Did I say that? Maybe…"

There was no maybe about the kiss she gave him.

MAYBE HER PROBLEM, all along, Katie decided, had been trust. She'd trusted herself, no one else. Now, trusting others made her feel vulnerable, yes, but also cherished.

In the cool temperatures of early morning, Aquila was up, playing and in a great mood— for a panther.

Taking out the notebook she'd put in her backpack, Katie marked the time and what Aquila was doing. Then she skirted his enclosure, searching for anything that didn't belong. Captive cats were territorial and tended to take issue with any change in their environment. Something as small as a plastic cup or towel could change Aquila's mood. While she trusted Aquila, she was also aware that instinct was a powerful motivator.

And she was very aware of the number of years it had been since she'd last worked with exotic cats.

Once she'd verified the enclosure was secure, she enticed Aquila with food: four pounds of chicken, per Fred's orders. Then she got him into his holding pen while she cleaned his night house and emptied his exhibit.

In that moment, as she leaned on the rake and brushed away flies, Katie realized *she'd done it.*

Scattered on the ground were horse ribs. Aquila was eating. In the air was the undeniable scent of a cat marking his territory.

Aquila was back!

And so was Katie.

Luke stopped by about seven. She met him at the cage door, gave him a quick kiss and then shooed him off. Right now, this close, he was interference—just as much as a plastic cup or towel would be. She had work to do, and so did he.

"Rexette at ten?" he said.

"It's a date."

The light in his eyes told her he was as ready as she was. There just might be plenty of dates in the coming days. Not just here at Bridget's with Rexette as a chaperone, but in the evenings, too.

Alone.

After Aquila finished his breakfast, Katie got him into the enclosure and once again sat on the log. He played, came to her and sniffed and played some more. She never lost sight of him. After about an hour, she left, careful to close and lock every door.

She almost, by habit, turned toward the infirmary, thinking she needed to check on Scoot. Her steps faltered at the last minute and instead she headed for Luke.

Katie found him in his office on the phone. He was both talking and typing on the computer. Careful not to disturb him, Katie went behind the desk to read the PDF file that listed the history of a leopard named Frisky.

There were lots of holes in the information.

Not good. She was pretty sure her father would have passed on an animal with a history as shoddy as this, and so would she.

"Tell him we can pick up Frisky as soon as the paperwork is approved." He moved the phone aside and mouthed, *It's Meredith.*

Katie raised an eyebrow. So they'd be getting a new leopard. Where would it go? Aquila's enclosure wasn't big enough. There was room for expansion but that cost money.

"Does Frisky still have his claws?" she asked.

Luke pointed to a line on his computer screen. By the word *claws* was the word *yes*.

"No, I trust you," Luke said into the phone. "And you've already talked this over with Ruth. So, if you say we should take the leopard, we'll take the leopard."

There was that word again. Trust.

When Luke hung up, he glanced at Katie. "I guess we'll be getting another leopard."

"I'm not sure it's a good idea."

"He's free. We have the space."

"No, we don't. Leopards are solitary. They need separate territories."

For a moment, indecision crossed Luke's face. Then his eyes went to the computer screen again. "I want to see him first," he said. "Want to drive to New Mexico with me?"

After almost two weeks, she'd just managed to get close to a panther she'd raised. No way did she want to get close to one she didn't know.

"No."

"Hey, if I sense there's any danger—"

"He's a wild animal. Of course there's danger."

"I mean anything out of the ordinary."

"When are you leaving?"

"Thursday. Fred has to come along, too.

Frisky will have to be medicated and monitored the whole trip."

He wasn't just going to see. Luke had already made up his mind.

"I'm heading to Dallas. Janie and I are going to get our things."

"Well, if I have to forgo your company on a one-day trip, I'm glad it's because you're packing up your old life and making us your new life."

"I'm still not sure I'm making the right decision." Especially after today.

He got up and came around the desk, reassuring her with one of those never-get-enough kisses. "Trust me, you are."

Did she trust him? Did he trust her? He'd accepted Meredith's and Ruth's opinions. But not hers.

Back at his desk, Luke took out his GPS and located Lordsburg. "Meredith says Frisky's all alone and not getting enough attention. At this point, we'll consider it a rescue. And who knows, this might be for the best. Two leopards are a better draw than one. And to get this one for free…"

"That is rare."

"Yes, very rare. Which is why I can't turn it down."

"How comfortable is Frisky with humans?"

Luke frowned. "Not as much as we would hope. The son, Tom, told Meredith that Frisky had already been fully grown when his dad purchased him and has always been unfriendly. Tom says he won't go near Frisky, he just throws meat over the top of the fence."

"Frisky's aggressive?"

"Meredith would never suggest we take him if he was dangerous. She believes it's more that he's solitary and just wants to be left alone. But she says he's gorgeous. And, again, the price is right. Ruth's a bit hesitant, because of the money it will take to house and feed him, but she says it's a good idea."

She wondered if Luke realized how much he relied on Ruth. Would his trust in her be shaken when he found out *she* was really in charge and not him, and that Ruth wanted to turn over some of the decision-making responsibility to Katie?

If it were up to Luke, he'd rescue every animal in the world, never worrying until after about how to feed them.

He needed Ruth in his life.

Or, better yet, Katie.

ON WEDNESDAY MORNING, Katie hugged Ruth goodbye. "We'll pack up what we want to keep and get rid of everything else. When we get back, we'll search for an apartment of our own."

Ruth pshawed. "Just stay with me. I'm close and the rent's affordable. I won't charge you at all."

Janie was willing.

Katie was not. She'd fought long and hard to stand on her own feet and gain control of her life.

She'd made a few mistakes, like forcing Janie to go to college. And closing herself off from the animals she loved.

That was changing now.

"Thanks, Ruth. We'll keep your offer in mind." That was the most Katie would consider.

Since Terrance's escape, Ruth had pulled back from Bridget's. She'd limited her duties to just Terrance and had passed everything else to Katie, though they hadn't discussed pay and schedules and such.

Oh, a vague offer had been put on the table, but Katie wasn't comfortable with it. Not at all.

"You just keep telling Aquila I'll be back," Katie said.

"I will," Ruth promised.

The drive from Scorpion Ridge to Dallas was very different than the one she'd taken almost two weeks ago. For one thing, Katie didn't want to leave Bridget's. She had so much to do. And no one could do it as well as she did.

Funny, she hadn't felt that way about her interpreter's position.

The good thing about the trip was the time with Janie. Now that she wasn't trying to guide Janie into making the right decisions, they could just enjoy each other's company.

Katie had to accept that college, right now, was not the right choice for her sister. She had to trust Janie. And after watching Adam and Janie work together, she had to admit that the girl could draw.

But, still, it wouldn't hurt to encourage her sister to maybe look into attending college here in Arizona, majoring in art with possibly an English minor.

Just in case.

"So," Janie said just before they made it to Tucson, "will I have a brother-in-law soon?"

"No! I've only known him for two weeks. Right now you can simply call him Sir Potential Boyfriend."

"Hmmm, that's a mouthful, but okay."

After a moment, Janie fired off her next question. "So, why can't we keep living with Ruth? She's all alone in that big house except for Yolanda. She enjoys the company. Plus, if you're always going to be out with Sir Potential Boyfriend, I should have a say in where we live."

"We can't impose."

"We're not imposing. She told me that until we came along, she was contemplating selling it."

Ruth hadn't shared that with Katie.

"Really?" Katie mused. "I wonder why."

"Why? It's way too big for one person."

Katie doubted that was the reason. Ruth had been alone for many years. And, Katie also knew, Ruth was proud of her home. She'd decorated it to perfection, she'd cared for Terrance there and it had that great back patio so she could drink coffee in the morning and watch the sun peep over the mountains.

Which meant the only reason Ruth would sell the house was if she needed money.

If Bridget's needed money, that is.

To hire Katie.

CHAPTER NINETEEN

TOM LONGTREE MET them at the front gate of a ranch that had long since stopped production. Stepping into the home's living room was like walking into the seventies, complete with shag carpeting and olive-green paint.

Tom had a firm handshake and reminded Luke a little bit of a much younger Jasper.

"Glad you men could make it." Tom had the raspy voice of a smoker. "I'm trying to figure out what to do with everything, and Frisky's definitely more than I can handle. I'm not even comfortable feeding him, so his enclosure hasn't been cleaned since my father died. That's not right."

A German shepherd stood guard at the man's side, making sure no one threatened his owner.

Tom obviously knew enough about animals to be bothered by how Frisky was living—and not to try something he wasn't capable of, like getting the cat in and out of the enclosure to clean it.

Tom led them past empty cages the size of

railroad cars, forming two lines leading all the way to the barn. From their cages, the animals could glimpse an expanse of grass and trees. If Luke had been a leopard, trapped in one of these cages, he'd have gone crazy staring at the freedom he couldn't access.

A horse neighed, the only sign of animal life besides the dog.

"That's my horse," Tom said. "When I realized I'd be here for a while, I brought him up. Hired someone to tend to my other five. I was afraid to hire someone, though, to take care of Frisky. If they got hurt, I'd never forgive myself. Heck, I can't even show the house until he's gone."

Luke hoped the other animals had gone to better places, places where there was grass and room to run and more toys. The bottom of these cages was just dirt. A few of the cages still held balls or small bones.

This was not the way animals, wild or domestic, should live. And if this man's father had cared for—Luke quickly counted nine cages on each side, eighteen in all—this many animals, he wouldn't have been able to give much individual attention to each animal.

The way Ruth gave to Terrance, or Meredith gave to Yoda, or Jasper gave to Ollie, or Luke gave to Rexette, or Katie gave to Aquila.

Frisky was in an enclosure outside the barn.

"How many big cats did your father have?" Fred asked, speaking up for the first time. His face mirrored Luke's opinion. He didn't like it here.

"What? Oh!" Tom's face went from quizzical to enlightened. "You think he had exotic animals in all those cages? No, no, he didn't. For years he ran a rescue for hurt and injured dogs. He inherited a very tame leopard from his father, my grandpa. When she died, Dad wanted another one. That's how he got Frisky. Answered an ad in the paper, of all things. Wasn't the same, though. My dad helped raise the first one. This guy should have been in the wild from the get-go. Maybe you can rehabilitate him and release him?"

When Luke saw Frisky, he wondered the same thing. He was beautiful. A golden color with unique black markings. He had the biggest feet Luke had ever seen on a leopard. But unfortunately it cost even more to rehabilitate and release than it did to rehabilitate and keep. And the statistics on survival rates for big cats released into the wild after being in captivity were dismal.

But Luke would do what he could for him; he would give Frisky a chance.

An hour later, he and Fred had Frisky sedated and in the back of the truck. They'd get to Bridget's around midnight, if they hurried.

And Luke was in a hurry. After all, he had someone to hurry home to.

"WELL, WHAT DID he say?" Janie asked after Katie hung up.

Checking the road behind her before changing lanes, Katie replied, "He and Fred got back late last night. They've put Frisky in a small temporary enclosure for now. Luke says Frisky's acting like he's woken up in the middle of a nightmare. He's hiding under the rocks and refusing to eat."

"So now we have two leopards that won't eat."

"Aquila's eating just fine. Frisky just has to get used to his new surroundings."

"Are they going to build a new enclosure?"

"I really doubt it. There's no money for that. It would be cheaper to extend Aquila's enclosure, and…" Katie's words tapered off. She had a thought, one her father would certainly have had, but one that probably hadn't crossed Luke's mind.

He was too animal-friendly, not business-oriented like Bob Vincent.

And Katie Vincent.

"What?" Janie asked.

Taking a breath, Katie speculated, "Given Terrance's age, I wonder if Luke's considered how soon there will be a whole area available, right next to Aquila."

Janie shook her head. "Luke wouldn't have the heart to even consider that."

It was Luke's heart, which would never dream of getting rid of the old for the new, that made her love him.

It was early morning, still dark, when Katie and Janie pulled into Ruth's driveway. Trying to be quiet, they left the car still packed and made their way inside and to bed.

Ruth knocked on Katie's door at seven the same morning. "Good to have you back."

"Thanks, it's good to be back."

"I've got coffee on the patio. Let's talk."

Katie grabbed her slippers and robe before following Ruth.

"You think over my offer?" Ruth said.

"The one where I take over as Bridget's chief executive officer?"

"That's the one."

"I've been thinking about it, yes, and I'm going to decline."

Ruth wasn't surprised. "What are you going to do instead?"

"I'll do the job—without the title. I'm going to work alongside Luke. And I'm also going to go back to school and learn all I can about animal science."

"That's a great plan," Ruth said.

"Does that mean you'll tell Luke you're the private, nonprofit society of one?"

"I'm going to have to. I'll do it after I insist he move Terrance into Aquila's enclosure, and place both Aquila and Frisky in Terrance's."

"But it's too small—"

"Terrance's area is big enough for both of the leopards. You've just not noticed because you've been too focused on Aquila and the bears and Luke."

Katie's phone buzzed. She checked her text message: Miss U Come Wrk.

"Let me get dressed, and I'll ride with you to Bridget's."

Janie met them downstairs. She wore old clothes and now she, too, sported a BAAA backpack. "I can't wait to see what Adam's done while I've been gone."

In the car, she sat in the backseat but continued to gush about Adam. "He's got a contract to paint a wall on some new building going up in Casa Grande. He says if I help, I can have half the proceeds. He's hoping it will mean even more commissions."

It wasn't a stable job, but it reassured Katie

a bit about Janie's future. She was learning to let go.

At Bridget's, Jasper was just walking in the entrance. Meredith's, Fred's and Luke's vehicles were in the parking lot.

Katie wished it were Luke waiting for them at the entrance. She'd already be in his arms.

Jasper was full of news. "We put Crisco in with George yesterday. George was afraid of the little guy at first. Now he's annoyed at him— George keeps moving away and Crisco keeps following."

"Let's hope Frisky acclimates that easily to a permanent enclosure," Ruth said.

"I haven't seen him yet," Jasper shared. "They got in late yesterday and Meredith was on duty."

"Where were you? It usually doesn't matter who's on duty when a new animal arrives."

"I was at home working in the backyard. I've been thinking, now that Katie's signing on to help out at Bridget's, I might work a little less. Ollie, George and Kobie are all familiar with her. They won't need me as much."

"How does everyone kn—" Katie stopped. Of course, Jasper had found out she was staying at Bridget's. The animal park was a small town in itself. "If anything, they'll need you more," she protested. "Especially when I go back to school."

"Imagine going to school willingly," Janie muttered.

"I'll help out, proud to, but I've got some things on my mind I want to get done." He was gazing at Ruth. She didn't look away.

Maybe selling the big house had more to do with Jasper than money, Katie hoped.

Jasper checked his watch and muttered something about a meeting. The cart arrived then, Luke at the wheel. He jumped out and made his way to Katie. When he got to her, he took her in his arms, raising her up and swinging her around.

"Man, I missed you."

"Not as much as I missed you," she teased.

"I was trapped in a truck with Fred and Frisky. They both snored the entire drive."

"Fred and Frisky, huh? It sounds like they should have a morning radio show."

His smiled, his eyes crinkling at the corners. "I love the way your mind works."

"I want to see the new leopard."

There wasn't room in the cart for everyone, so he turned it over to Ruth. Luke, Katie and Janie walked to the enclosure. They gave Luke a rundown of their drive to Dallas—the speeding ticket Janie got, and the good luck Katie had in being able to switch their lease to Billy and even get their deposit back.

Katie wanted to spend a few minutes watching Frisky, to discern if he was a good fit with Aquila. Then she'd head over to Aquila and start his morning routine.

"He's beautiful," Luke was saying as they got to the temporary enclosure.

Katie jerked to a halt.

"He's very beautiful," Katie choked out. "Even my father thought so. It's Tyre."

CHAPTER TWENTY

"YOU'RE KIDDING," Luke said.

Katie took a step backward and bumped into Janie. For once it was the little sister reaching out to steady the big sister. Katie spun, looking frantically down the road. She wanted to run, but Ruth was standing in her path.

"You brought Tyre here," she choked out. "He can't stay."

Luke stayed where he was, close to Katie but not touching her. "I had no idea he was Tyre. But we can't take him back to New Mexico."

"Yes, you can. There's always a clause for returns if an animal doesn't work out. That's what you told me, remember?"

"You don't have to take him anywhere," Janie said. "It's okay. I'm really okay."

"But Katie's not," Luke said. He took her by the arms then and shook her gently. "Hey, look at me. Not at Frisky. At me."

Katie tried, she really tried, but Tyre filled her vision. Even from a distance his angry expression seemed out of place on his too-perfect features.

"We'll get through this," Luke promised.

"When did his name change to Frisky?" Katie asked the question but didn't expect an answer. She'd read the PDF file on the computer screen. Noticed herself the holes in Frisky's history.

She faced Luke. "What are you going to do?"

"I don't know," Luke admitted. "I have to think."

Wrong answer. She didn't want a man who *had to think* about a dangerous animal. She wanted a man who would take action if an animal threatened those he loved. She wanted a man who would step between her and Tyre and make the past go away.

For a brief moment, she'd believed Luke was that man. She'd trusted him.

"What's to think about? Take him back."

"I can't. There's no 'back' to take him to."

"Katie," Janie said. "It's all right. He's not going to hurt me."

Luke's fingers tightened around her arms, but she could still easily walk away.

"Have you ever wondered," he said, voice husky, "why you're so afraid of Tyre? Jasper told me you were the most natural animal handler he'd ever met. And you made that impression on him when you were ten. You know animals, how to touch them, talk to them, work with them. What exactly did Tyre do?"

She closed her eyes. He was well aware just what Tyre had done.

"If your father hadn't sent you and Janie away, if you'd stayed and lived out the rest of your childhood at Bob's Animal Kingdom, would your dad have gotten rid of Tyre?"

Katie opened her eyes. She'd asked herself all kinds of what-ifs? But she'd never really imagined her life staying exactly the same. None of her daydreams included Tyre.

"Dad sold him to pay for Janie's surgery."

"Your dad could have found the money somewhere."

"Tyre couldn't be trusted."

"Why?"

Anger replaced fear. "He couldn't be trained. He attacked Janie."

"He acted like a leopard. Janie came into his territory."

"That doesn't matter—"

"Yes, it does." Luke put his hands on her cheeks and drew her close. "If you work with animals, you take chances. But those chances keep entire species alive."

Katie reflected on her new morning routine with Aquila, searching his enclosure before entering because something as trivial as a plastic

cup or towel could transform him from con-
tented feline to unpredictable weapon.

She swallowed, and it hurt.

"If you walk away, Katie, I'll follow. I wonder, though, if walking away will make you
happy."

Tears streamed down her face. He moved his
hands and wiped the dampness off her cheeks.

"If you'd spent your life with your father,
working with the animals, with Tyre, what
would have happened?"

She didn't answer, couldn't.

"Do what I'm going to do," he suggested.
"Mull it over. Janie, you won't go near Tyre,
will you?"

Katie had forgotten that anyone else was
there. It had seemed for a moment that it was
just her, Luke and Tyre.

"I won't." Janie shook her head quickly. The
young, teasing girl of the past few years was
gone, a grown-up woman in her place. "I promise, I won't." Janie glanced over at Tyre as she
said the words, no fear whatsoever on her face.

Luke nudged Katie toward the cart. "Let's
get you something to drink and into the shade."

Katie dug her feet in.

She remembered all those drawings Janie had
done over the years.

"Janie," Katie said, "you're always drawing leopards. Why?"

"I like leopards."

Katie had liked leopards once, too. Until the attack. And since then, she'd not been able to forgive herself, or to forget her own failures. "I'm going to go—" she was surprised she had the ability to talk "—check on Aquila. Can I take the cart?"

He walked over to it, removed a bag from the back and helped her in.

"If you need me," he said, "I'm a phone call away."

As she drove down the pathway, the air was heavy, harsh, hot. She drove by Aquila's enclosure, but didn't stop. Ollie blew kisses as she went by. George didn't even notice her.

For the animals, it was a perfect day at Bridget's. If not for Tyre, it'd be a perfect day for her, too.

She drove around, trying to decide what she wanted.

She wanted to get away, be by herself, right? But she had to be here.

Her demons were here. They kept popping up, taunting her, just when she believed she'd squashed them. But was that because she hadn't really let go of them? Was her anger holding her back, as Jasper had warned?

Katie had never let herself heal, but here, she had that chance. The chance Luke gave to everyone and everything—the chance to live.

She wound up at the old cabin. It should have been empty because Bridget's wasn't open yet, but there was another cart and two mules tied up outside. She heard laughter.

She didn't want to be alone.

Wiping at her eyes, she got off and headed inside.

"Hey," Jasper said, "what made you decide to come up here?"

If he noticed her red eyes, he didn't say anything. He probably hadn't been by to check out the new acquisition. The girls weren't so subtle. "You cry?" they signed. "What wrong?"

The girls insisted on taking her for a tour. It gave Katie time to calm down, time to think and time to remember how good it felt to trust.

Good wasn't always easy.

They'd just finished the tour when Luke walked in.

"Boyfriend," one of the girls signed, and they all giggled. Then they frowned, as if suddenly remembering her red eyes. "You okay?"

She signed back that she was fine. Luke took in the spiderwebs, giant spiders and fake blood already scattered across the room.

"Just checking on things," he said.

Amanda couldn't stop smiling. She inserted herself between Luke and Katie and asked Katie to sign while she explained things to Luke.

The main room, the one they'd been in, was a holding room for guests to wait for their turn to go into the haunted house. Then each room would have a different theme. There was the vampire room, the werewolf room, the witch room—the kitchen, of course—and last, the coffin room.

It wasn't much, but it was enough.

When she was finished, Katie followed Luke from the cabin. She reached for him, welcoming the strength and warmth he offered.

"I've spent the last thirty minutes in my office, going over our options. You were right, I acted purely from my heart. I should have trusted your judgment. We'll find a new home for Tyre."

Every creature deserved a home. Katie'd found one.

She'd take his heart over her logic right now. She'd wanted a man who would step between her and Tyre and make the past go away. Instead, he'd helped her accept her past and, in the process, given her a future.

Did Tyre deserve any less?

For a moment, she didn't think the words would come. Her throat closed. There was so much she wanted, needed, to say. Finally, she managed, "Let's give him a chance. Then we can talk about the best place for him."

"Deal."

The resulting kiss, probably the best so far in her life, was interrupted by a very red Jasper clearing his throat.

"Ahem," he said. Beside him on the cabin porch were the five teenage girls. "Seems Amanda enjoys decorating. She's offering, after we take down the Halloween decorations, to transform the cabin into a wedding chapel. I told her I'd ask the question."

"I guess that means I'd better ask the question, too," Luke said in her ear.

"You already know my answer," she said, and he bent to kiss her again.

* * * * *

REQUEST YOUR FREE BOOKS!
2 FREE WHOLESOME ROMANCE NOVELS
IN LARGER PRINT
PLUS 2
FREE
MYSTERY GIFTS

✽✽✽✽✽✽✽✽✽✽✽✽✽✽✽✽✽✽✽✽✽✽✽✽

HEARTWARMING™
✿✿✿✿✿✿✿✿✿✿✿✿✿✿✿✿✿✿✿✿✿✿✿✿

Wholesome, tender romances

YES! Please send me 2 FREE Harlequin® Heartwarming Larger-Print novels and my 2 FREE mystery gifts (gifts worth about $10). After receiving them, if I don't wish to receive any more books, I can return the shipping statement marked "cancel." If I don't cancel, I will receive 4 brand-new larger-print novels every month and be billed just $4.99 per book in the U.S. or $5.74 per book in Canada. That's a savings of at least 23% off the cover price. It's quite a bargain! Shipping and handling is just 50¢ per book in the U.S. and 75¢ per book in Canada.* I understand that accepting the 2 free books and gifts places me under no obligation to buy anything. I can always return a shipment and cancel at any time. Even if I never buy another book, the two free books and gifts are mine to keep forever.

161/361 IDN F47N

Name _____ (PLEASE PRINT) _____

Address _____ Apt. #

City _____ State/Prov. _____ Zip/Postal Code

Signature (if under 18, a parent or guardian must sign)

Mail to the **Harlequin® Reader Service:**
IN U.S.A.: P.O. Box 1867, Buffalo, NY 14240-1867
IN CANADA: P.O. Box 609, Fort Erie, Ontario L2A 5X3

* Terms and prices subject to change without notice. Prices do not include applicable taxes. Sales tax applicable in N.Y. Canadian residents will be charged applicable taxes. Offer not valid in Quebec. This offer is limited to one order per household. Not valid for current subscribers to Harlequin Heartwarming larger-print books. All orders subject to credit approval. Credit or debit balances in a customer's account(s) may be offset by any other outstanding balance owed by or to the customer. Please allow 4 to 6 weeks for delivery. Offer available while quantities last.

Your Privacy—The Harlequin® Reader Service is committed to protecting your privacy. Our Privacy Policy is available online at www.ReaderService.com or upon request from the Harlequin Reader Service.

We make a portion of our mailing list available to reputable third parties that offer products we believe may interest you. If you prefer that we not exchange your name with third parties, or if you wish to clarify or modify your communication preferences, please visit us at www.ReaderService.com/consumerschoice or write to us at Harlequin Reader Service Preference Service, P.O. Box 9062, Buffalo, NY 14269. Include your complete name and address.

HWDIR13R